STAR TREK™ PICARD COUNTDOWN

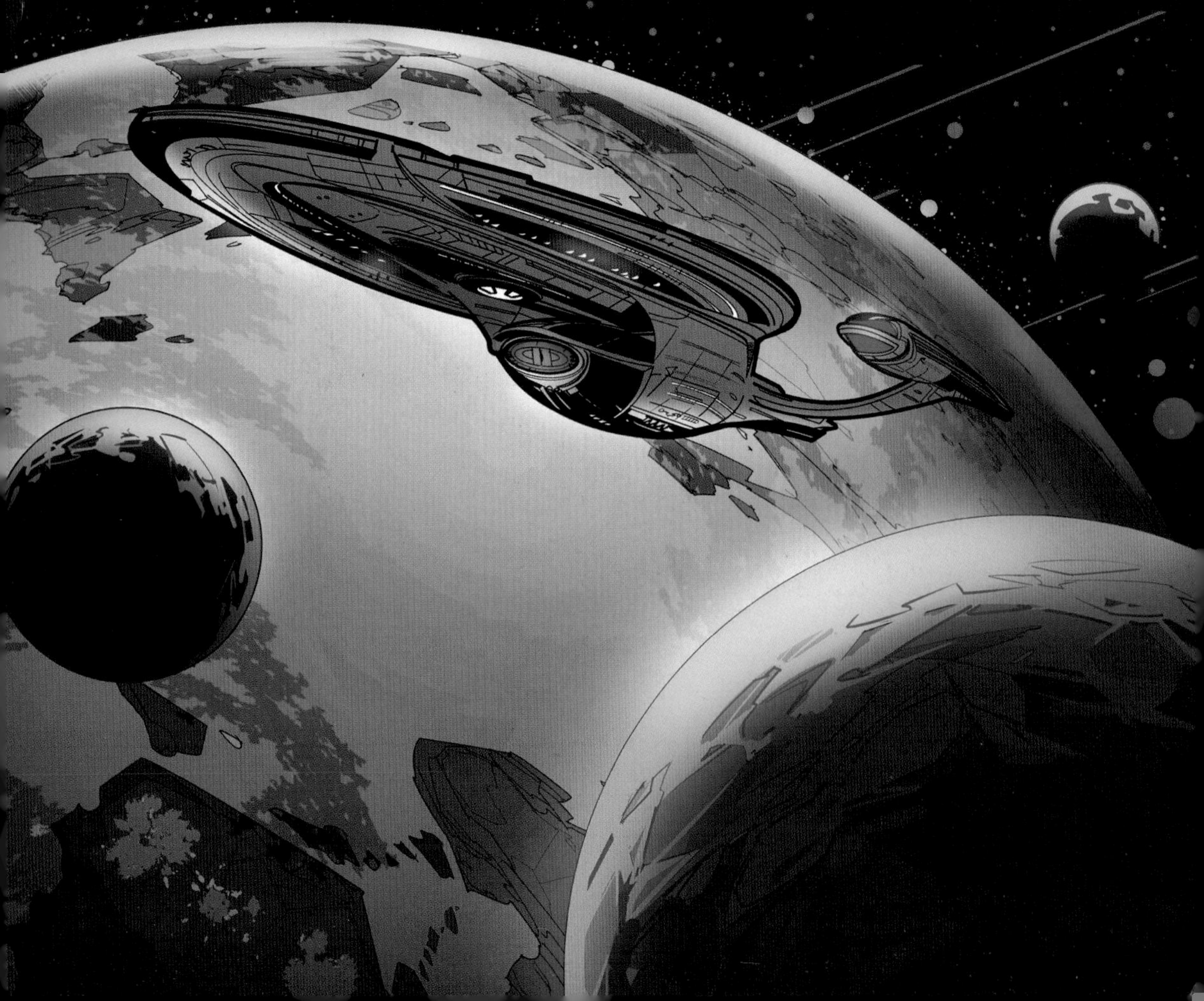

IDW

Facebook: **facebook.com/idwpublishing**
Twitter: **@idwpublishing**
YouTube: **youtube.com/idwpublishing**
Tumblr: **tumblr.idwpublishing.com**
Instagram: **instagram.com/idwpublishing**

ISBN: 978-1-68405-694-1 23 22 21 20 1 2 3 4

Cover Artist
JIM SALVATI

Series Editor
CHASE MAROTZ

Collection Editors
ALONZO SIMON
and ZAC BOONE

Collection Designer
MARCONI TORRES

STAR TREK: PICARD: COUNTDOWN. AUGUST 2020. FIRST PRINTING. IDW Publishing, a division of Idea and Design Works, LLC. Editorial offices: 2765 Truxtun Road, San Diego, CA 92106.

Printed in Korea.

Originally published as STAR TREK: PICARD: COUNTDOWN issues #1–3.

Chris Ryall, President & Publisher/CCO
Cara Morrison, Chief Financial Officer
Matthew Ruzicka, Chief Accounting Officer
John Barber, Editor-in-Chief
Justin Eisinger, Editorial Director, Graphic Novels & Collections
Scott Dunbier, Director, Special Projects
Jerry Bennington, VP of New Product Development
Lorelei Bunjes, VP of Technology & Information Services
Jud Meyers, Sales Director
Anna Morrow, Marketing Director
Tara McCrillis, Director of Design & Production
Mike Ford, Director of Operations
Shauna Monteforte, Manufacturing Operations Director
Rebekah Cahalin, General Manager

Ted Adams and Robbie Robbins, IDW Founders

SPECIAL THANKS TO RISA KESSLER, MARIAN CORDRY, DAYTON WARD, AND JOHN VAN CITTERS OF CBS CONSUMER PRODUCTS FOR THEIR INVALUABLE ASSISTANCE.

STAR TREK™
PICARD
COUNTDOWN

Written by
Kirsten Beyer
& Mike Johnson

Art by
Angel Hernandez

Colors by
Joana Lafuente

Letters by
Neil Uyetake

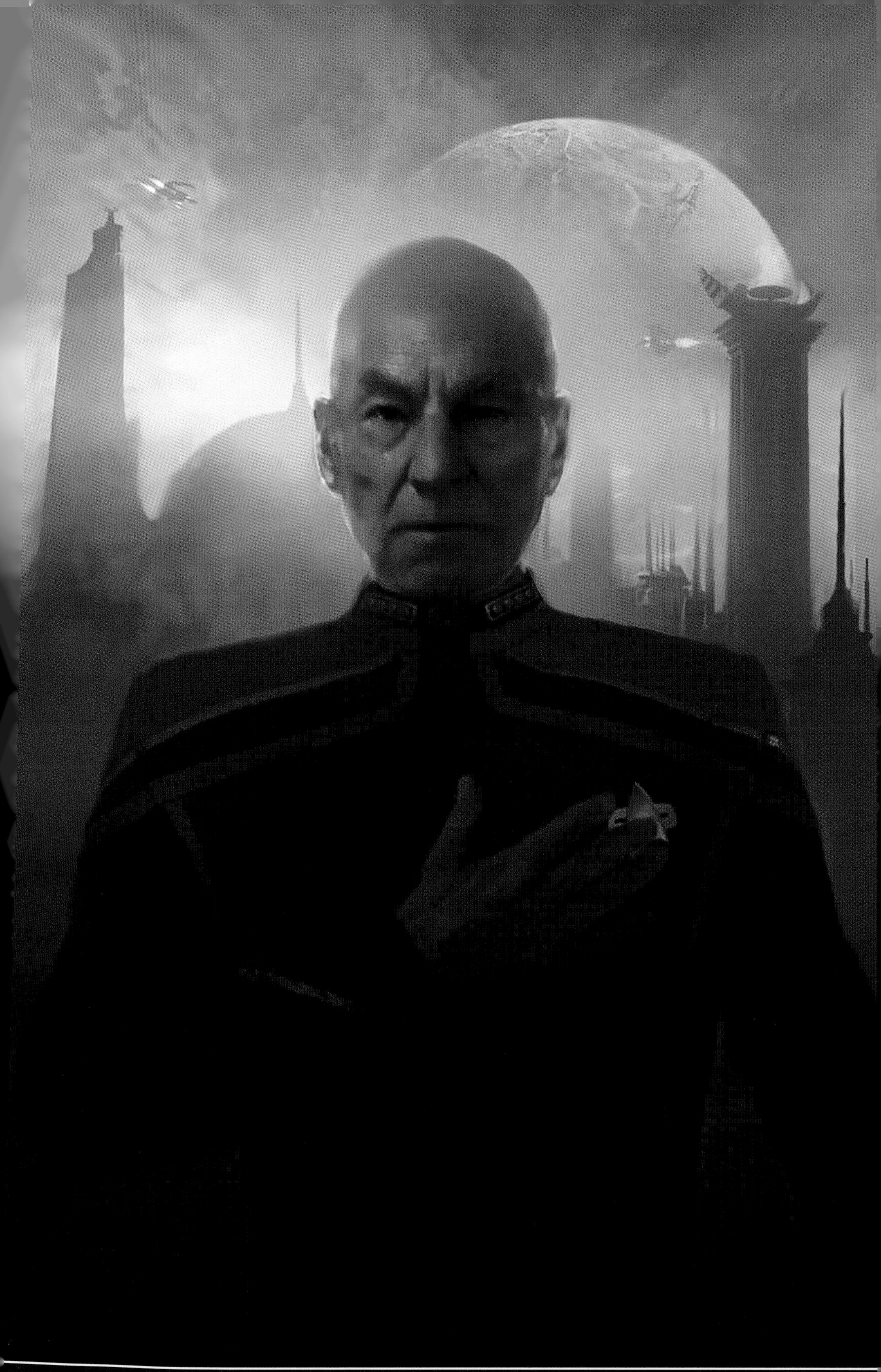

art by MICHAEL PANGRAZIO

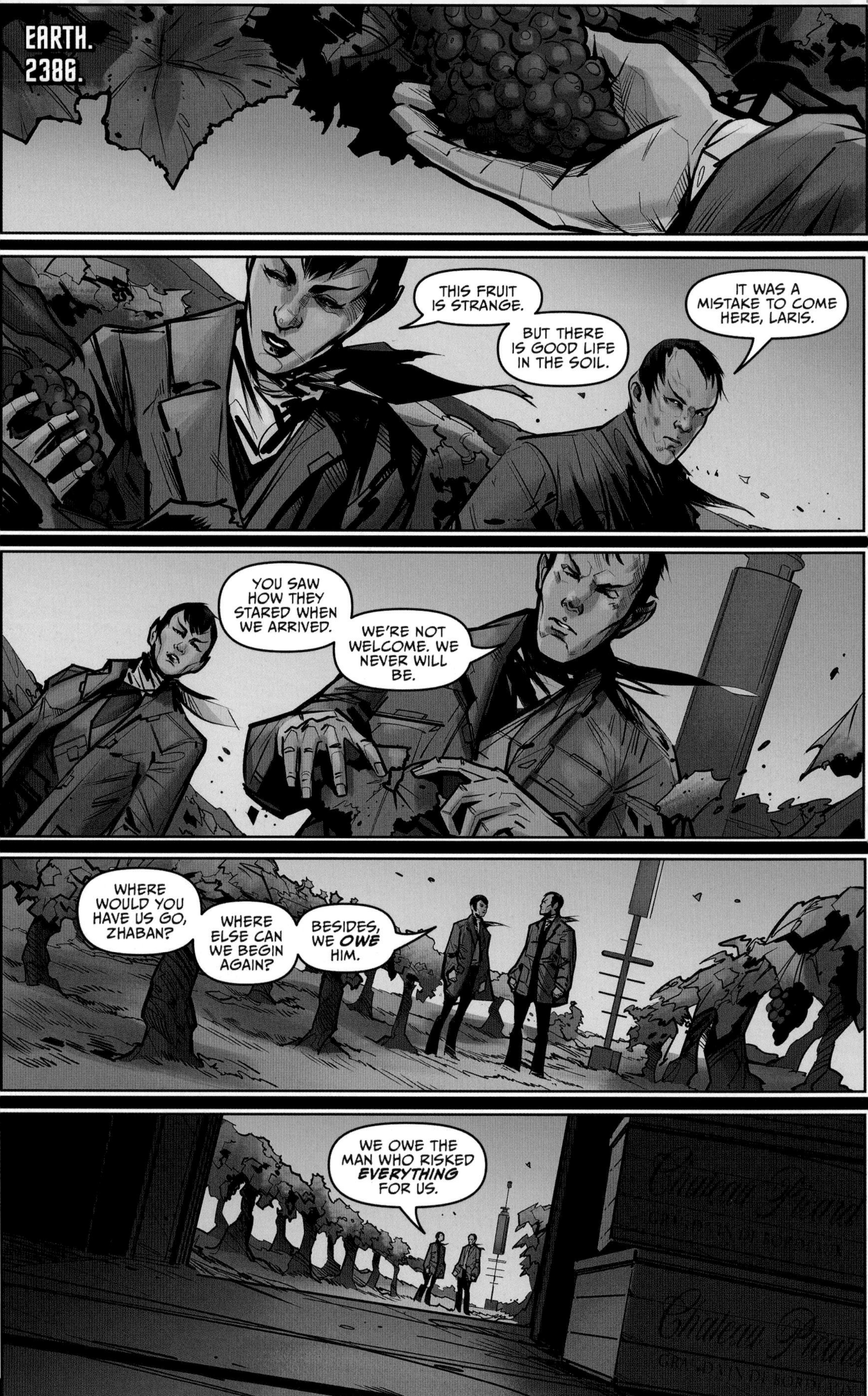
EARTH. 2386.
THIS FRUIT IS STRANGE.
BUT THERE IS GOOD LIFE IN THE SOIL.
IT WAS A MISTAKE TO COME HERE, LARIS.
YOU SAW HOW THEY STARED WHEN WE ARRIVED.
WE'RE NOT WELCOME. WE NEVER WILL BE.
WHERE WOULD YOU HAVE US GO, ZHABAN?
WHERE ELSE CAN WE BEGIN AGAIN?
BESIDES, WE OWE HIM.
WE OWE THE MAN WHO RISKED EVERYTHING FOR US.

MARS.

ONE YEAR BEFORE.

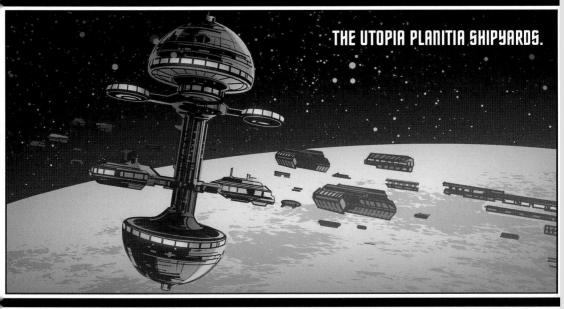

THE UTOPIA PLANITIA SHIPYARDS.

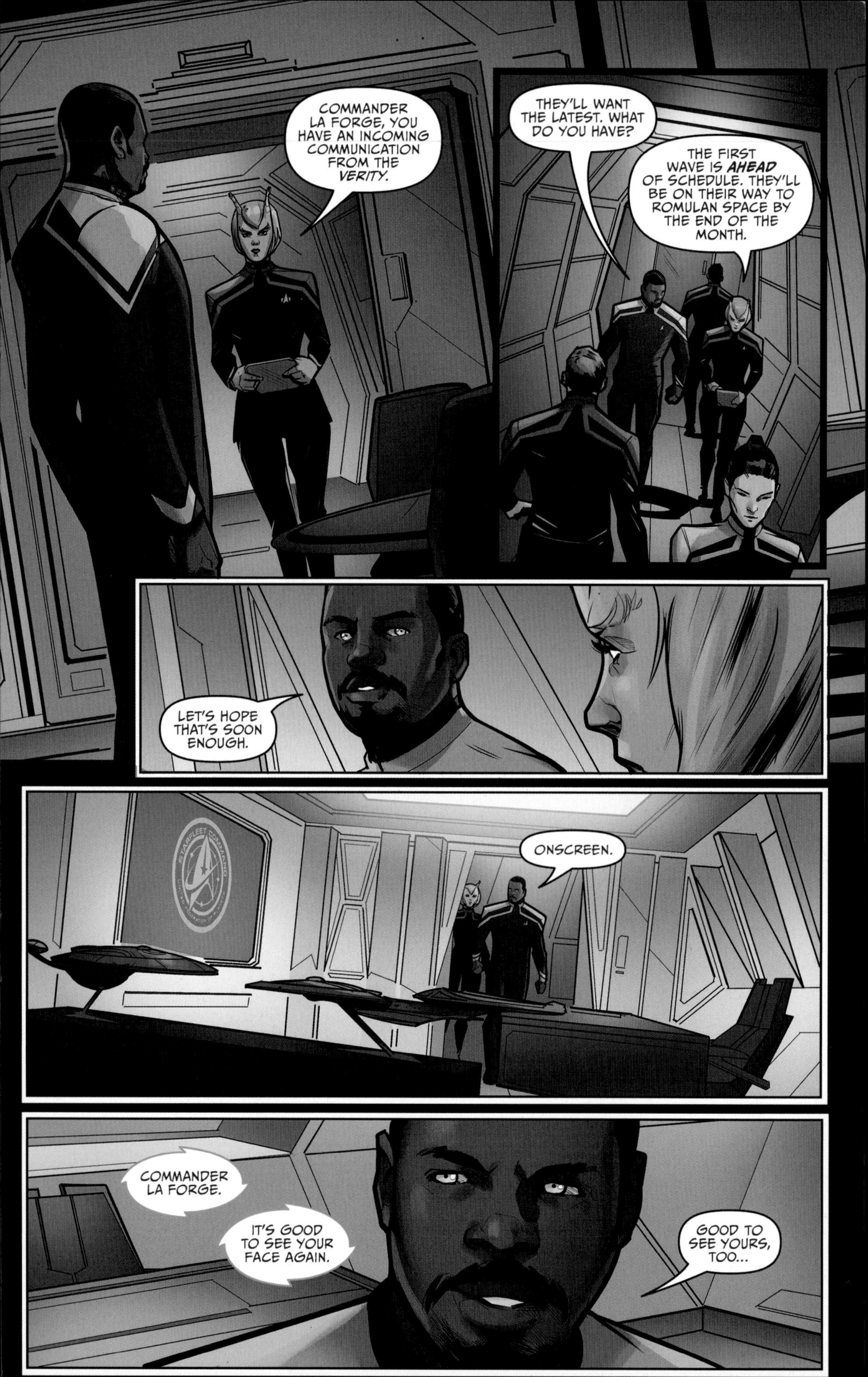
COMMANDER LA FORGE, YOU HAVE AN INCOMING COMMUNICATION FROM THE *VERITY.*
THEY'LL WANT THE LATEST. WHAT DO YOU HAVE?
THE FIRST WAVE IS ***AHEAD*** OF SCHEDULE. THEY'LL BE ON THEIR WAY TO ROMULAN SPACE BY THE END OF THE MONTH.
LET'S HOPE THAT'S SOON ENOUGH.
ONSCREEN.
COMMANDER LA FORGE.
IT'S GOOD TO SEE YOUR FACE AGAIN.
GOOD TO SEE YOURS, TOO...

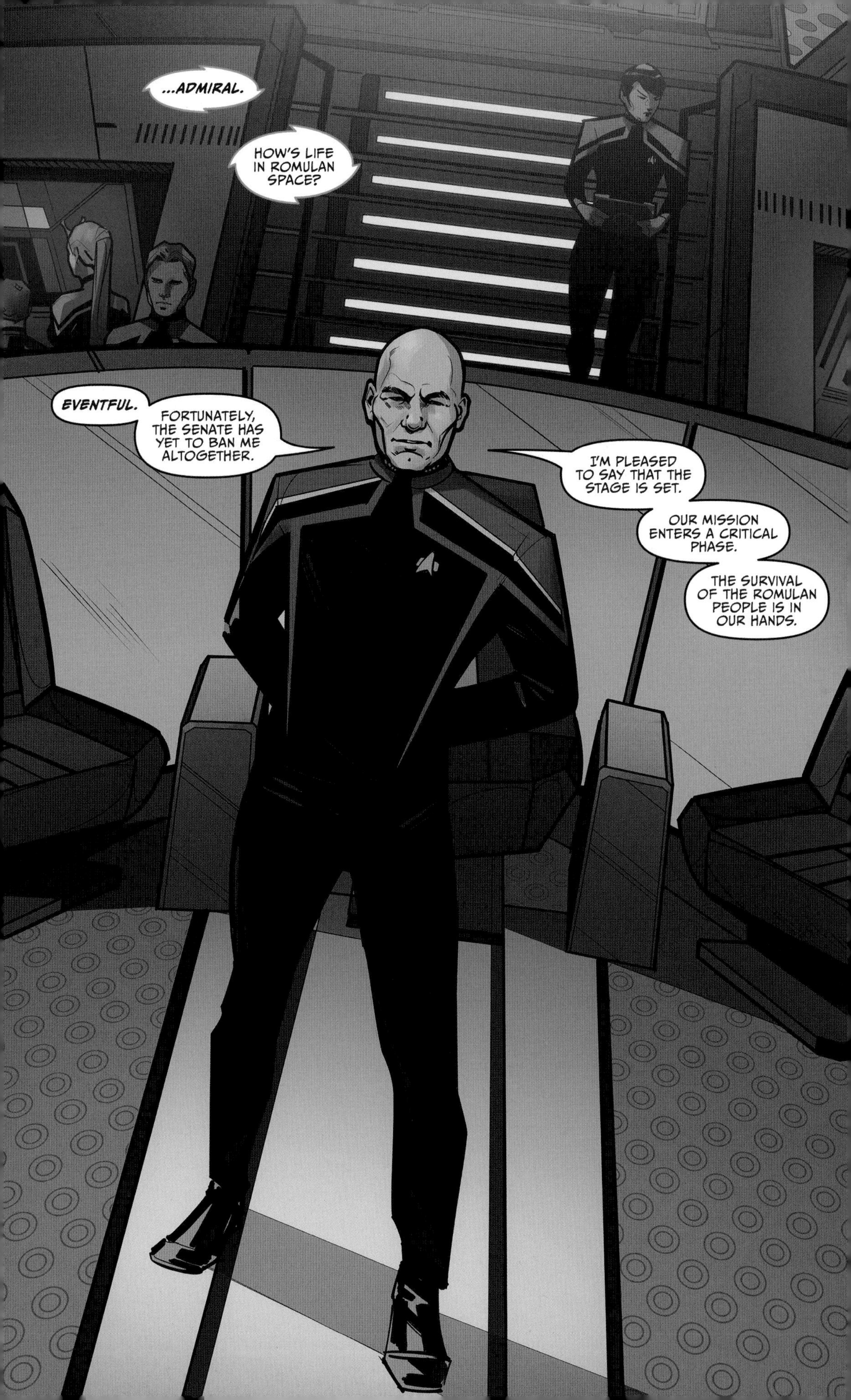
...ADMIRAL.
HOW'S LIFE IN ROMULAN SPACE?
EVENTFUL.
FORTUNATELY, THE SENATE HAS YET TO BAN ME ALTOGETHER.
I'M PLEASED TO SAY THAT THE STAGE IS SET.
OUR MISSION ENTERS A CRITICAL PHASE.
THE SURVIVAL OF THE ROMULAN PEOPLE IS IN OUR HANDS.

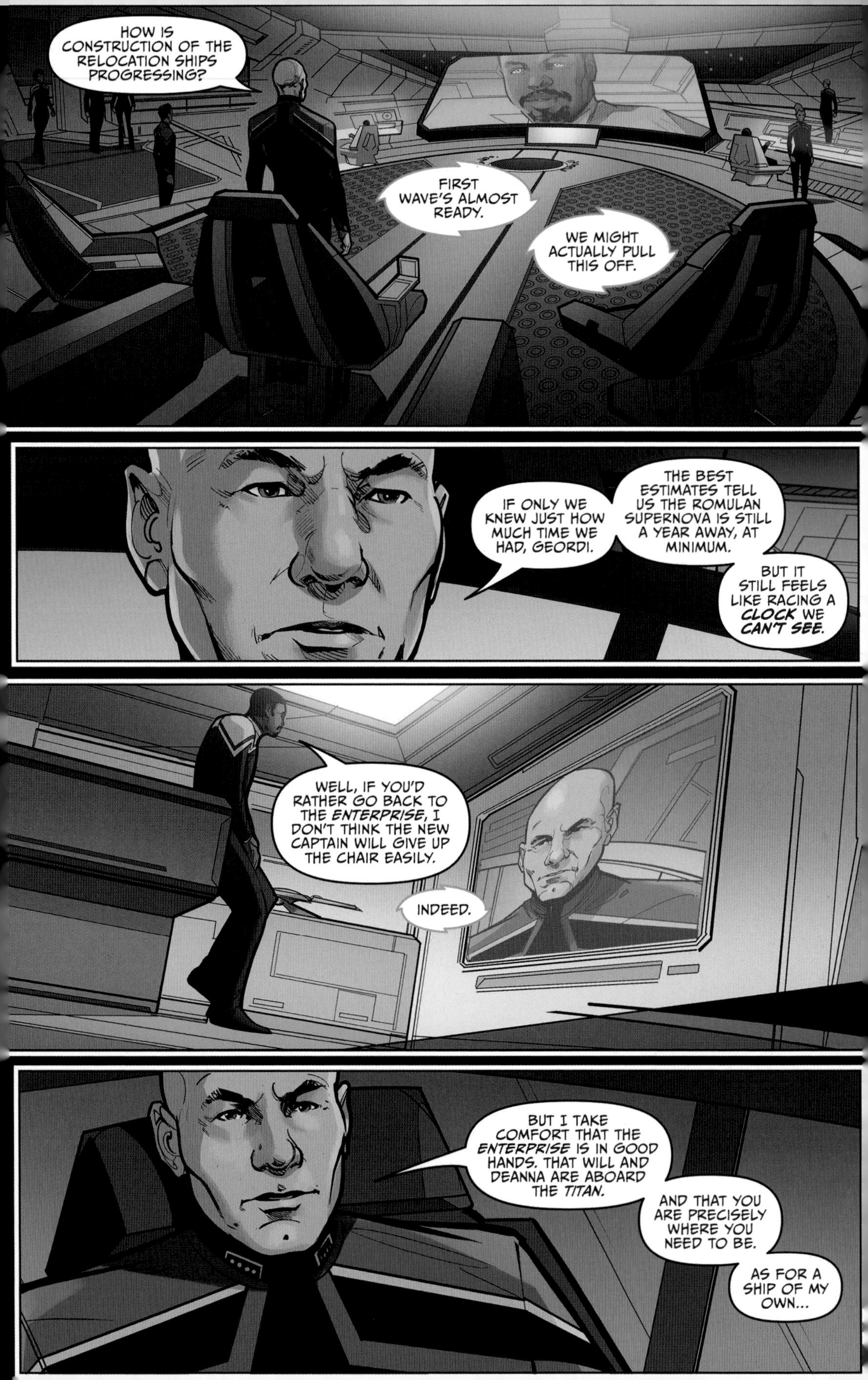
HOW IS CONSTRUCTION OF THE RELOCATION SHIPS PROGRESSING?
FIRST WAVE'S ALMOST READY.
WE MIGHT ACTUALLY PULL THIS OFF.
IF ONLY WE KNEW JUST HOW MUCH TIME WE HAD, GEORDI.
THE BEST ESTIMATES TELL US THE ROMULAN SUPERNOVA IS STILL A YEAR AWAY, AT MINIMUM.
BUT IT STILL FEELS LIKE RACING A ***CLOCK*** WE ***CAN'T SEE***.
WELL, IF YOU'D RATHER GO BACK TO THE *ENTERPRISE*, I DON'T THINK THE NEW CAPTAIN WILL GIVE UP THE CHAIR EASILY.
INDEED.
BUT I TAKE COMFORT THAT THE *ENTERPRISE* IS IN GOOD HANDS. THAT WILL AND DEANNA ARE ABOARD THE *TITAN*.
AND THAT YOU ARE PRECISELY WHERE YOU NEED TO BE.
AS FOR A SHIP OF MY OWN...

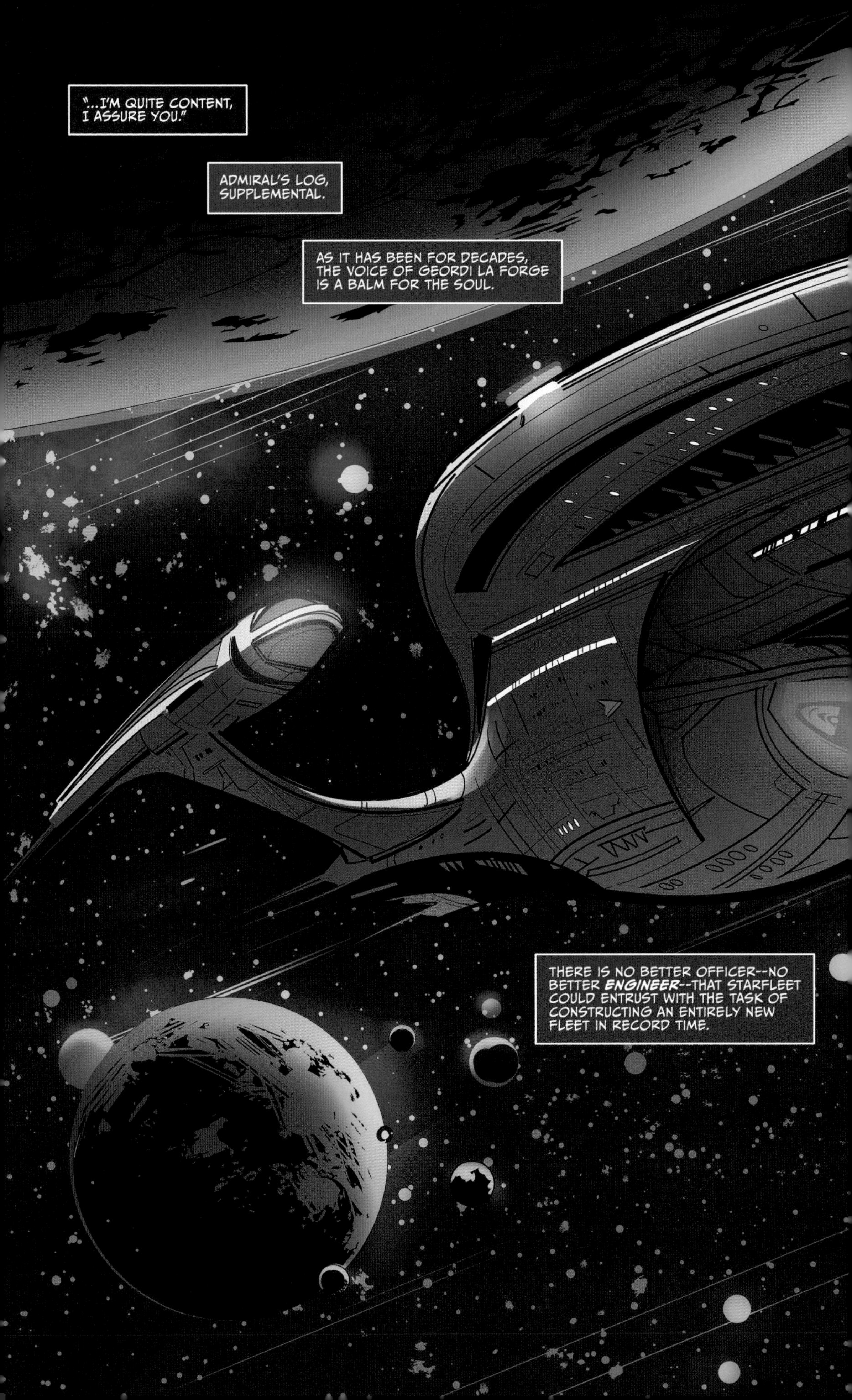
"...I'M QUITE CONTENT, I ASSURE YOU."
ADMIRAL'S LOG, SUPPLEMENTAL.
AS IT HAS BEEN FOR DECADES, THE VOICE OF GEORDI LA FORGE IS A BALM FOR THE SOUL.
THERE IS NO BETTER OFFICER--NO BETTER ENGINEER--THAT STARFLEET COULD ENTRUST WITH THE TASK OF CONSTRUCTING AN ENTIRELY NEW FLEET IN RECORD TIME.

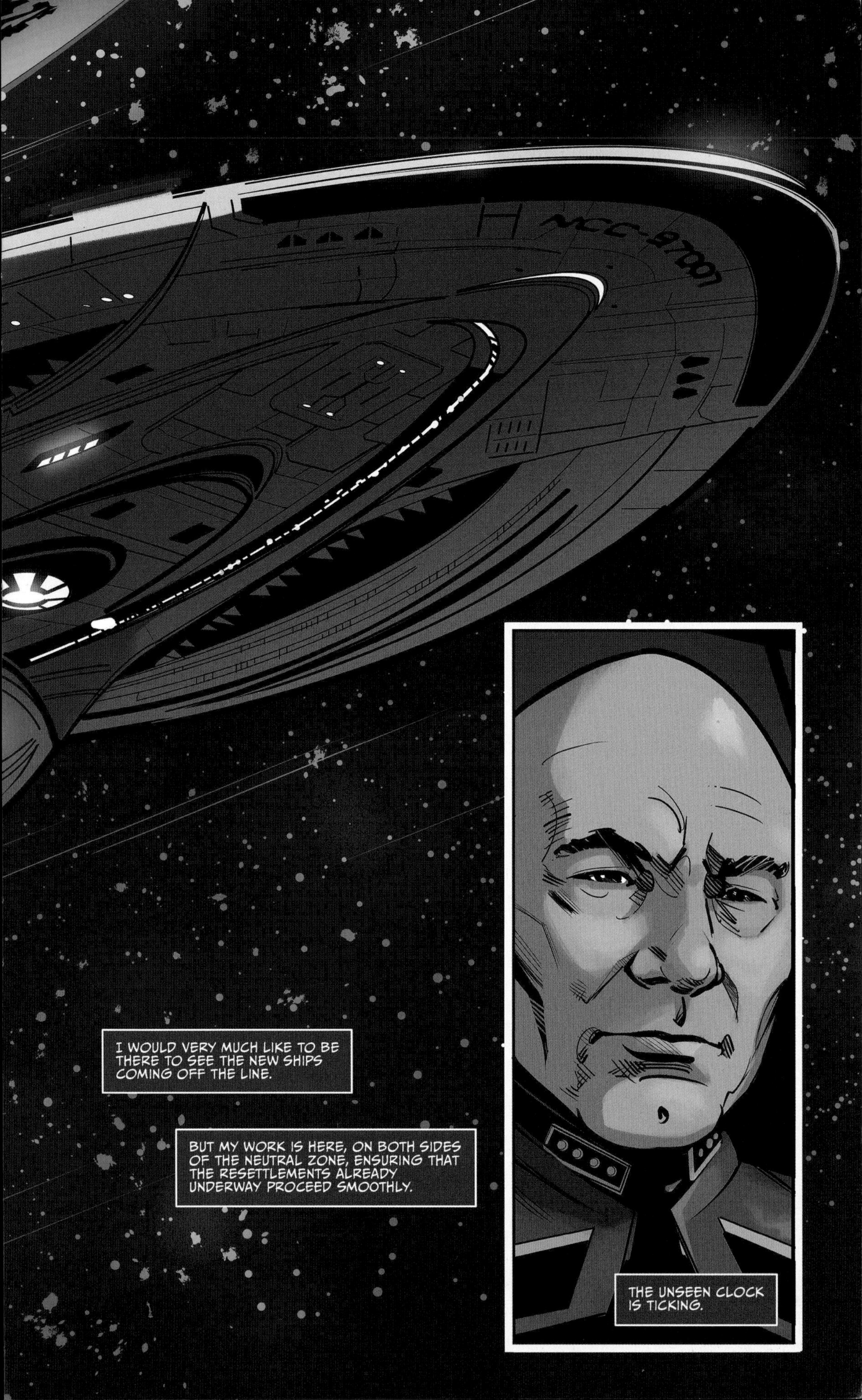
NCC-97001
I WOULD VERY MUCH LIKE TO BE THERE TO SEE THE NEW SHIPS COMING OFF THE LINE.
BUT MY WORK IS HERE, ON BOTH SIDES OF THE NEUTRAL ZONE, ENSURING THAT THE RESETTLEMENTS ALREADY UNDERWAY PROCEED SMOOTHLY.
THE UNSEEN CLOCK IS TICKING.

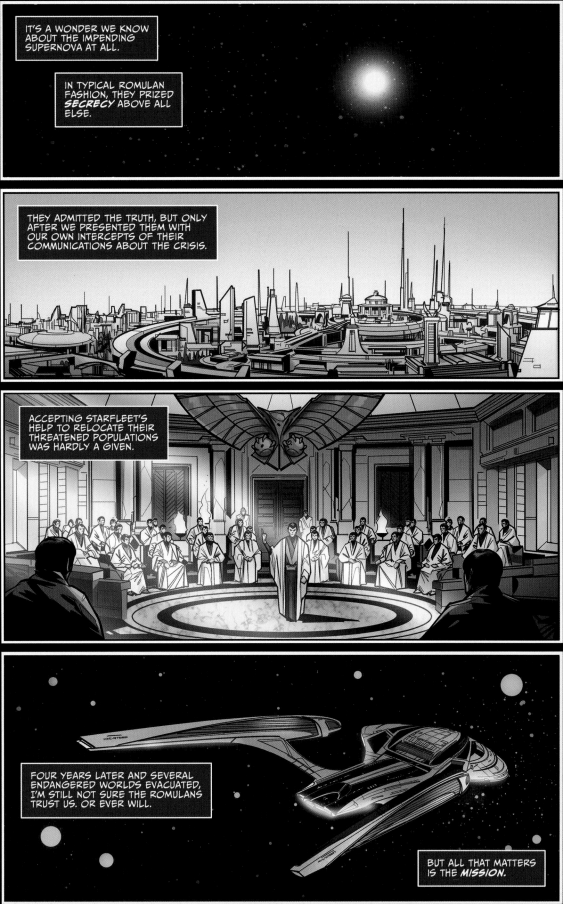

IT'S A WONDER WE KNOW ABOUT THE IMPENDING SUPERNOVA AT ALL.

IN TYPICAL ROMULAN FASHION, THEY PRIZED *SECRECY* ABOVE ALL ELSE.

THEY ADMITTED THE TRUTH, BUT ONLY AFTER WE PRESENTED THEM WITH OUR OWN INTERCEPTS OF THEIR COMMUNICATIONS ABOUT THE CRISIS.

ACCEPTING STARFLEET'S HELP TO RELOCATE THEIR THREATENED POPULATIONS WAS HARDLY A GIVEN.

FOUR YEARS LATER AND SEVERAL ENDANGERED WORLDS EVACUATED, I'M STILL NOT SURE THE ROMULANS TRUST US. OR EVER WILL.

BUT ALL THAT MATTERS IS THE *MISSION.*

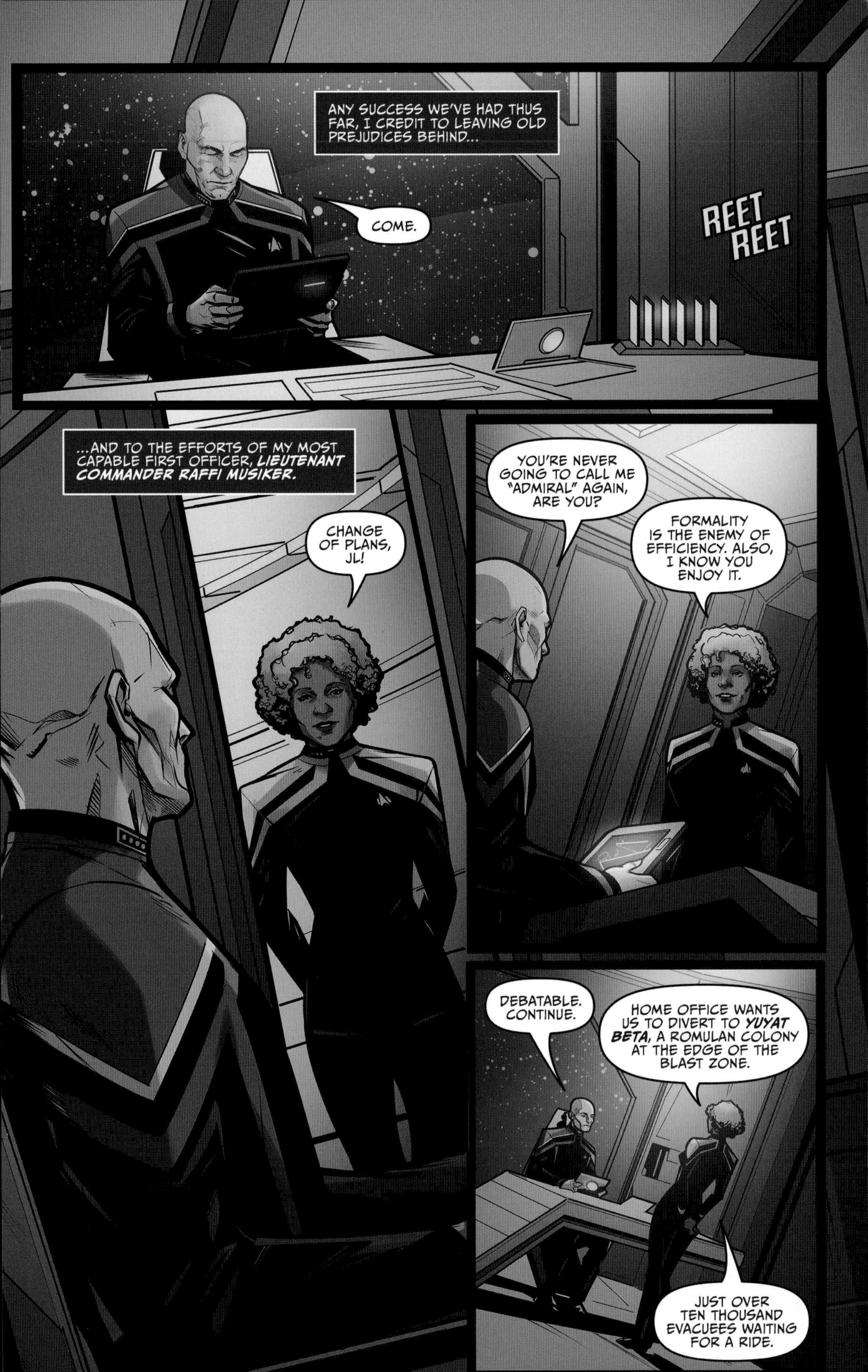
ANY SUCCESS WE'VE HAD THUS FAR, I CREDIT TO LEAVING OLD PREJUDICES BEHIND...
REET REET
COME.
...AND TO THE EFFORTS OF MY MOST CAPABLE FIRST OFFICER, *LIEUTENANT COMMANDER RAFFI MUSIKER.*
CHANGE OF PLANS, JL!
YOU'RE NEVER GOING TO CALL ME "ADMIRAL" AGAIN, ARE YOU?
FORMALITY IS THE ENEMY OF EFFICIENCY. ALSO, I KNOW YOU ENJOY IT.
DEBATABLE. CONTINUE.
HOME OFFICE WANTS US TO DIVERT TO *YUYAT BETA*, A ROMULAN COLONY AT THE EDGE OF THE BLAST ZONE.
JUST OVER TEN THOUSAND EVACUEES WAITING FOR A RIDE.

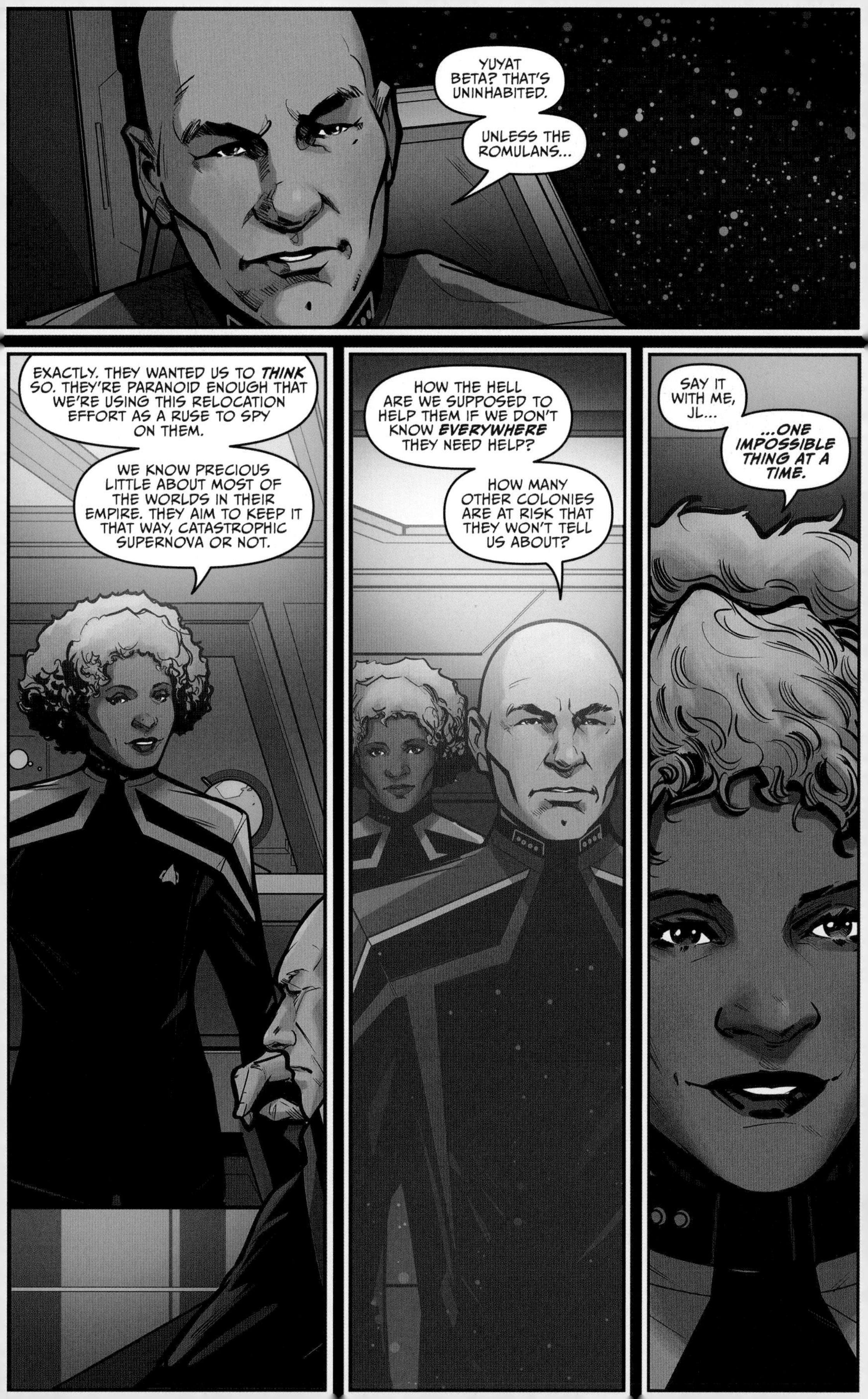
YUYAT BETA? THAT'S UNINHABITED.
UNLESS THE ROMULANS...
EXACTLY. THEY WANTED US TO *THINK* SO. THEY'RE PARANOID ENOUGH THAT WE'RE USING THIS RELOCATION EFFORT AS A RUSE TO SPY ON THEM.
WE KNOW PRECIOUS LITTLE ABOUT MOST OF THE WORLDS IN THEIR EMPIRE. THEY AIM TO KEEP IT THAT WAY, CATASTROPHIC SUPERNOVA OR NOT.
HOW THE HELL ARE WE SUPPOSED TO HELP THEM IF WE DON'T KNOW **EVERYWHERE** THEY NEED HELP?
HOW MANY OTHER COLONIES ARE AT RISK THAT THEY WON'T TELL US ABOUT?
SAY IT WITH ME, JL...
...ONE IMPOSSIBLE THING AT A TIME.

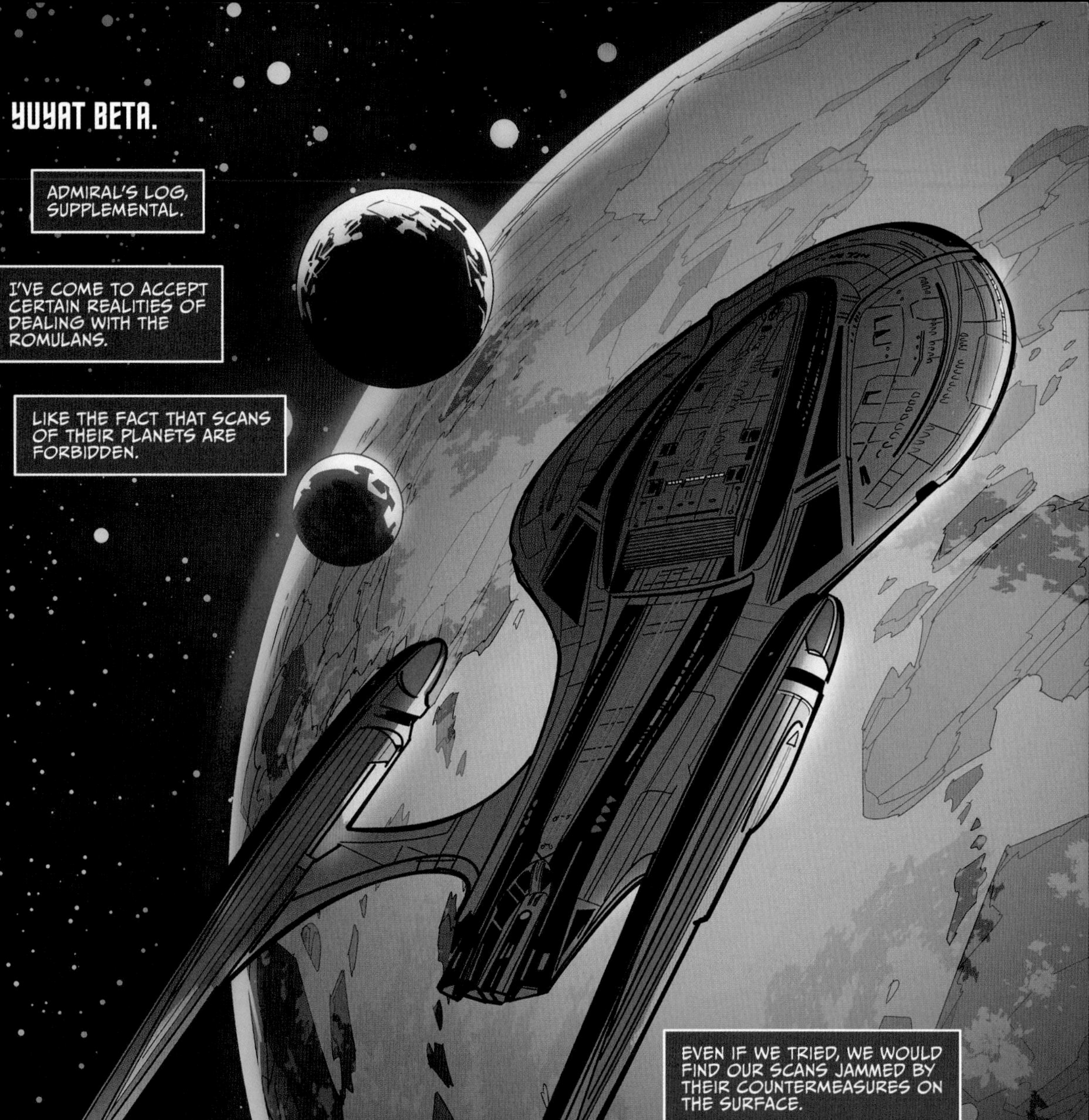
YUYAT BETA.
ADMIRAL'S LOG, SUPPLEMENTAL.
I'VE COME TO ACCEPT CERTAIN REALITIES OF DEALING WITH THE ROMULANS.
LIKE THE FACT THAT SCANS OF THEIR PLANETS ARE FORBIDDEN.
EVEN IF WE TRIED, WE WOULD FIND OUR SCANS JAMMED BY THEIR COUNTERMEASURES ON THE SURFACE.
SECRETS WITHIN SECRETS. SCHEMES WITHIN SCHEMES.
WE MUST SIMPLY EMBRACE OUR ROLE AS HUMBLE GUESTS.

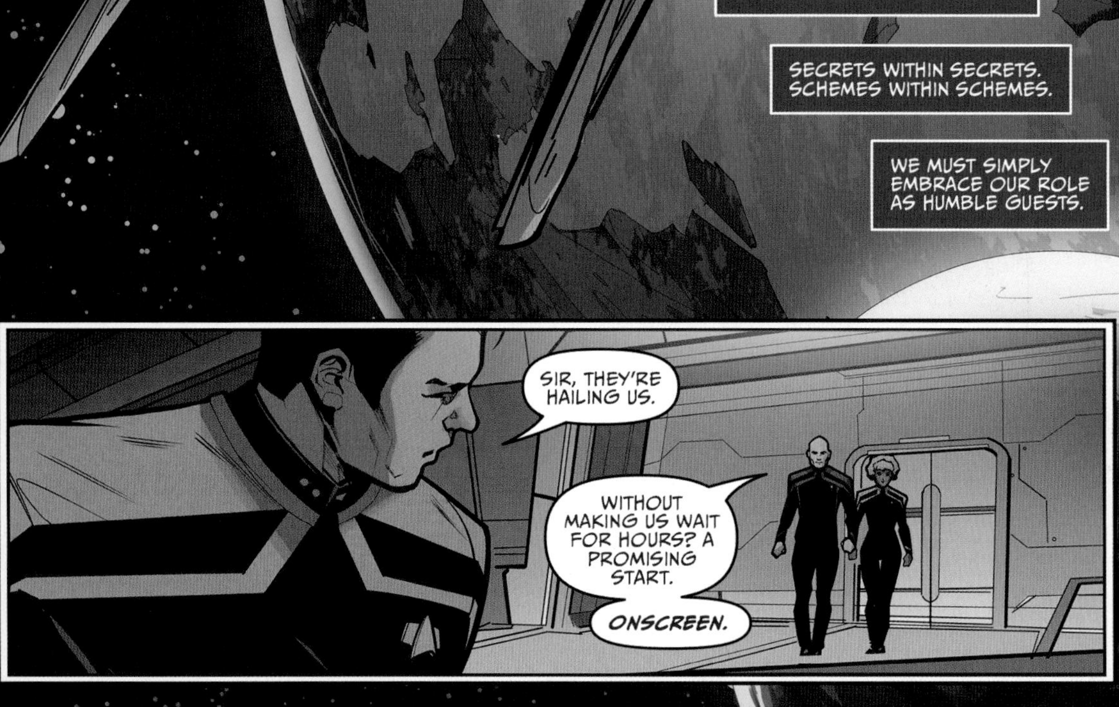
SIR, THEY'RE HAILING US.
WITHOUT MAKING US WAIT FOR HOURS? A PROMISING START.
ONSCREEN.

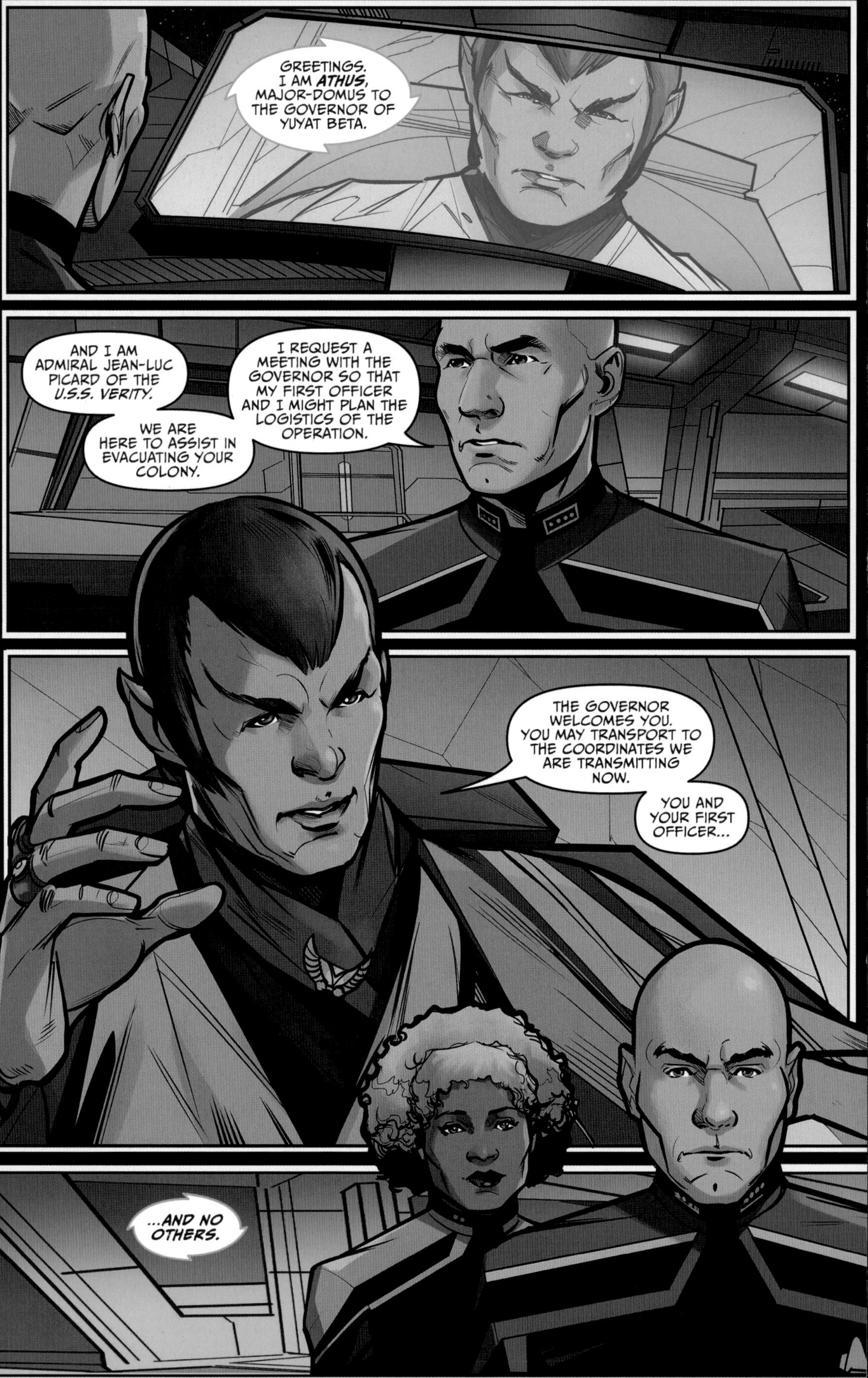
GREETINGS. I AM ATHUS, MAJOR-DOMUS TO THE GOVERNOR OF YUYAT BETA.
AND I AM ADMIRAL JEAN-LUC PICARD OF THE U.S.S. VERITY.
WE ARE HERE TO ASSIST IN EVACUATING YOUR COLONY.
I REQUEST A MEETING WITH THE GOVERNOR SO THAT MY FIRST OFFICER AND I MIGHT PLAN THE LOGISTICS OF THE OPERATION.
THE GOVERNOR WELCOMES YOU. YOU MAY TRANSPORT TO THE COORDINATES WE ARE TRANSMITTING NOW.
YOU AND YOUR FIRST OFFICER...
...AND NO OTHERS.

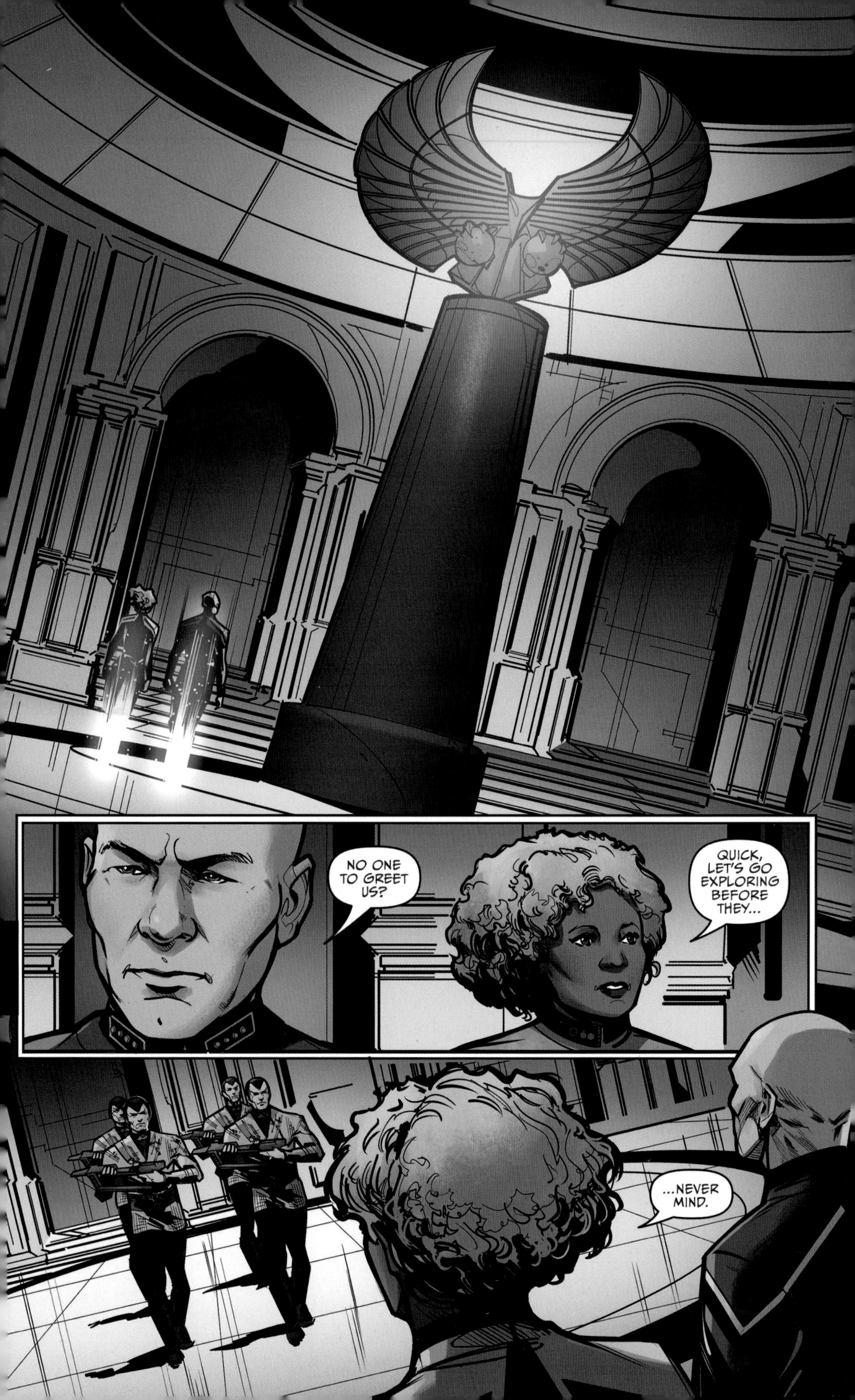
NO ONE TO GREET US?
QUICK, LET'S GO EXPLORING BEFORE THEY...
...NEVER MIND.

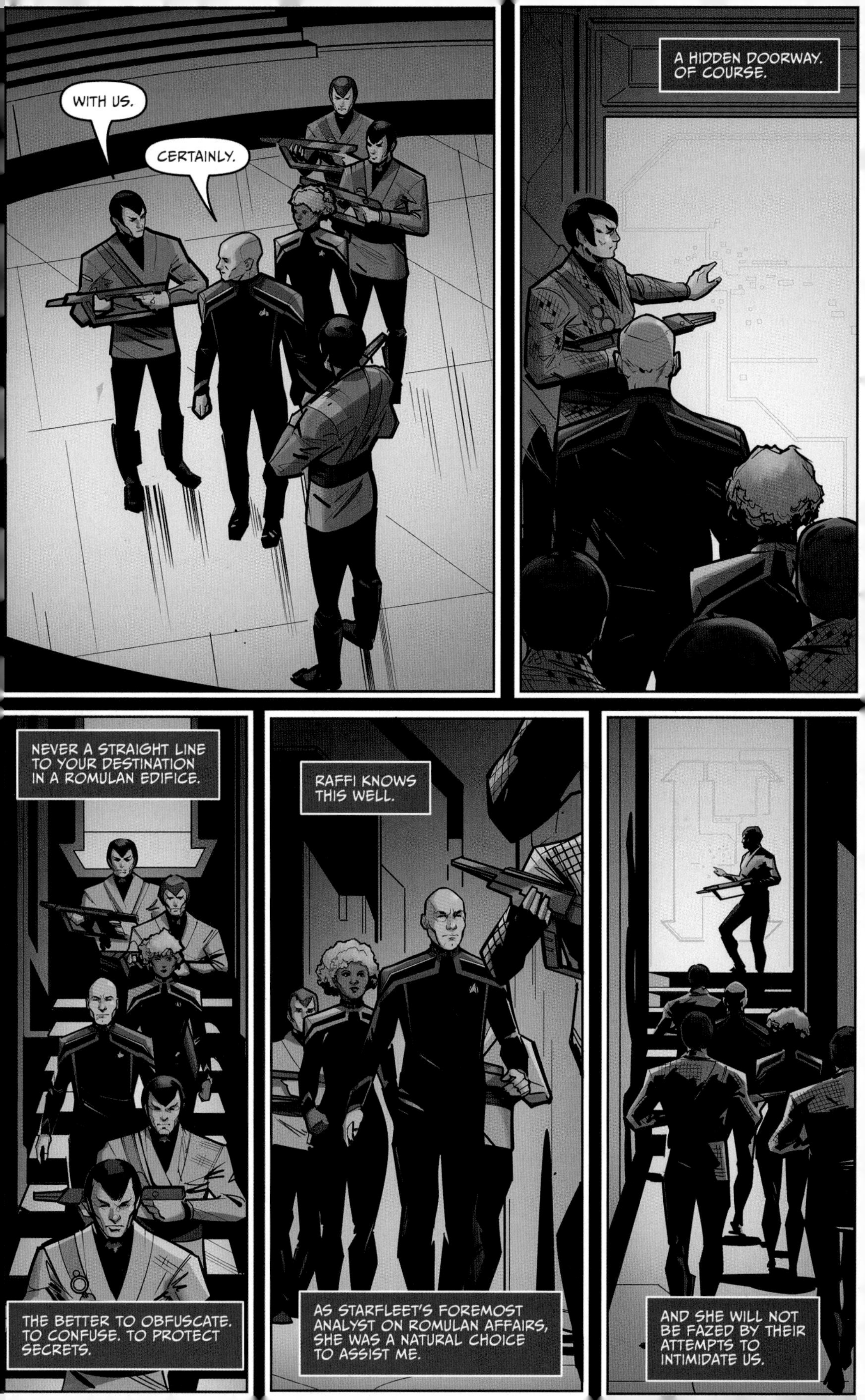
WITH US.
CERTAINLY.
A HIDDEN DOORWAY. OF COURSE.
NEVER A STRAIGHT LINE TO YOUR DESTINATION IN A ROMULAN EDIFICE.
THE BETTER TO OBFUSCATE. TO CONFUSE. TO PROTECT SECRETS.
RAFFI KNOWS THIS WELL.
AS STARFLEET'S FOREMOST ANALYST ON ROMULAN AFFAIRS, SHE WAS A NATURAL CHOICE TO ASSIST ME.
AND SHE WILL NOT BE FAZED BY THEIR ATTEMPTS TO INTIMIDATE US.

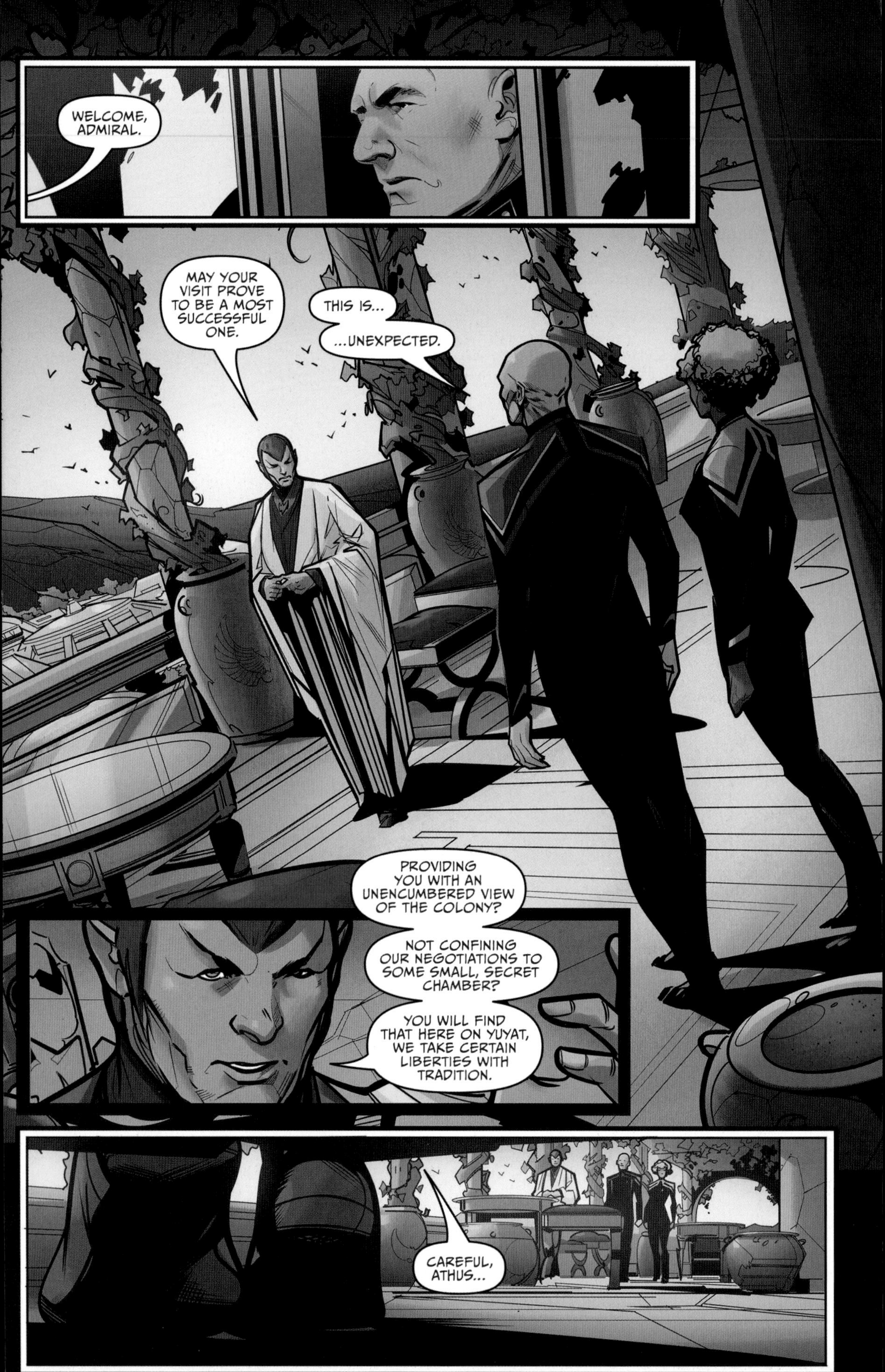
WELCOME, ADMIRAL.
MAY YOUR VISIT PROVE TO BE A MOST SUCCESSFUL ONE.
THIS IS...
...UNEXPECTED.
PROVIDING YOU WITH AN UNENCUMBERED VIEW OF THE COLONY?
NOT CONFINING OUR NEGOTIATIONS TO SOME SMALL, SECRET CHAMBER?
YOU WILL FIND THAT HERE ON YUYAT, WE TAKE CERTAIN LIBERTIES WITH TRADITION.
CAREFUL, ATHUS...

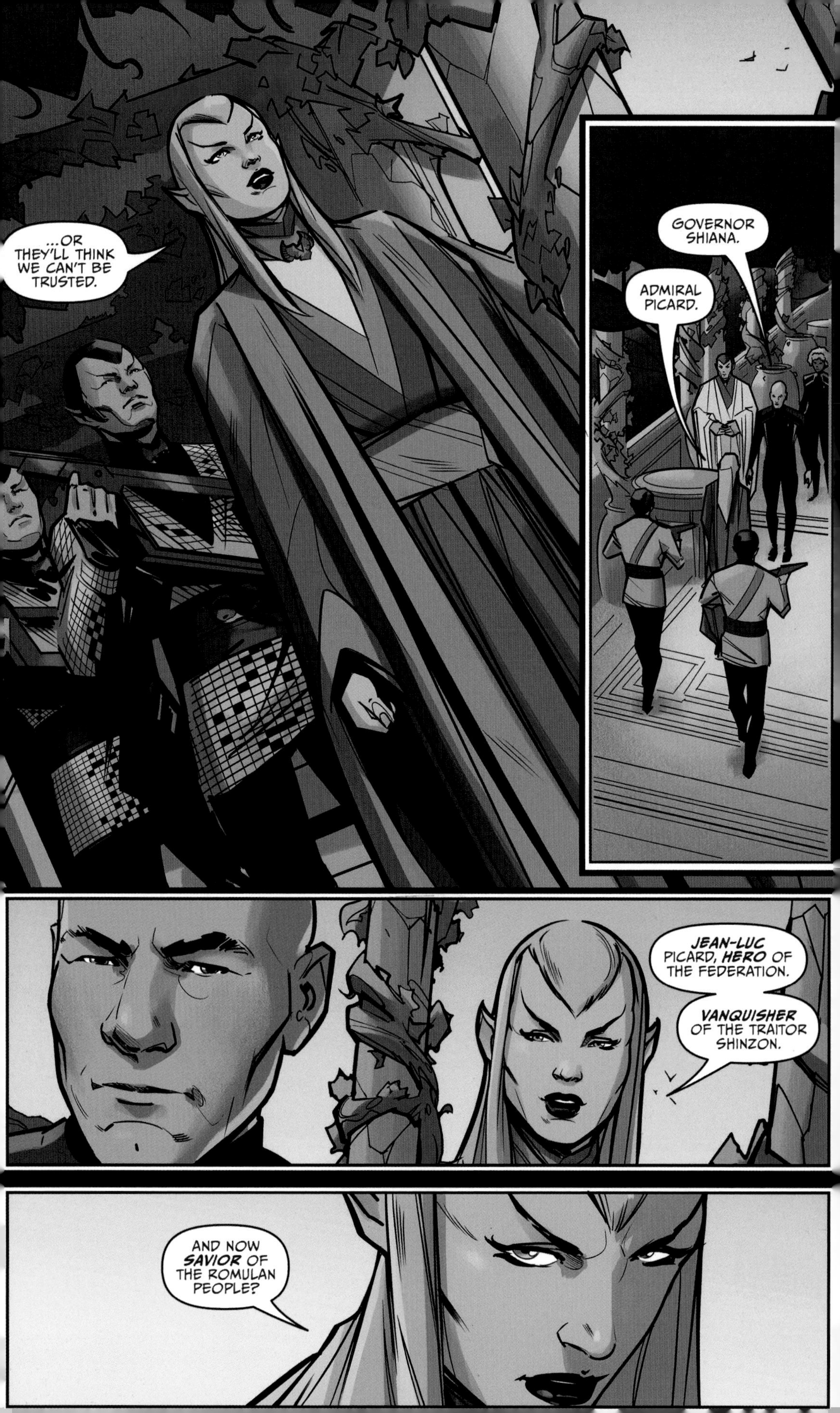

...OR THEY'LL THINK WE CAN'T BE TRUSTED.
GOVERNOR SHIANA.
ADMIRAL PICARD.
JEAN-LUC PICARD, HERO OF THE FEDERATION.
VANQUISHER OF THE TRAITOR SHINZON.
AND NOW SAVIOR OF THE ROMULAN PEOPLE?

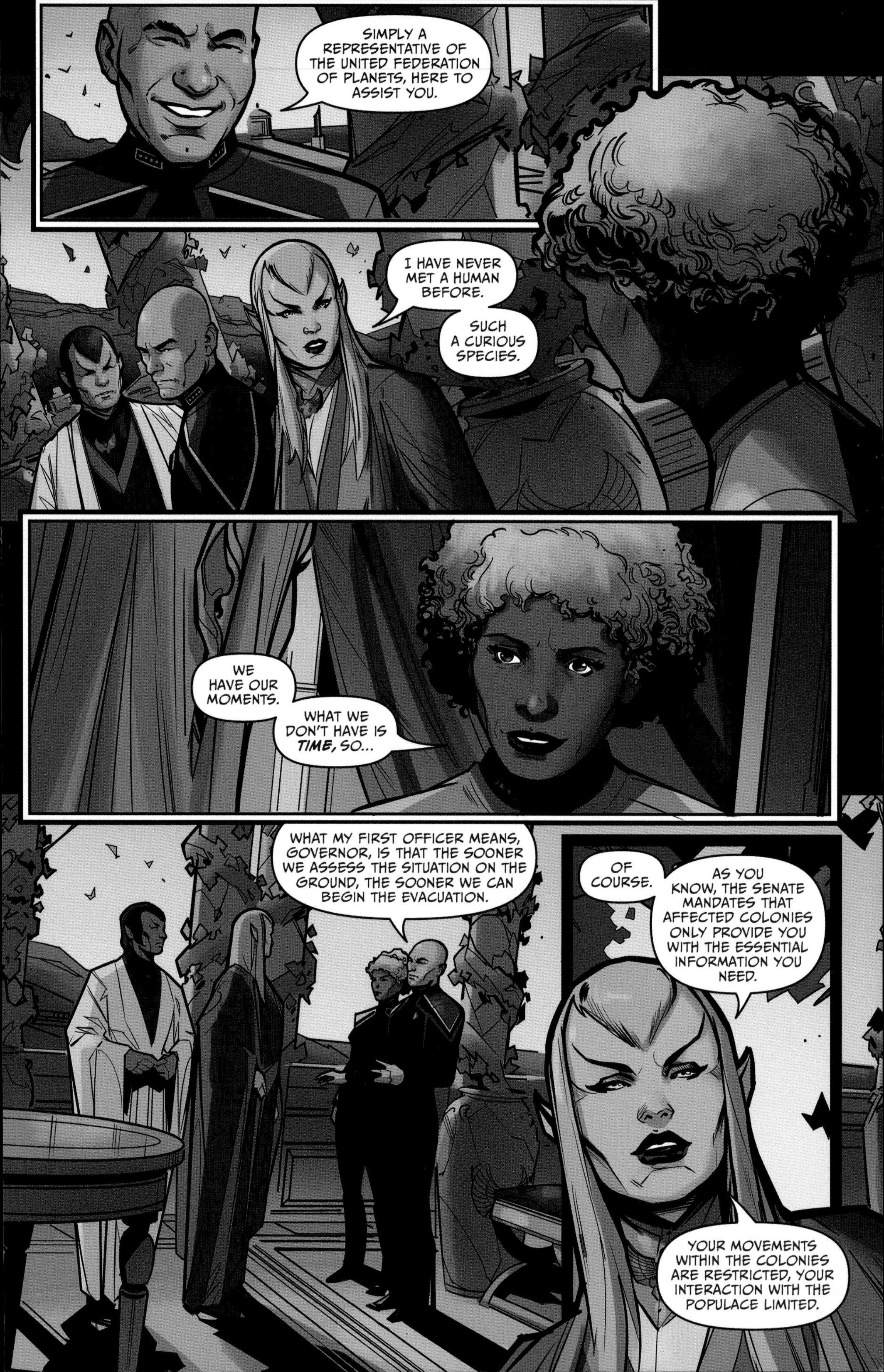
SIMPLY A REPRESENTATIVE OF THE UNITED FEDERATION OF PLANETS, HERE TO ASSIST YOU.
I HAVE NEVER MET A HUMAN BEFORE.
SUCH A CURIOUS SPECIES.
WE HAVE OUR MOMENTS.
WHAT WE DON'T HAVE IS *TIME*, SO...
WHAT MY FIRST OFFICER MEANS, GOVERNOR, IS THAT THE SOONER WE ASSESS THE SITUATION ON THE GROUND, THE SOONER WE CAN BEGIN THE EVACUATION.
OF COURSE.
AS YOU KNOW, THE SENATE MANDATES THAT AFFECTED COLONIES ONLY PROVIDE YOU WITH THE ESSENTIAL INFORMATION YOU NEED.
YOUR MOVEMENTS WITHIN THE COLONIES ARE RESTRICTED, YOUR INTERACTION WITH THE POPULACE LIMITED.

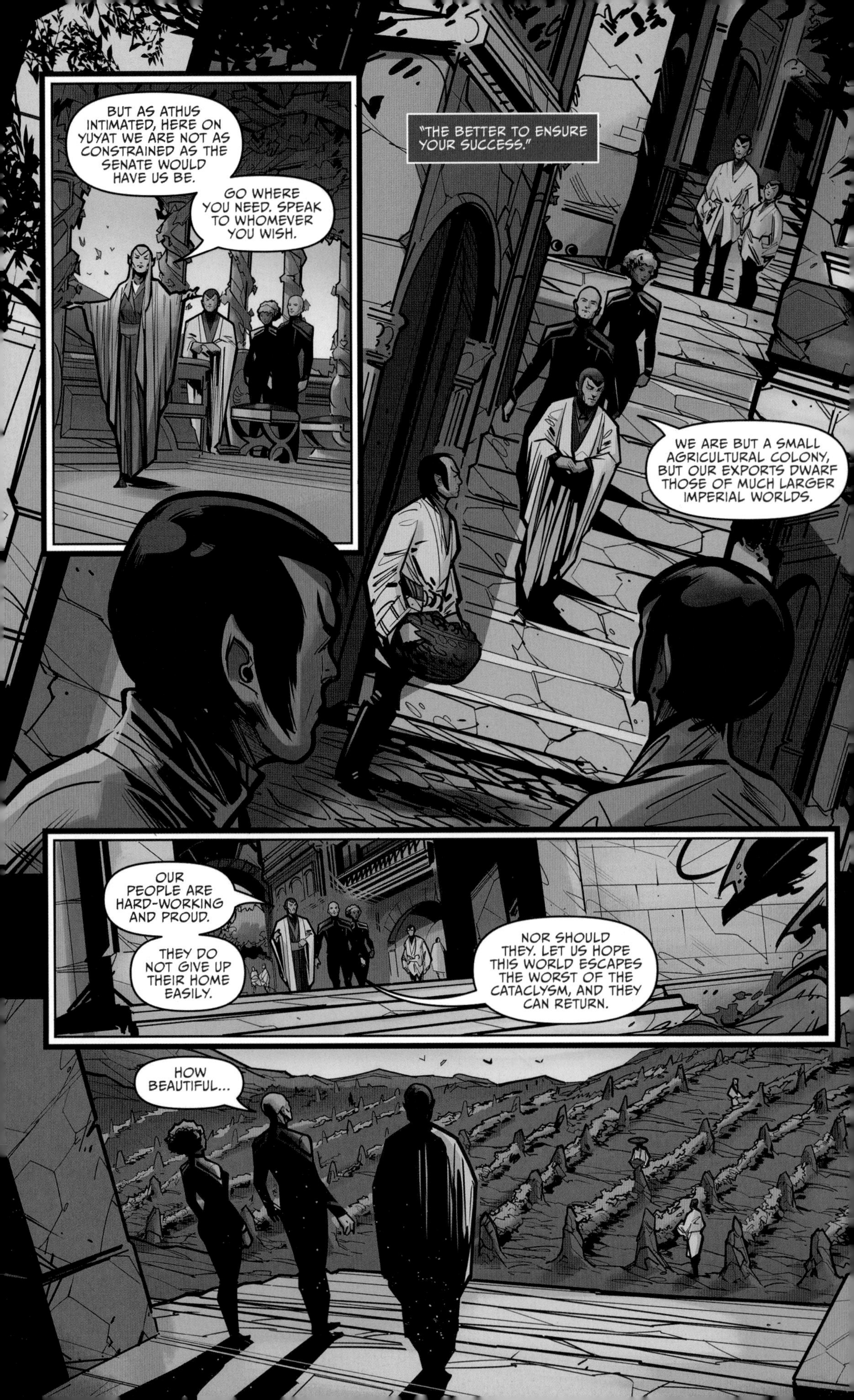
BUT AS ATHUS INTIMATED, HERE ON YUYAT WE ARE NOT AS CONSTRAINED AS THE SENATE WOULD HAVE US BE.
GO WHERE YOU NEED. SPEAK TO WHOMEVER YOU WISH.
"THE BETTER TO ENSURE YOUR SUCCESS."
WE ARE BUT A SMALL AGRICULTURAL COLONY, BUT OUR EXPORTS DWARF THOSE OF MUCH LARGER IMPERIAL WORLDS.
OUR PEOPLE ARE HARD-WORKING AND PROUD.
THEY DO NOT GIVE UP THEIR HOME EASILY.
NOR SHOULD THEY. LET US HOPE THIS WORLD ESCAPES THE WORST OF THE CATACLYSM, AND THEY CAN RETURN.
HOW BEAUTIFUL...

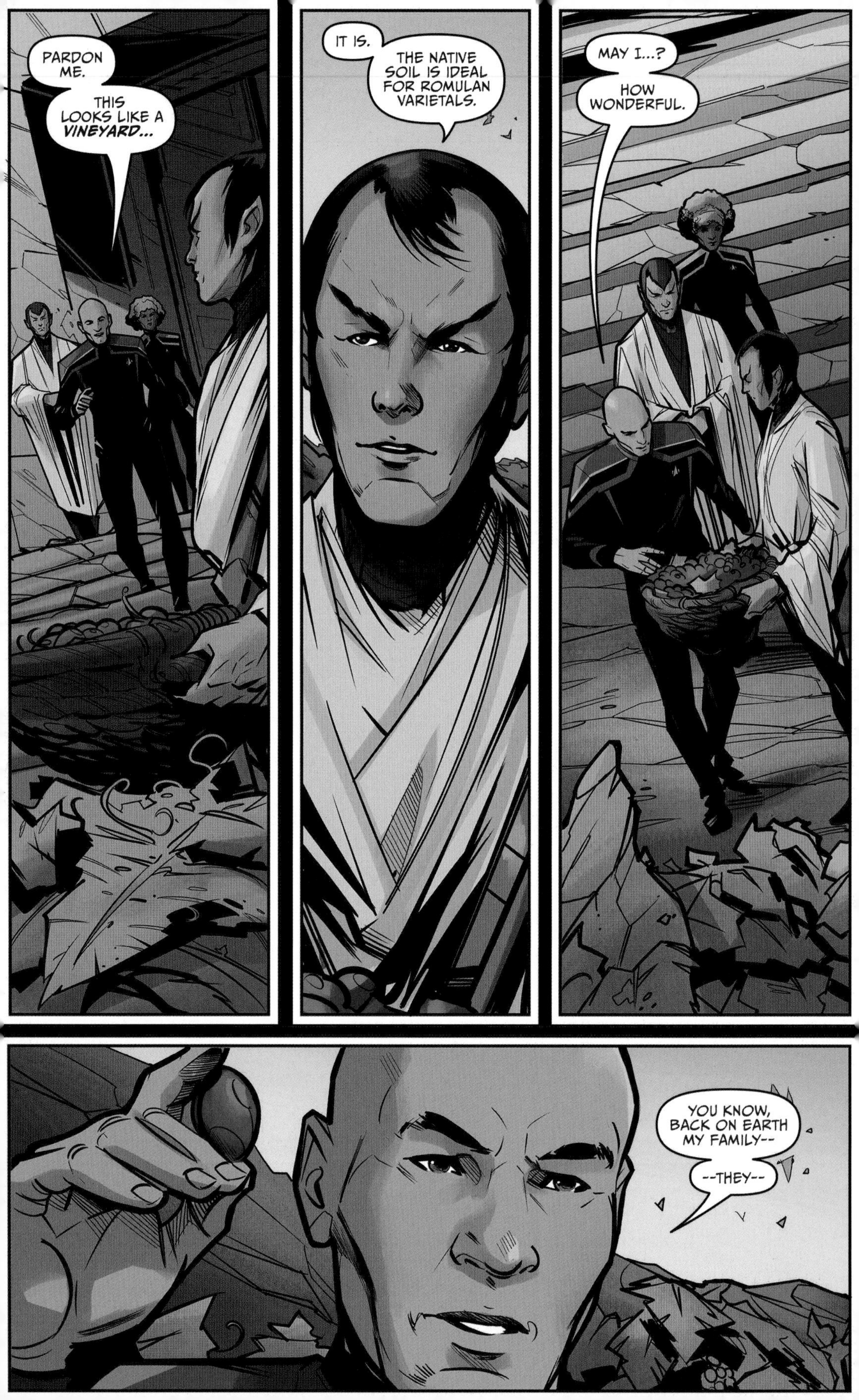
PARDON ME.
THIS LOOKS LIKE A *VINEYARD*...
IT IS.
THE NATIVE SOIL IS IDEAL FOR ROMULAN VARIETALS.
MAY I...?
HOW WONDERFUL.
YOU KNOW, BACK ON EARTH MY FAMILY--
--THEY--

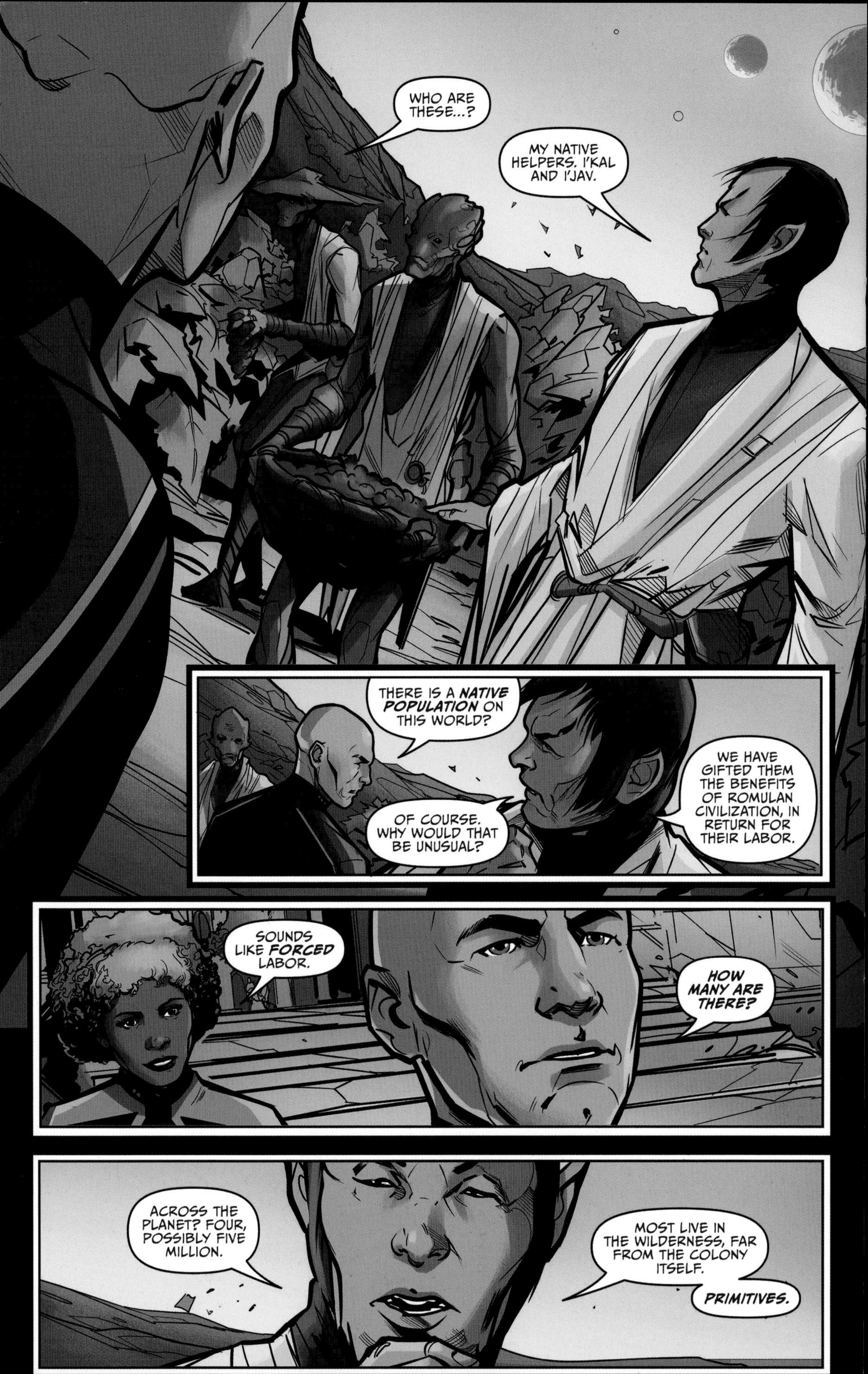
WHO ARE THESE...?
MY NATIVE HELPERS. I'KAL AND I'JAV.
THERE IS A *NATIVE POPULATION* ON THIS WORLD?
OF COURSE. WHY WOULD THAT BE UNUSUAL?
WE HAVE GIFTED THEM THE BENEFITS OF ROMULAN CIVILIZATION, IN RETURN FOR THEIR LABOR.
SOUNDS LIKE *FORCED* LABOR.
HOW MANY ARE THERE?
ACROSS THE PLANET? FOUR, POSSIBLY FIVE MILLION.
MOST LIVE IN THE WILDERNESS, FAR FROM THE COLONY ITSELF.
PRIMITIVES.

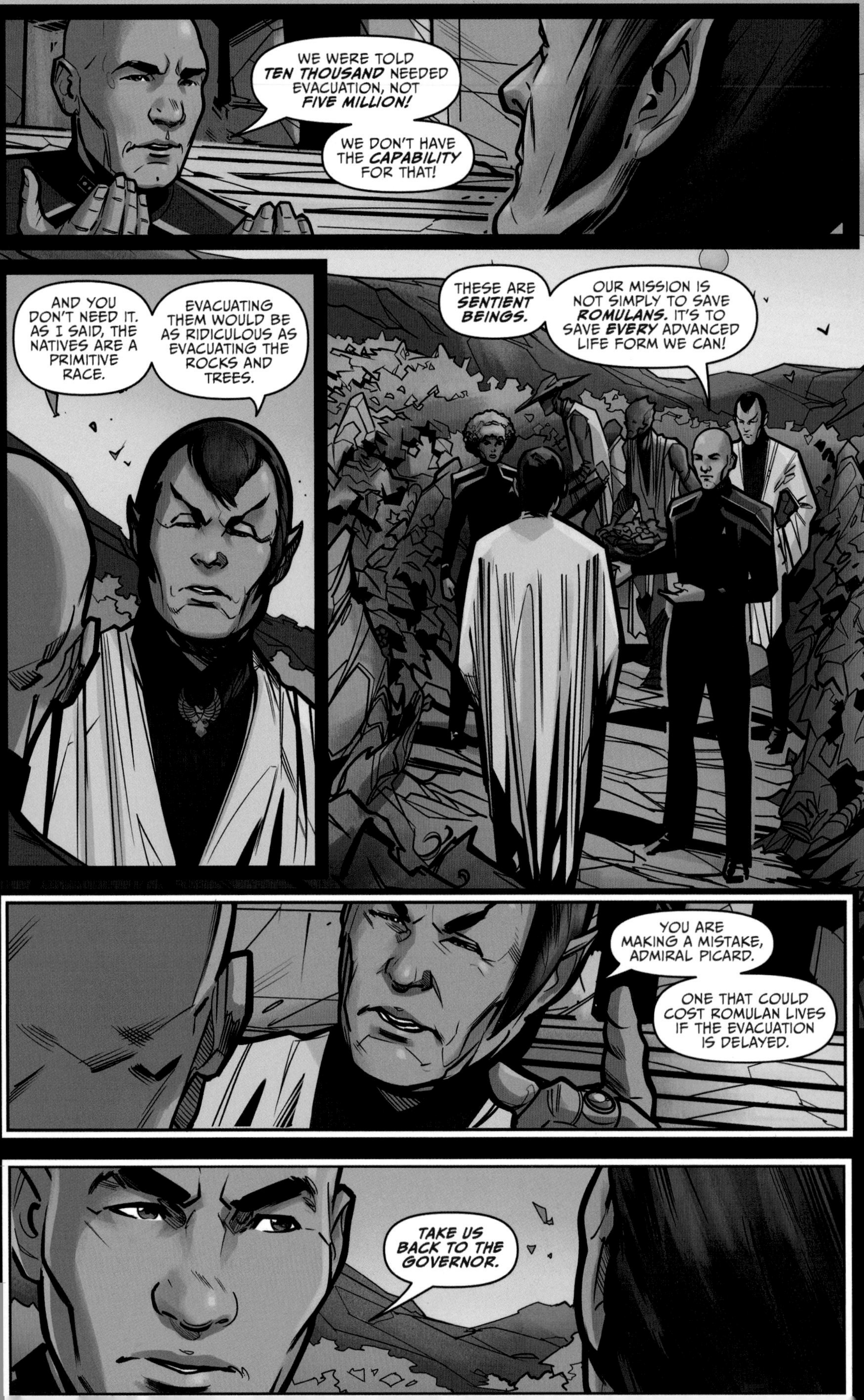
WE WERE TOLD TEN THOUSAND NEEDED EVACUATION, NOT FIVE MILLION!
WE DON'T HAVE THE CAPABILITY FOR THAT!
AND YOU DON'T NEED IT. AS I SAID, THE NATIVES ARE A PRIMITIVE RACE.
EVACUATING THEM WOULD BE AS RIDICULOUS AS EVACUATING THE ROCKS AND TREES.
THESE ARE SENTIENT BEINGS.
OUR MISSION IS NOT SIMPLY TO SAVE ROMULANS. IT'S TO SAVE EVERY ADVANCED LIFE FORM WE CAN!
YOU ARE MAKING A MISTAKE, ADMIRAL PICARD.
ONE THAT COULD COST ROMULAN LIVES IF THE EVACUATION IS DELAYED.
TAKE US BACK TO THE GOVERNOR.

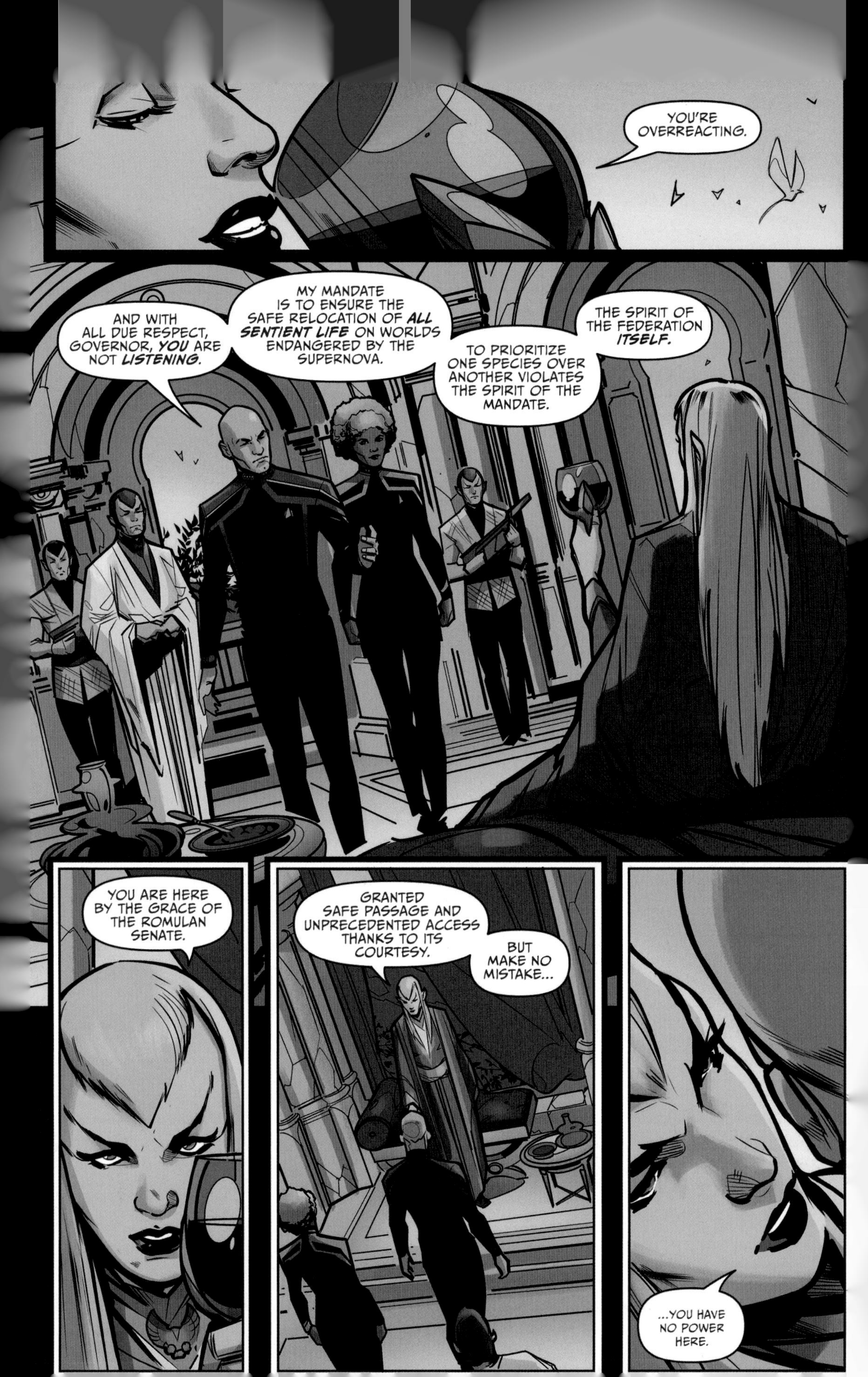
YOU'RE OVERREACTING.
AND WITH ALL DUE RESPECT, GOVERNOR, *YOU* ARE NOT *LISTENING*.
MY MANDATE IS TO ENSURE THE SAFE RELOCATION OF *ALL SENTIENT LIFE* ON WORLDS ENDANGERED BY THE SUPERNOVA.
TO PRIORITIZE ONE SPECIES OVER ANOTHER VIOLATES THE SPIRIT OF THE MANDATE.
THE SPIRIT OF THE FEDERATION *ITSELF*.
YOU ARE HERE BY THE GRACE OF THE ROMULAN SENATE.
GRANTED SAFE PASSAGE AND UNPRECEDENTED ACCESS THANKS TO ITS COURTESY.
BUT MAKE NO MISTAKE...
...YOU HAVE NO POWER HERE.

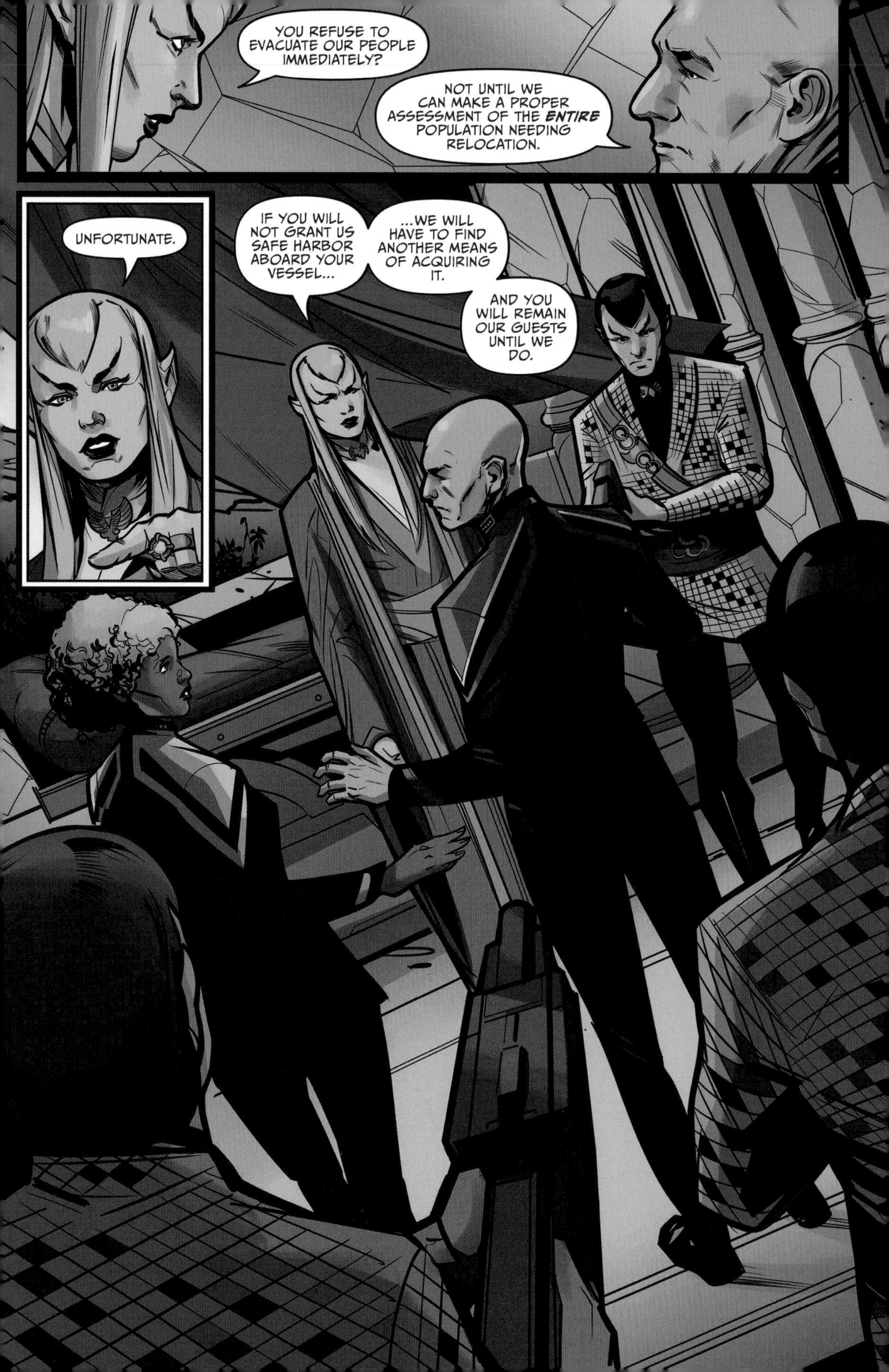
YOU REFUSE TO EVACUATE OUR PEOPLE IMMEDIATELY?
NOT UNTIL WE CAN MAKE A PROPER ASSESSMENT OF THE *ENTIRE* POPULATION NEEDING RELOCATION.
UNFORTUNATE.
IF YOU WILL NOT GRANT US SAFE HARBOR ABOARD YOUR VESSEL...
...WE WILL HAVE TO FIND ANOTHER MEANS OF ACQUIRING IT.
AND YOU WILL REMAIN OUR GUESTS UNTIL WE DO.

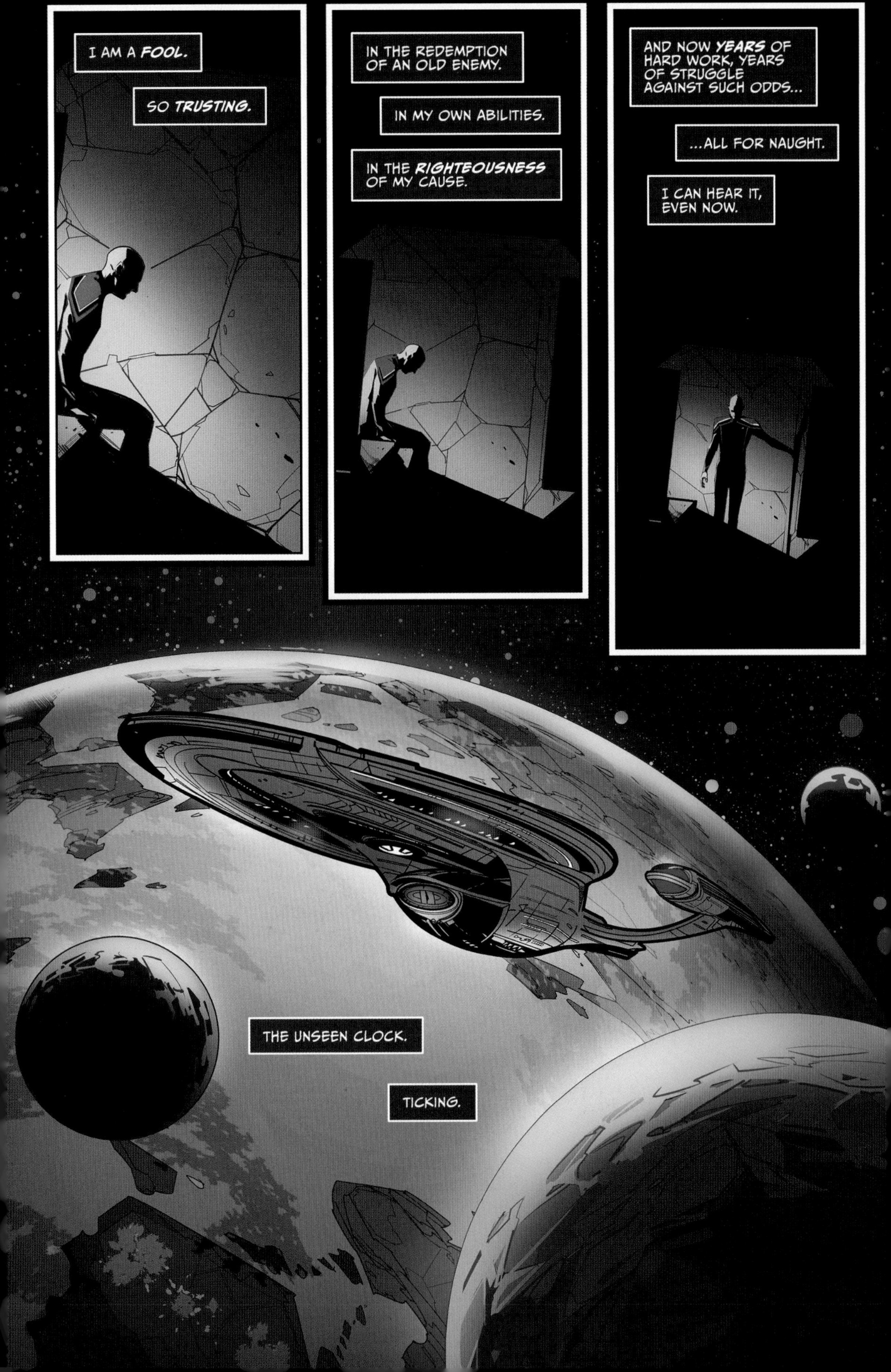
I AM A FOOL.
SO TRUSTING.
IN THE REDEMPTION OF AN OLD ENEMY.
IN MY OWN ABILITIES.
IN THE RIGHTEOUSNESS OF MY CAUSE.
AND NOW YEARS OF HARD WORK, YEARS OF STRUGGLE AGAINST SUCH ODDS...
...ALL FOR NAUGHT.
I CAN HEAR IT, EVEN NOW.
THE UNSEEN CLOCK.
TICKING.

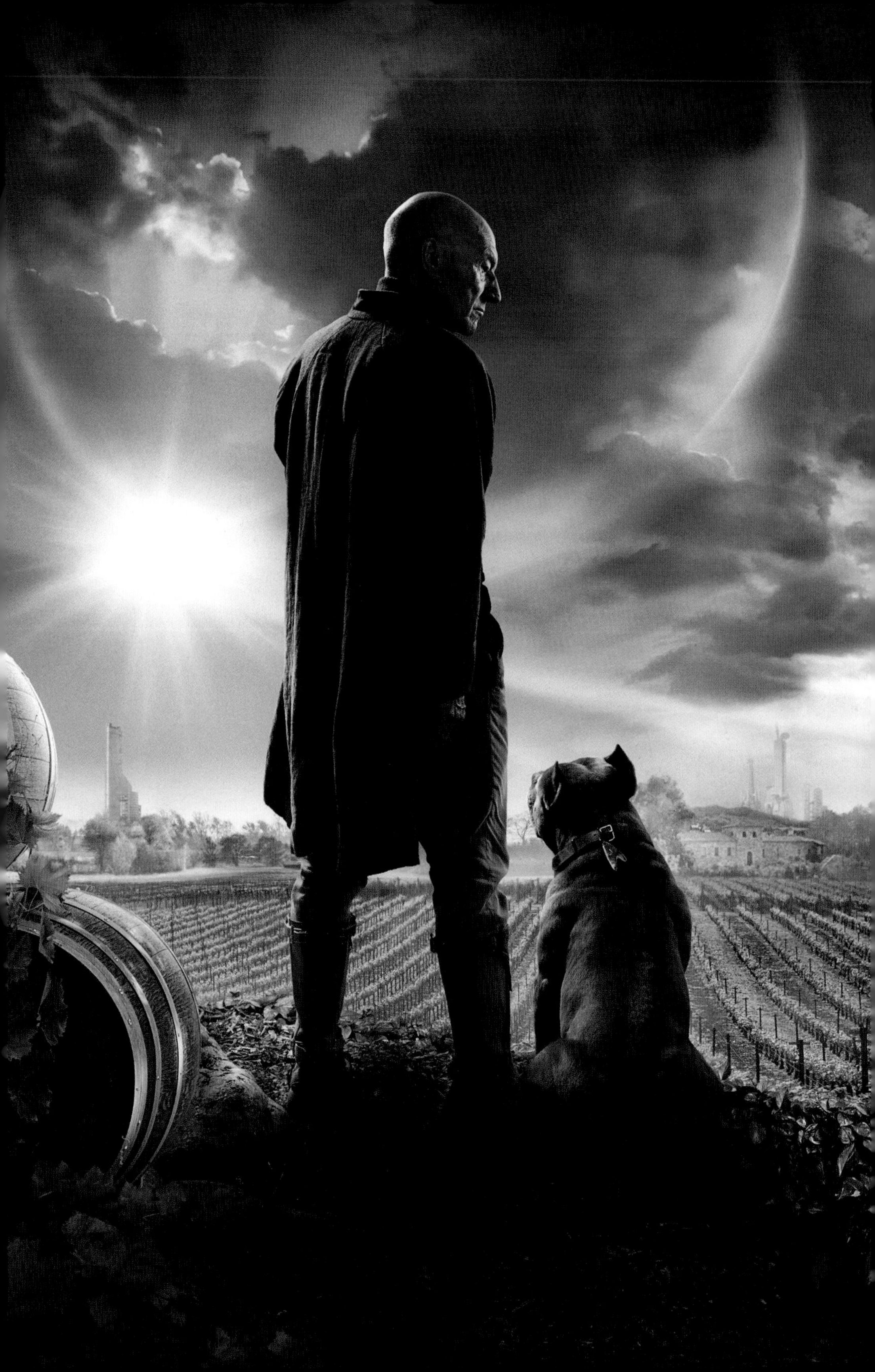

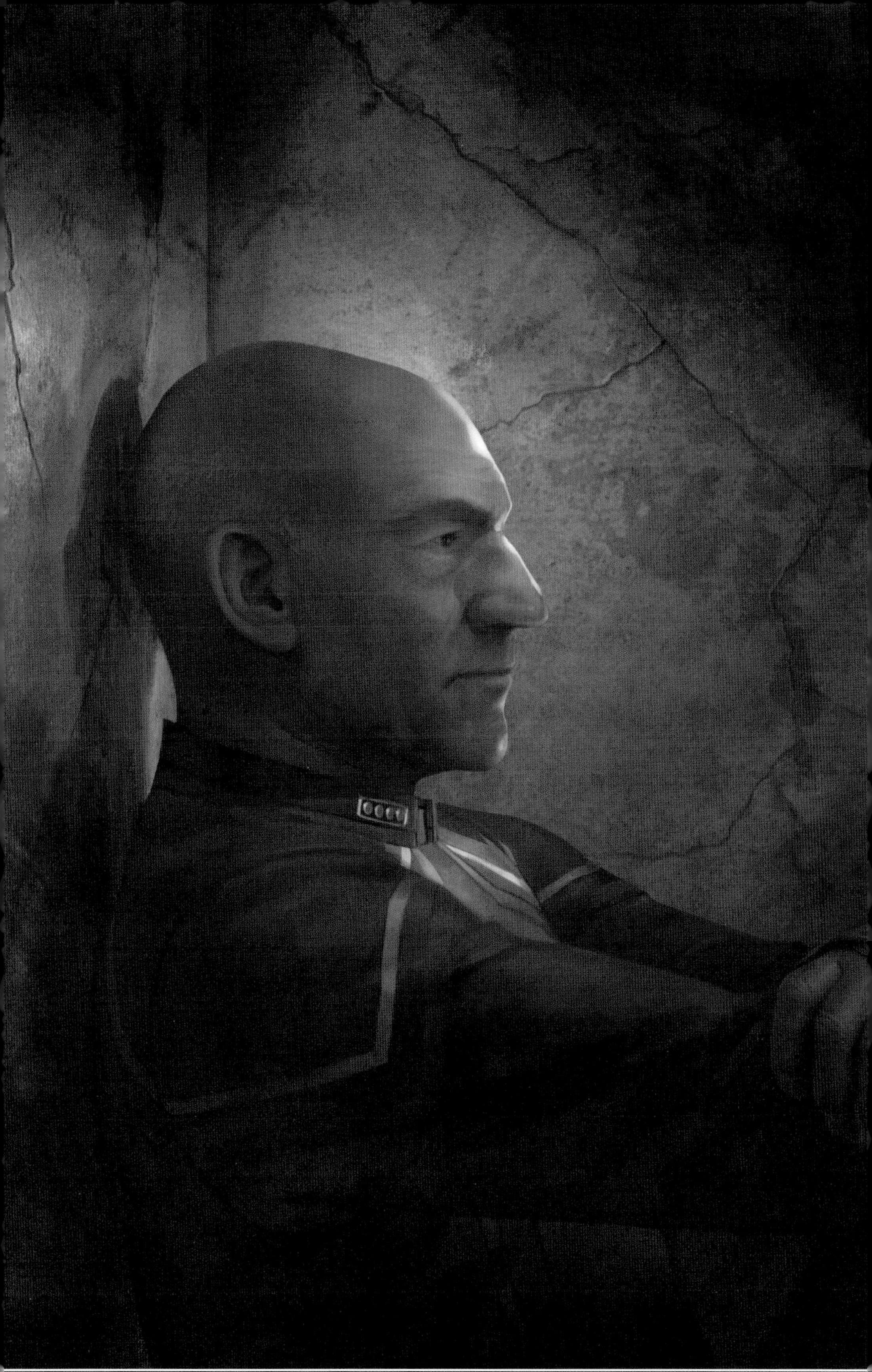

art by SARA PITRE-DUROCHER

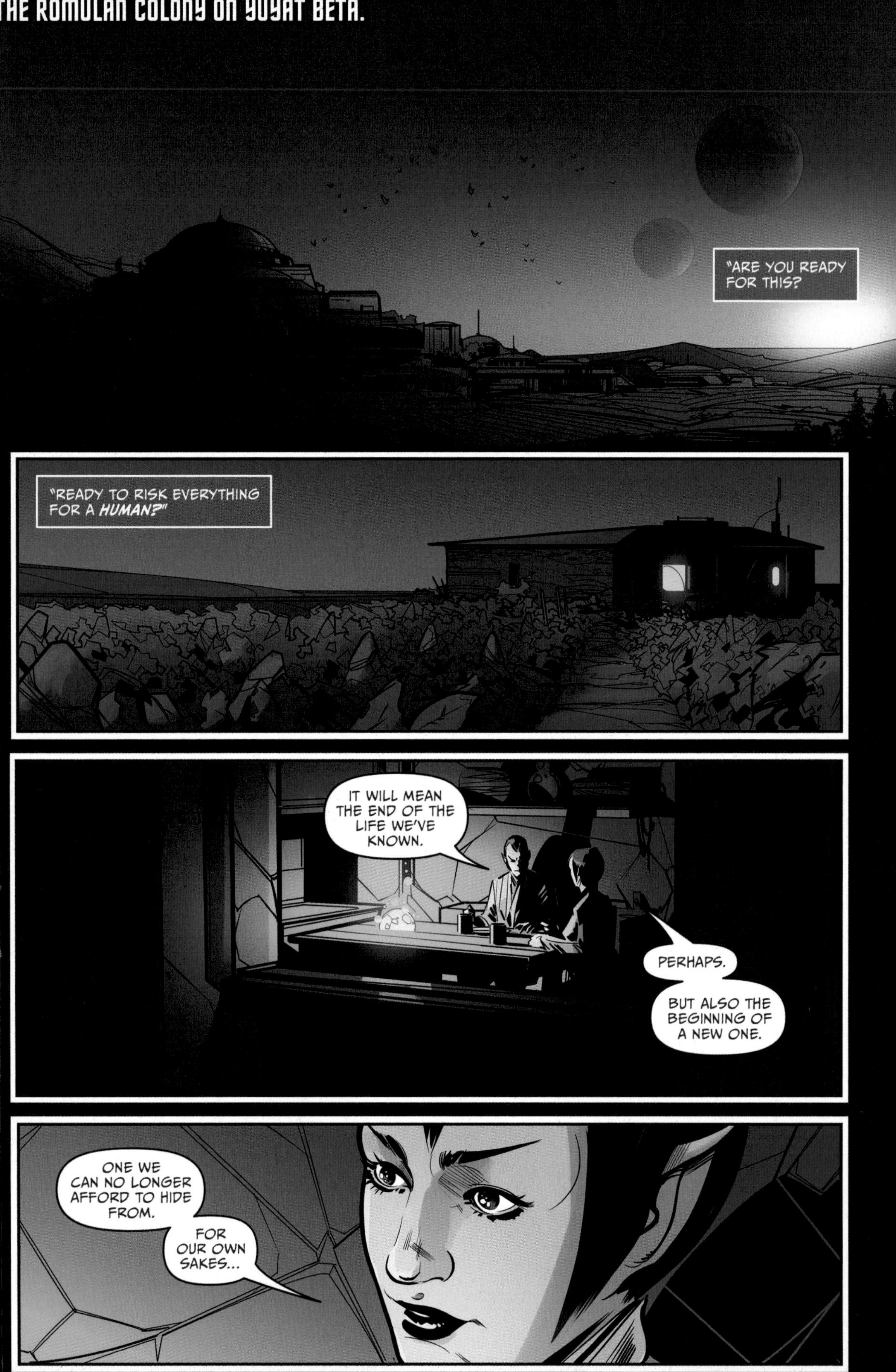
THE ROMULAN COLONY ON YUYAT BETA.
"ARE YOU READY FOR THIS?
"READY TO RISK EVERYTHING FOR A *HUMAN?*"
IT WILL MEAN THE END OF THE LIFE WE'VE KNOWN.
PERHAPS.
BUT ALSO THE BEGINNING OF A NEW ONE.
ONE WE CAN NO LONGER AFFORD TO HIDE FROM.
FOR OUR OWN SAKES...

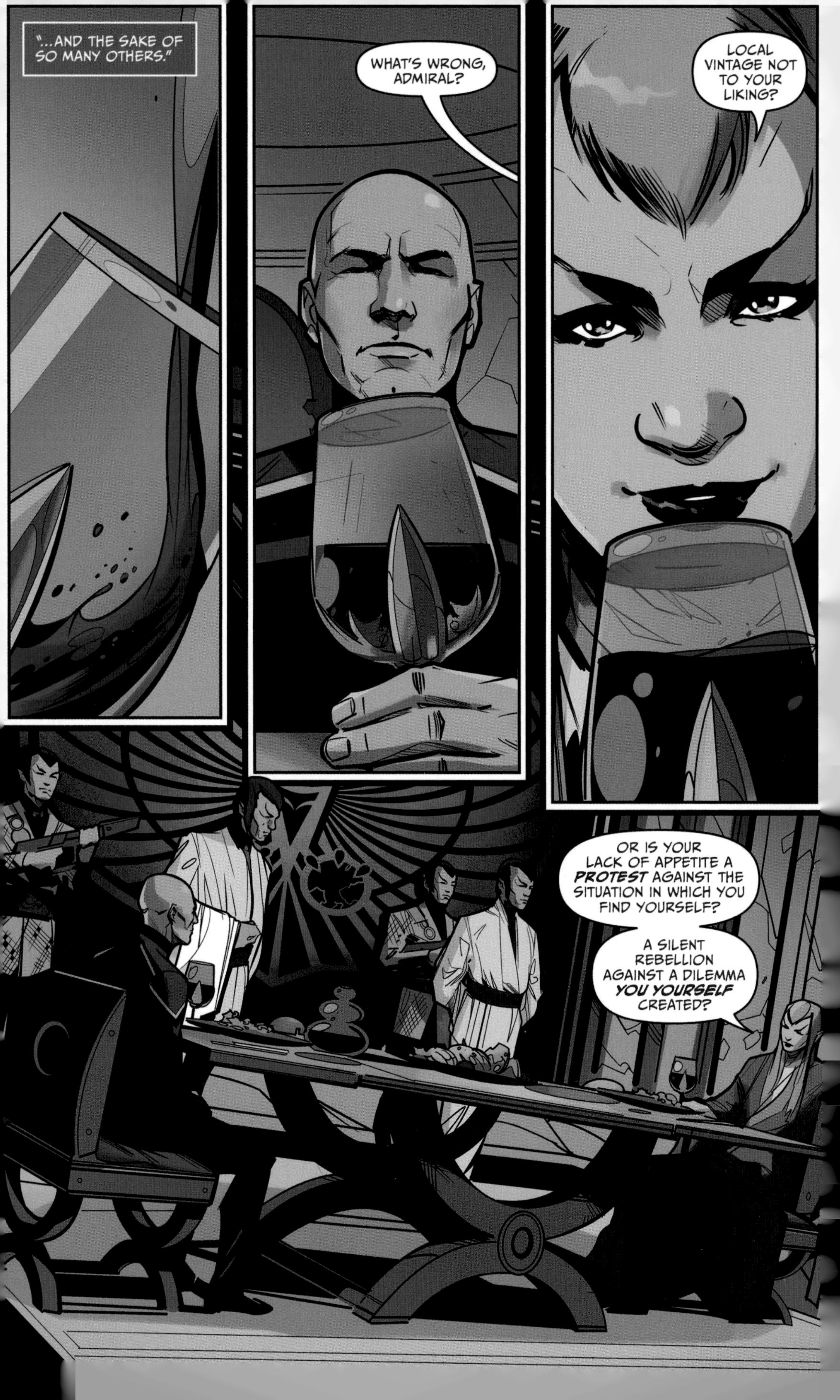
"...AND THE SAKE OF SO MANY OTHERS."
WHAT'S WRONG, ADMIRAL?
LOCAL VINTAGE NOT TO YOUR LIKING?
OR IS YOUR LACK OF APPETITE A **PROTEST** AGAINST THE SITUATION IN WHICH YOU FIND YOURSELF?
A SILENT REBELLION AGAINST A DILEMMA ***YOU YOURSELF*** CREATED?

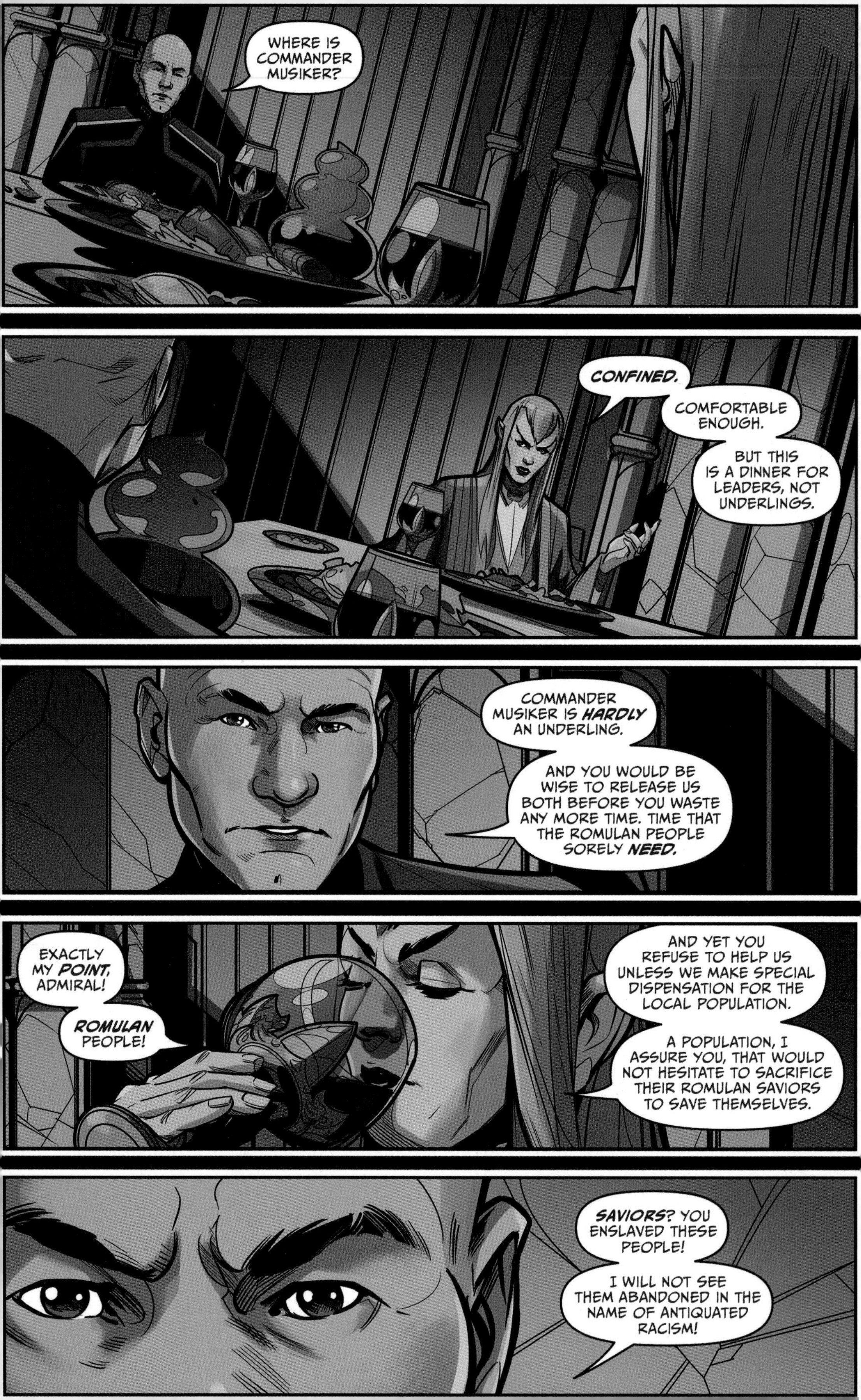
WHERE IS COMMANDER MUSIKER?
CONFINED.
COMFORTABLE ENOUGH.
BUT THIS IS A DINNER FOR LEADERS, NOT UNDERLINGS.
COMMANDER MUSIKER IS HARDLY AN UNDERLING.
AND YOU WOULD BE WISE TO RELEASE US BOTH BEFORE YOU WASTE ANY MORE TIME. TIME THAT THE ROMULAN PEOPLE SORELY NEED.
EXACTLY MY POINT, ADMIRAL!
ROMULAN PEOPLE!
AND YET YOU REFUSE TO HELP US UNLESS WE MAKE SPECIAL DISPENSATION FOR THE LOCAL POPULATION.
A POPULATION, I ASSURE YOU, THAT WOULD NOT HESITATE TO SACRIFICE THEIR ROMULAN SAVIORS TO SAVE THEMSELVES.
SAVIORS? YOU ENSLAVED THESE PEOPLE!
I WILL NOT SEE THEM ABANDONED IN THE NAME OF ANTIQUATED RACISM!

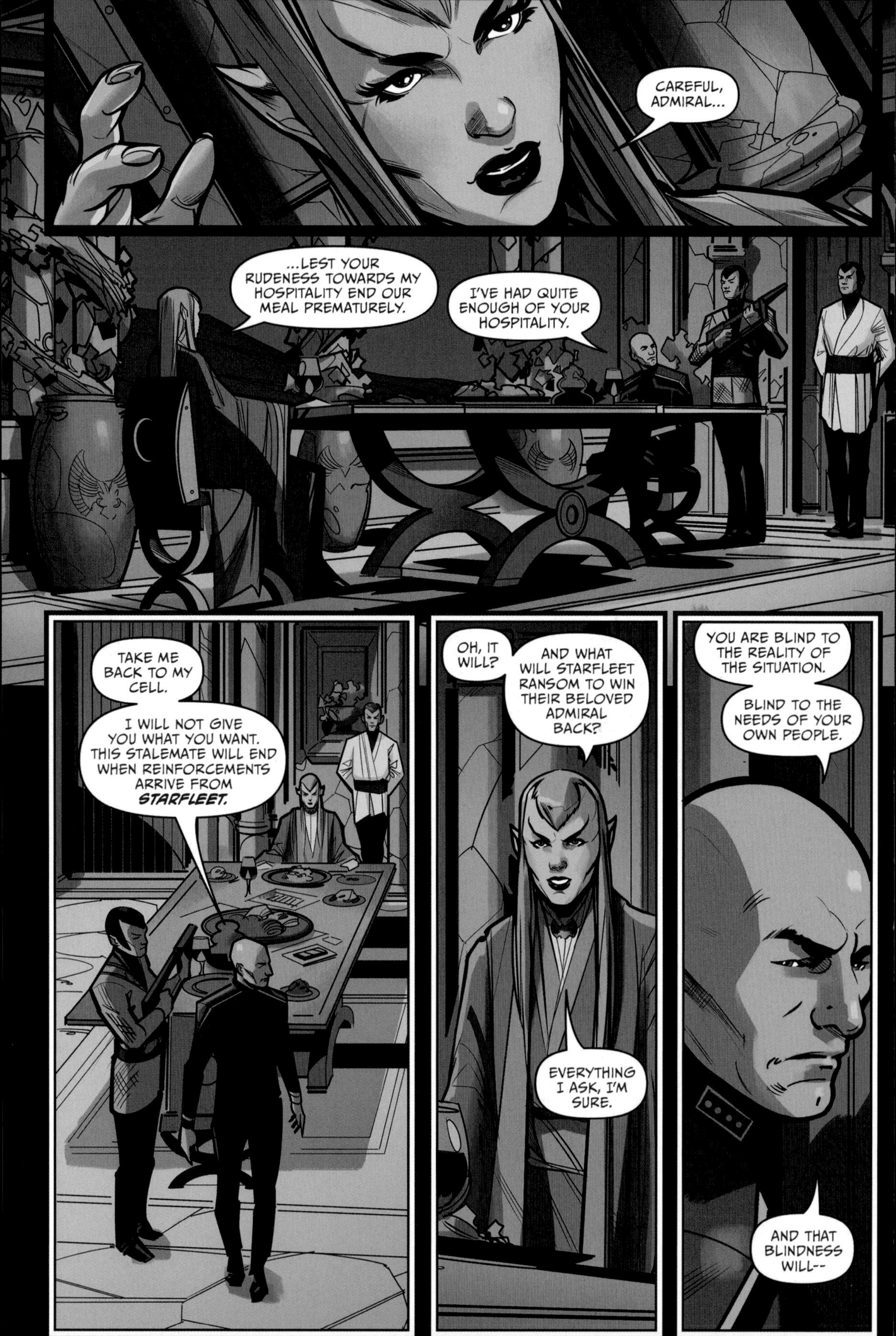
CAREFUL, ADMIRAL...
...LEST YOUR RUDENESS TOWARDS MY HOSPITALITY END OUR MEAL PREMATURELY.
I'VE HAD QUITE ENOUGH OF YOUR HOSPITALITY.
TAKE ME BACK TO MY CELL.
I WILL NOT GIVE YOU WHAT YOU WANT. THIS STALEMATE WILL END WHEN REINFORCEMENTS ARRIVE FROM *STARFLEET.*
OH, IT WILL?
AND WHAT WILL STARFLEET RANSOM TO WIN THEIR BELOVED ADMIRAL BACK?
EVERYTHING I ASK, I'M SURE.
YOU ARE BLIND TO THE REALITY OF THE SITUATION.
BLIND TO THE NEEDS OF YOUR OWN PEOPLE.
AND THAT BLINDNESS WILL--

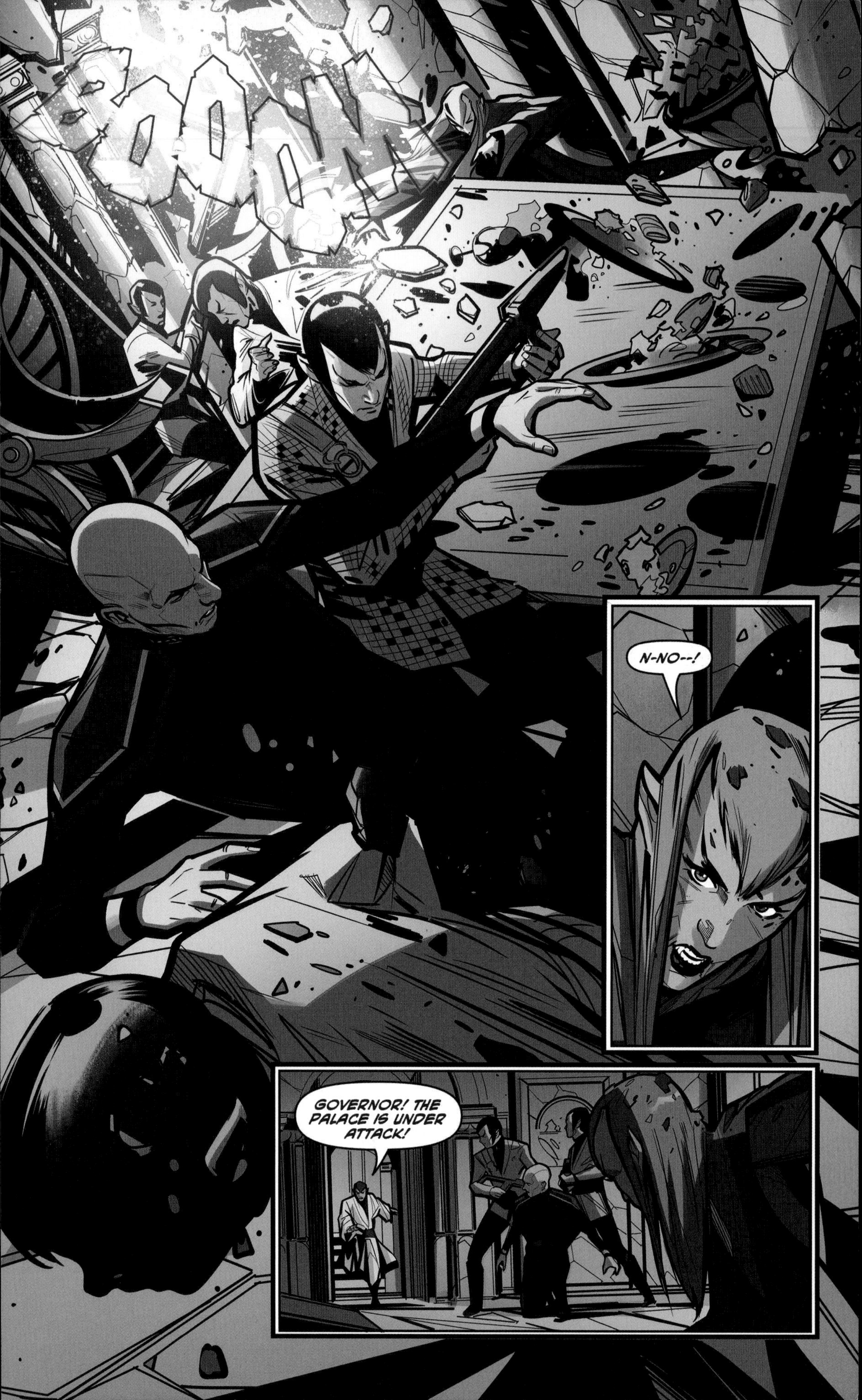
BOOM
N-NO--!
GOVERNOR! THE PALACE IS UNDER ATTACK!

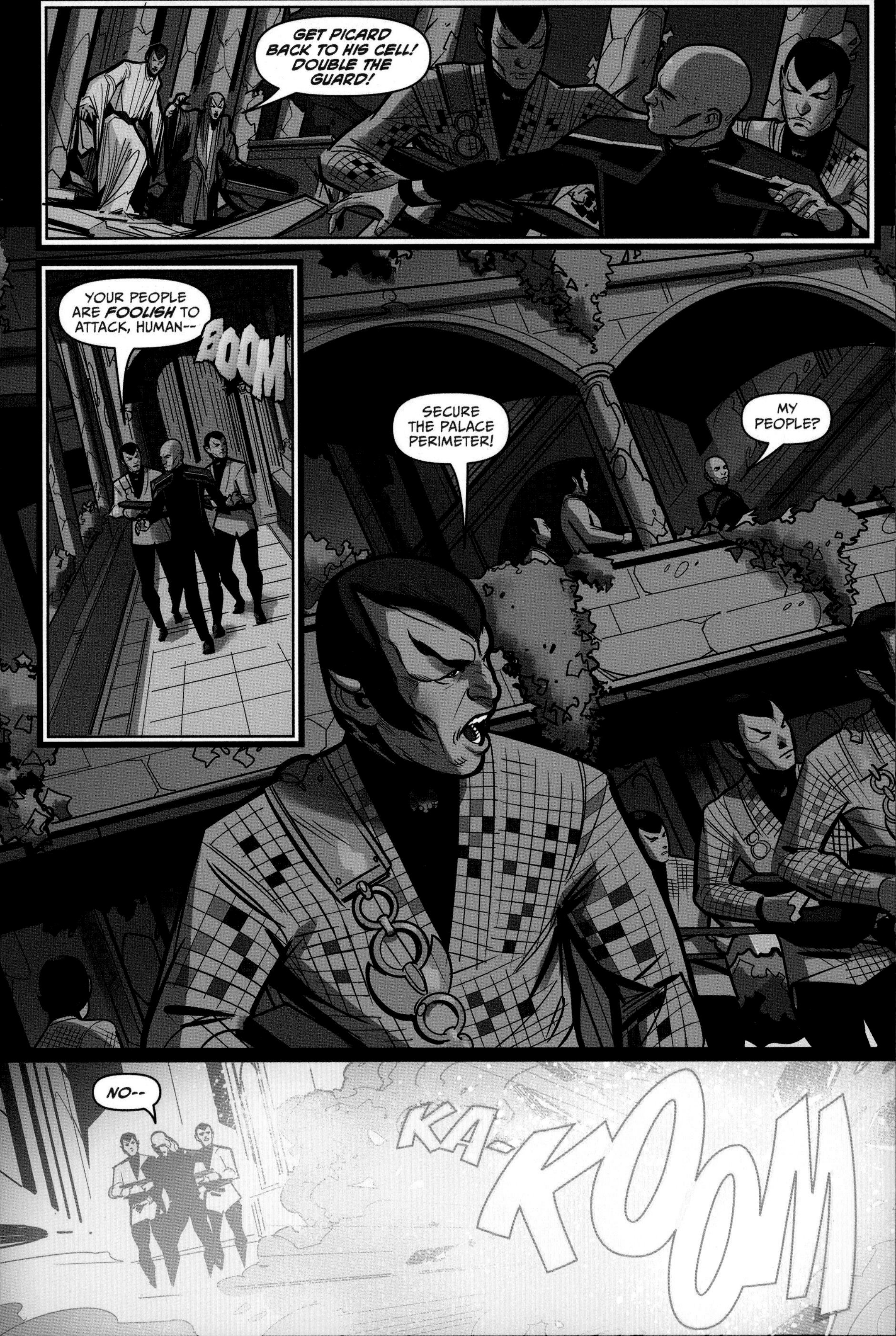
GET PICARD BACK TO HIS CELL! DOUBLE THE GUARD!
YOUR PEOPLE ARE FOOLISH TO ATTACK, HUMAN--
BOOM
SECURE THE PALACE PERIMETER!
MY PEOPLE?
NO--
KA-KOOOM

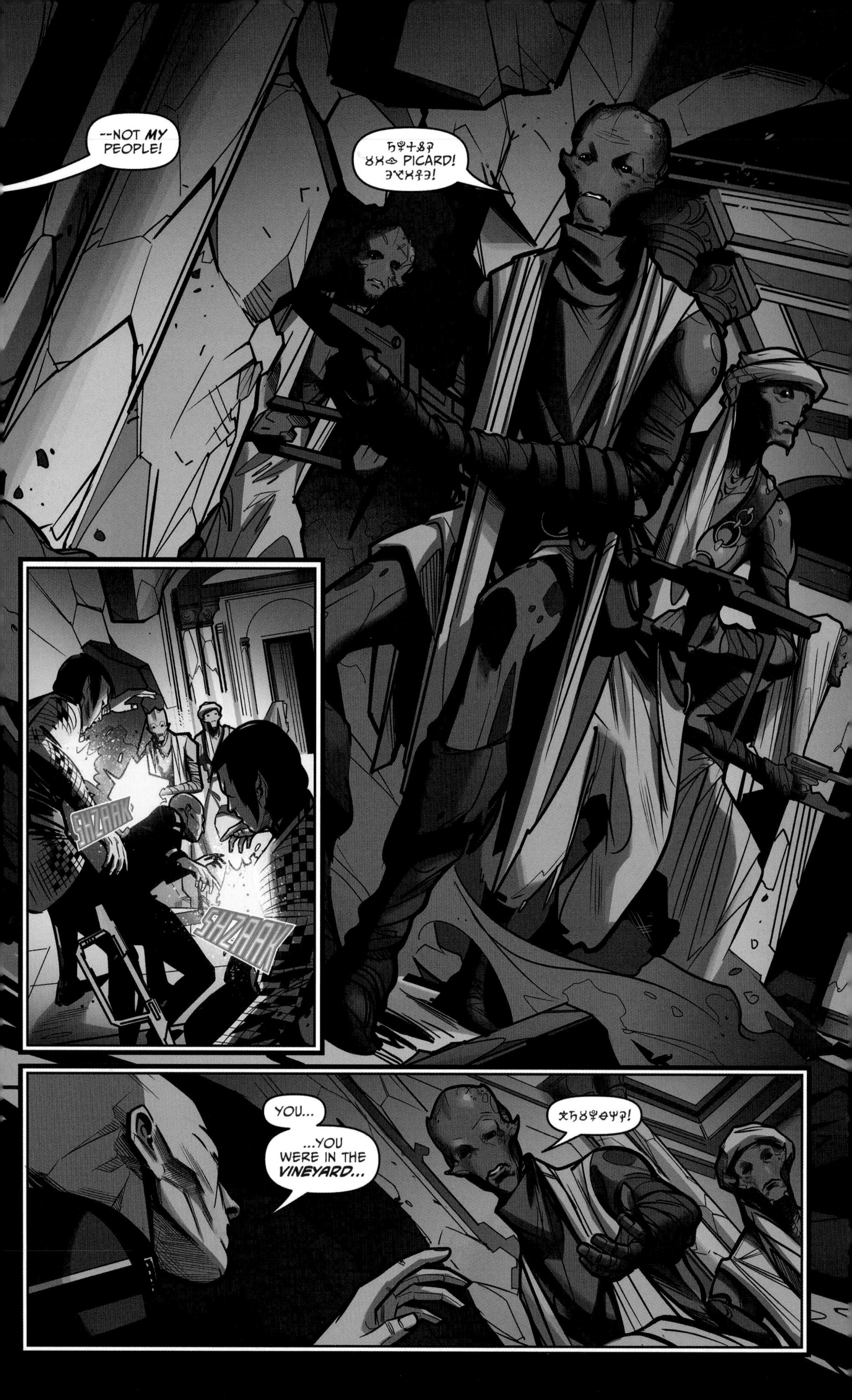
--NOT MY PEOPLE!
PICARD!
SHZAAK
SHZAAK
YOU...
...YOU WERE IN THE VINEYARD...

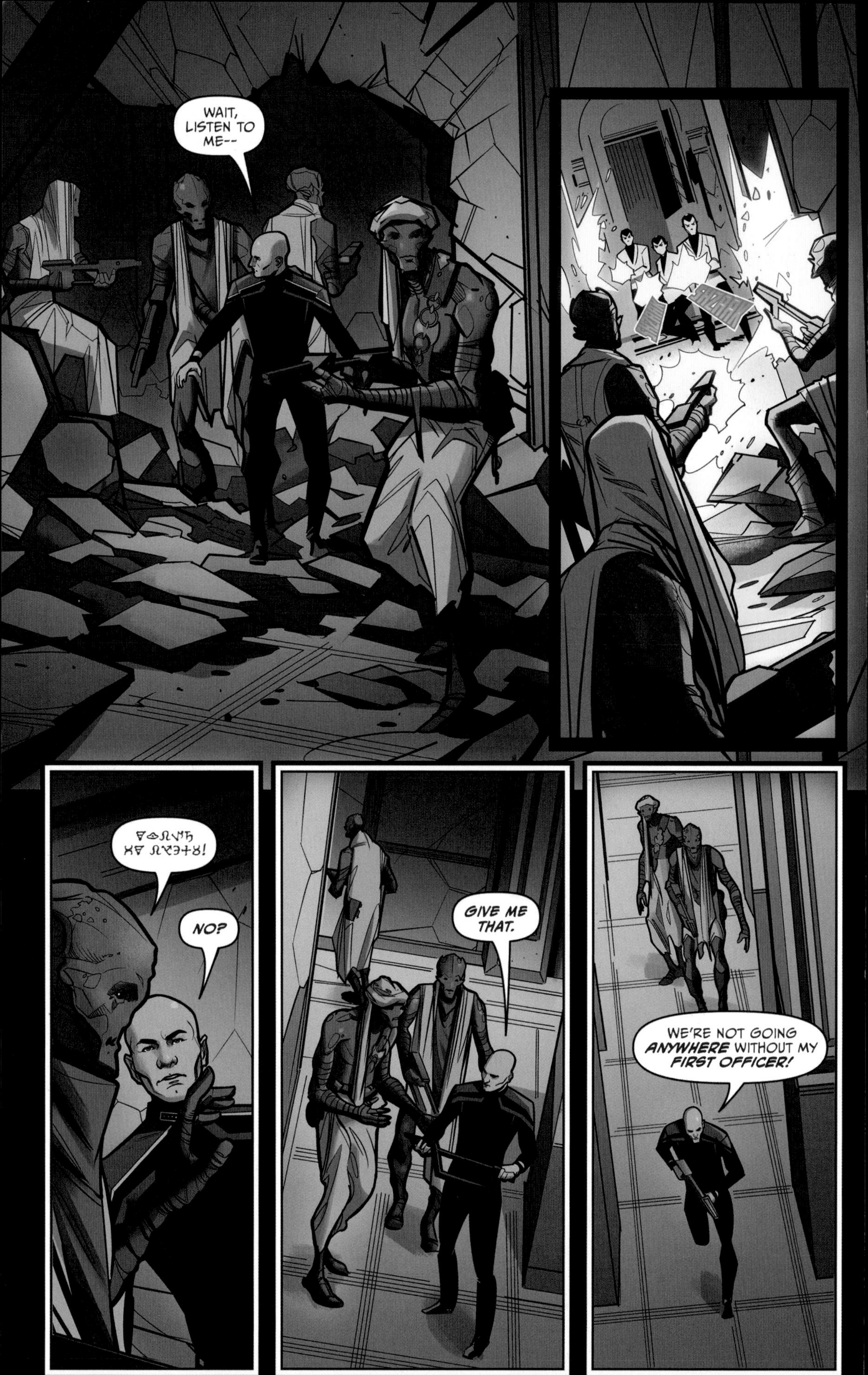
WAIT, LISTEN TO ME--
NO?
GIVE ME THAT.
WE'RE NOT GOING ANYWHERE WITHOUT MY FIRST OFFICER!

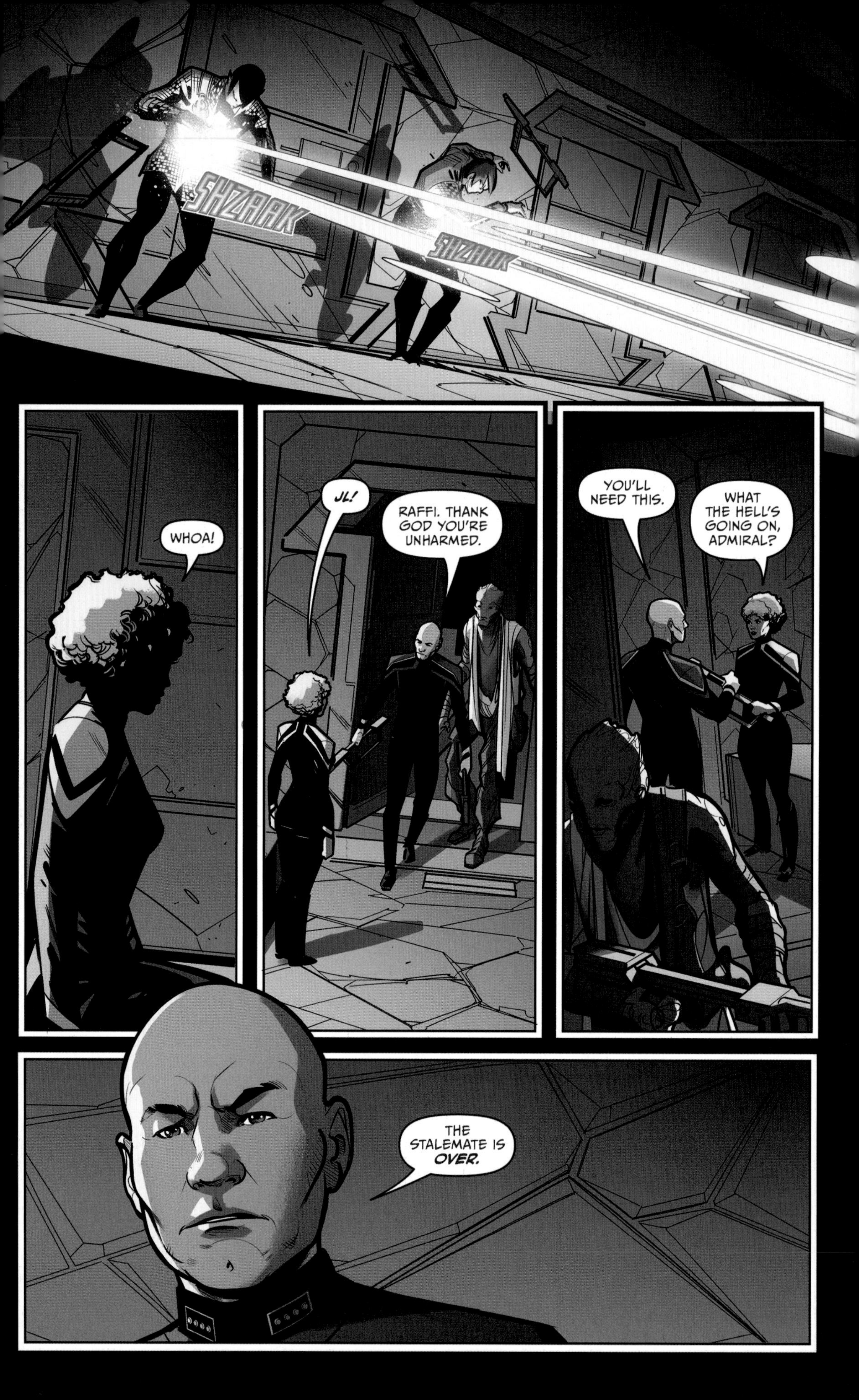
SHZAAK
SHZAAK
WHOA!
JL!
RAFFI. THANK GOD YOU'RE UNHARMED.
YOU'LL NEED THIS.
WHAT THE HELL'S GOING ON, ADMIRAL?
THE STALEMATE IS *OVER.*

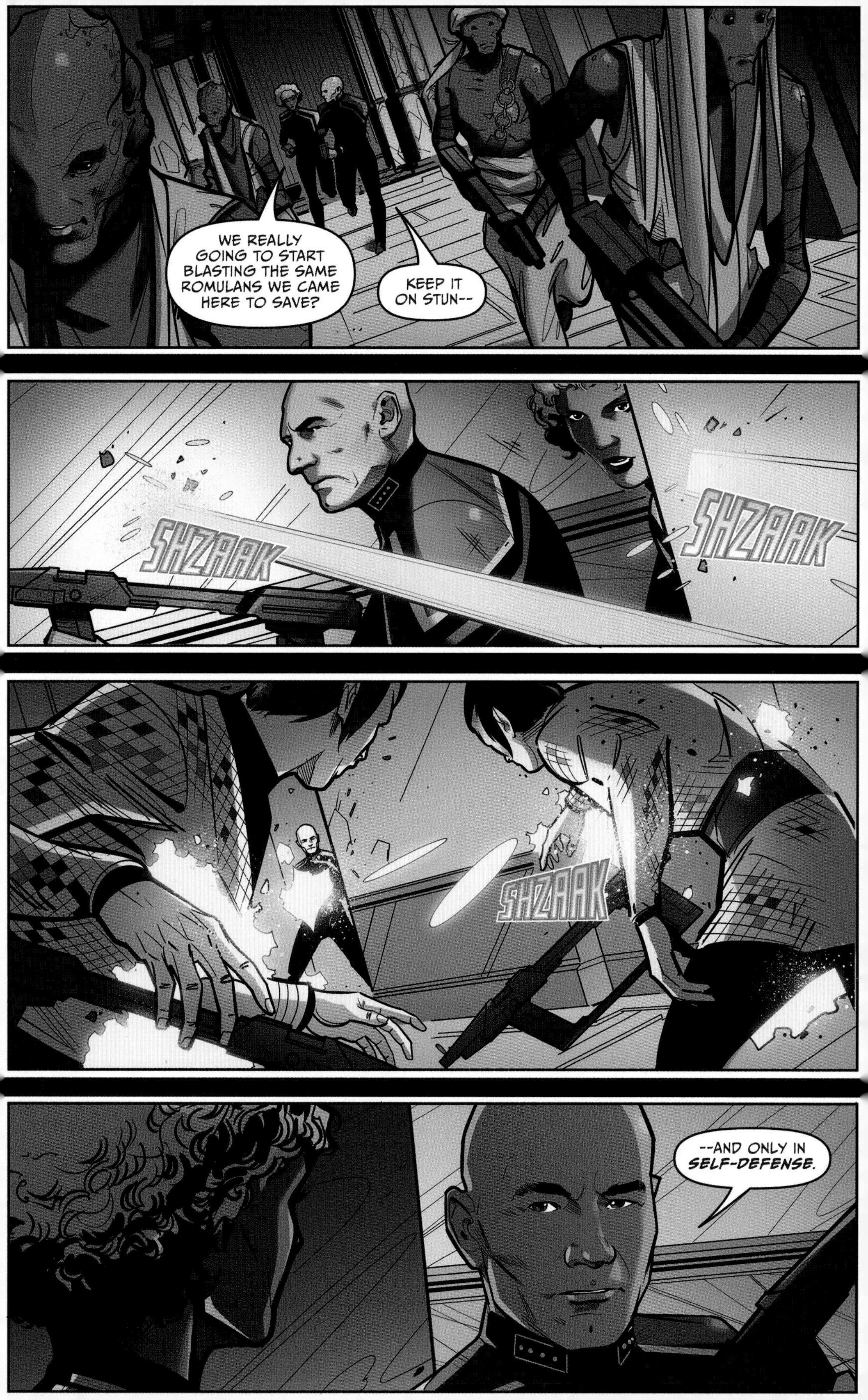
WE REALLY GOING TO START BLASTING THE SAME ROMULANS WE CAME HERE TO SAVE?
KEEP IT ON STUN--
SHZAAK
SHZAAK
SHZAAK
--AND ONLY IN *SELF-DEFENSE*.

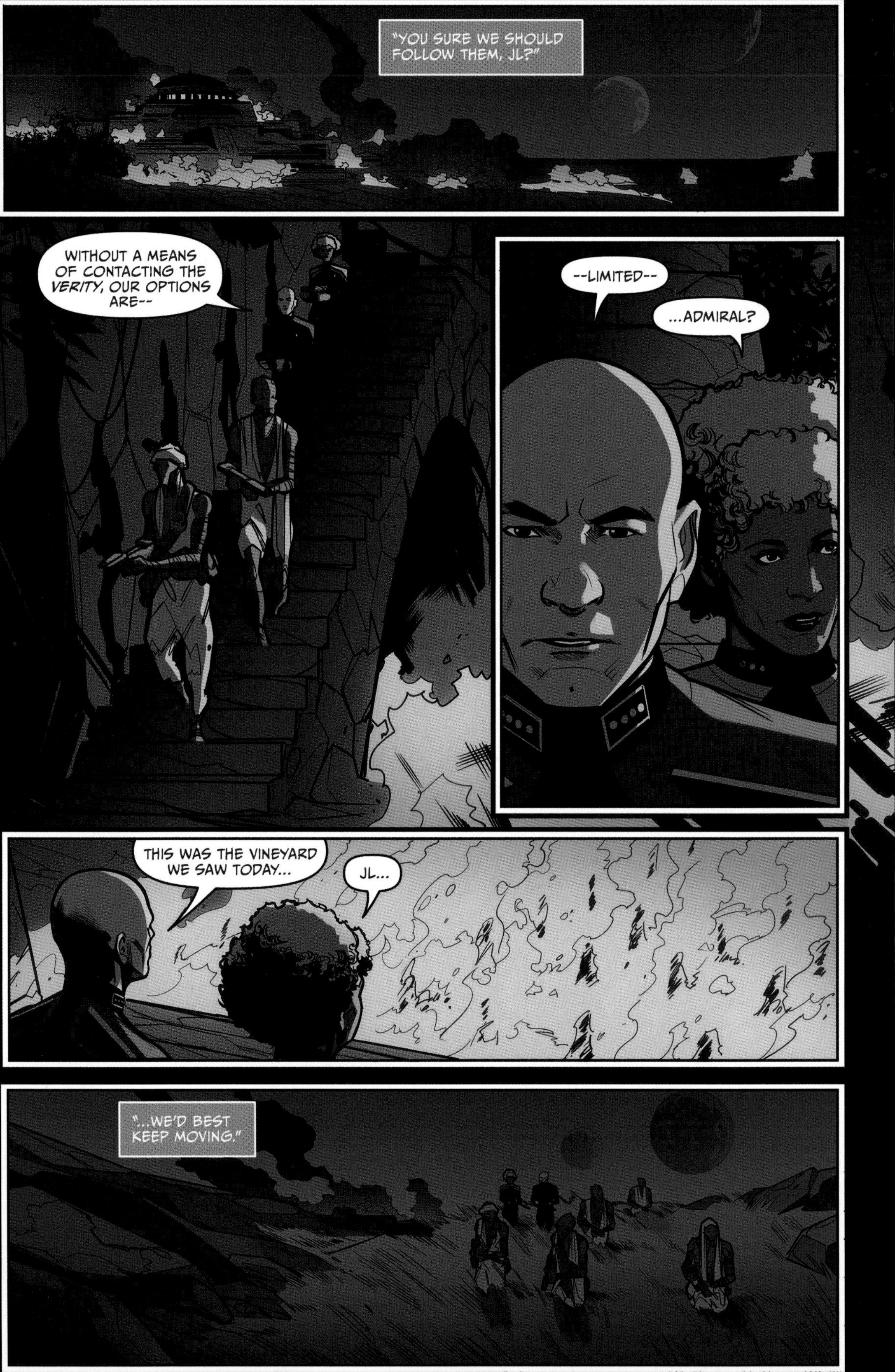
"YOU SURE WE SHOULD FOLLOW THEM, JL?"
WITHOUT A MEANS OF CONTACTING THE *VERITY*, OUR OPTIONS ARE--
--LIMITED--
...ADMIRAL?
THIS WAS THE VINEYARD WE SAW TODAY...
JL...
"...WE'D BEST KEEP MOVING."

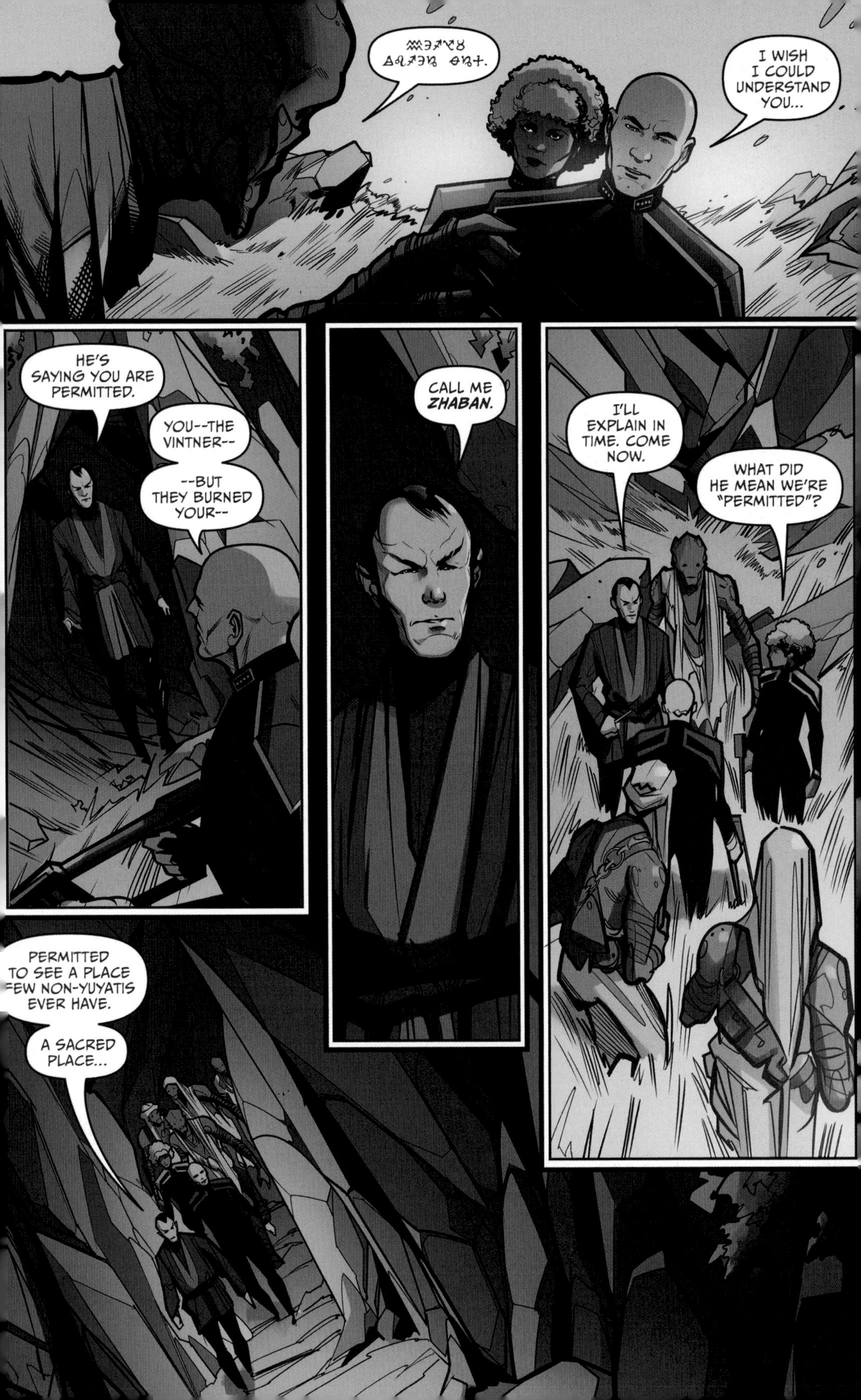
I WISH I COULD UNDERSTAND YOU...
HE'S SAYING YOU ARE PERMITTED.
YOU--THE VINTNER--
--BUT THEY BURNED YOUR--
CALL ME ZHABAN.
I'LL EXPLAIN IN TIME. COME NOW.
WHAT DID HE MEAN WE'RE "PERMITTED"?
PERMITTED TO SEE A PLACE FEW NON-YUYATIS EVER HAVE.
A SACRED PLACE...

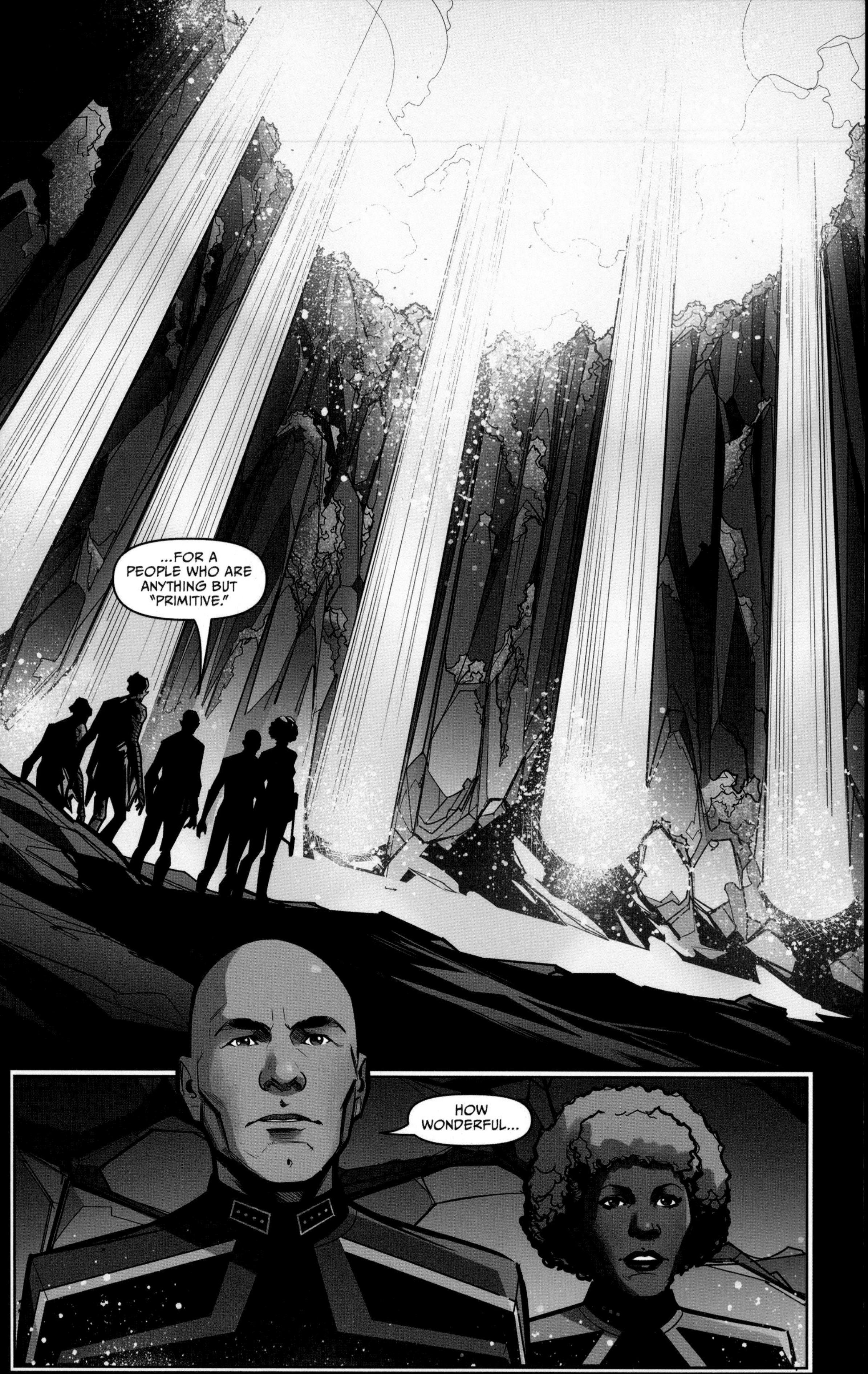
...FOR A PEOPLE WHO ARE ANYTHING BUT "PRIMITIVE."
HOW WONDERFUL...

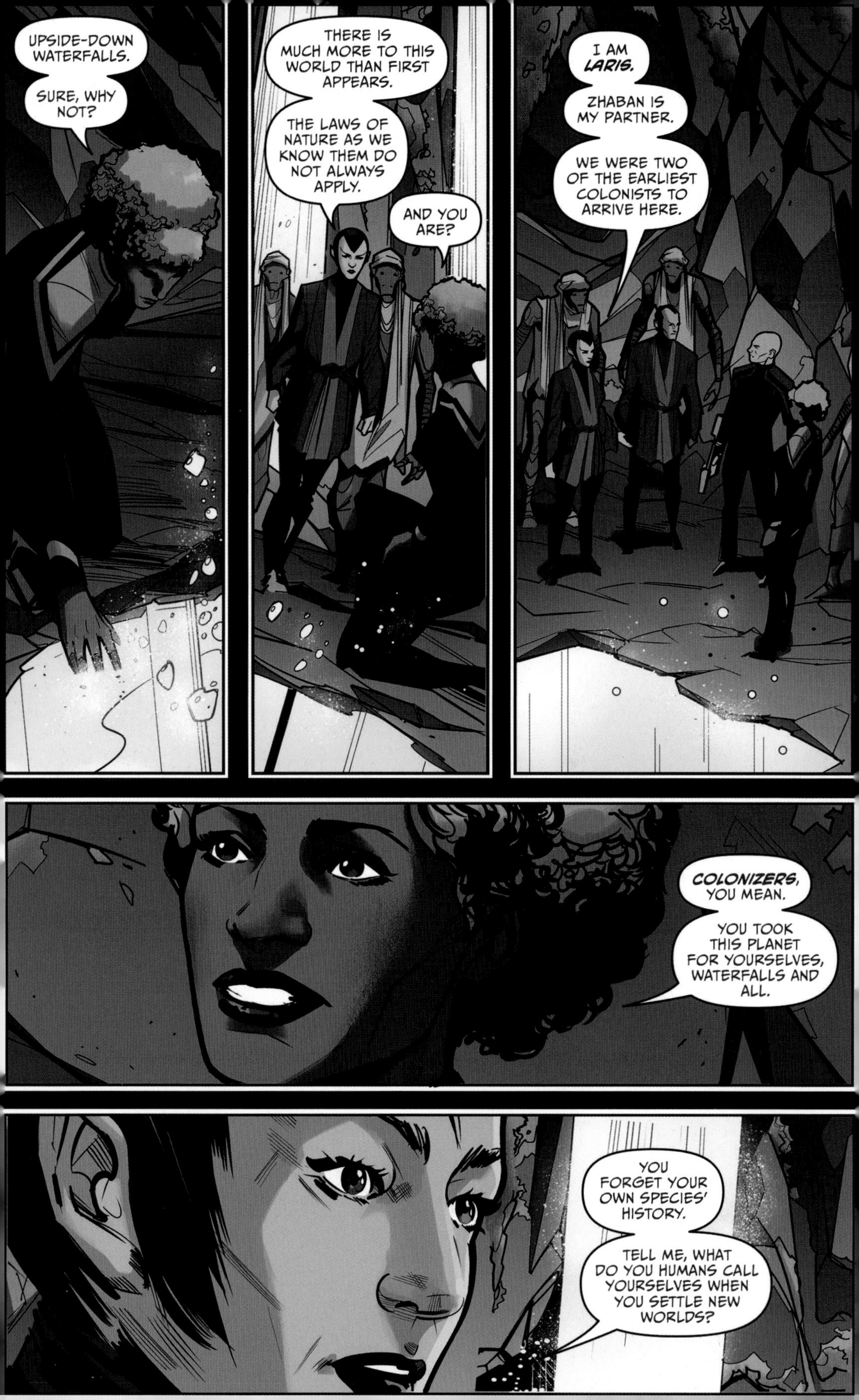

UPSIDE-DOWN WATERFALLS.
SURE, WHY NOT?
THERE IS MUCH MORE TO THIS WORLD THAN FIRST APPEARS.
THE LAWS OF NATURE AS WE KNOW THEM DO NOT ALWAYS APPLY.
AND YOU ARE?
I AM *LARIS.*
ZHABAN IS MY PARTNER.
WE WERE TWO OF THE EARLIEST COLONISTS TO ARRIVE HERE.
COLONIZERS, YOU MEAN.
YOU TOOK THIS PLANET FOR YOURSELVES, WATERFALLS AND ALL.
YOU FORGET YOUR OWN SPECIES' HISTORY.
TELL ME, WHAT DO YOU HUMANS CALL YOURSELVES WHEN YOU SETTLE NEW WORLDS?

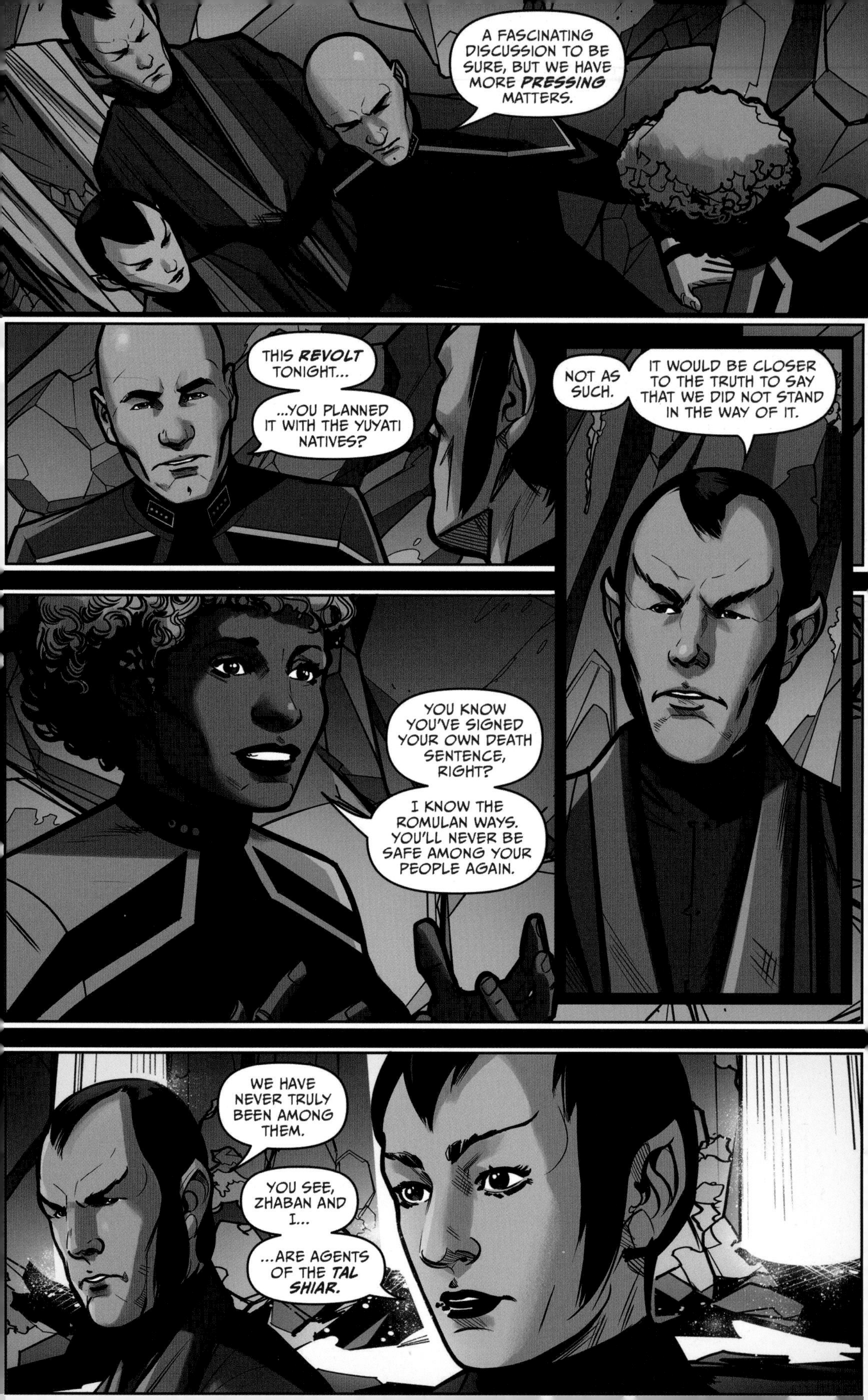
A FASCINATING DISCUSSION TO BE SURE, BUT WE HAVE MORE PRESSING MATTERS.
THIS REVOLT TONIGHT...
...YOU PLANNED IT WITH THE YUYATI NATIVES?
NOT AS SUCH.
IT WOULD BE CLOSER TO THE TRUTH TO SAY THAT WE DID NOT STAND IN THE WAY OF IT.
YOU KNOW YOU'VE SIGNED YOUR OWN DEATH SENTENCE, RIGHT?
I KNOW THE ROMULAN WAYS. YOU'LL NEVER BE SAFE AMONG YOUR PEOPLE AGAIN.
WE HAVE NEVER TRULY BEEN AMONG THEM.
YOU SEE, ZHABAN AND I...
...ARE AGENTS OF THE TAL SHIAR.

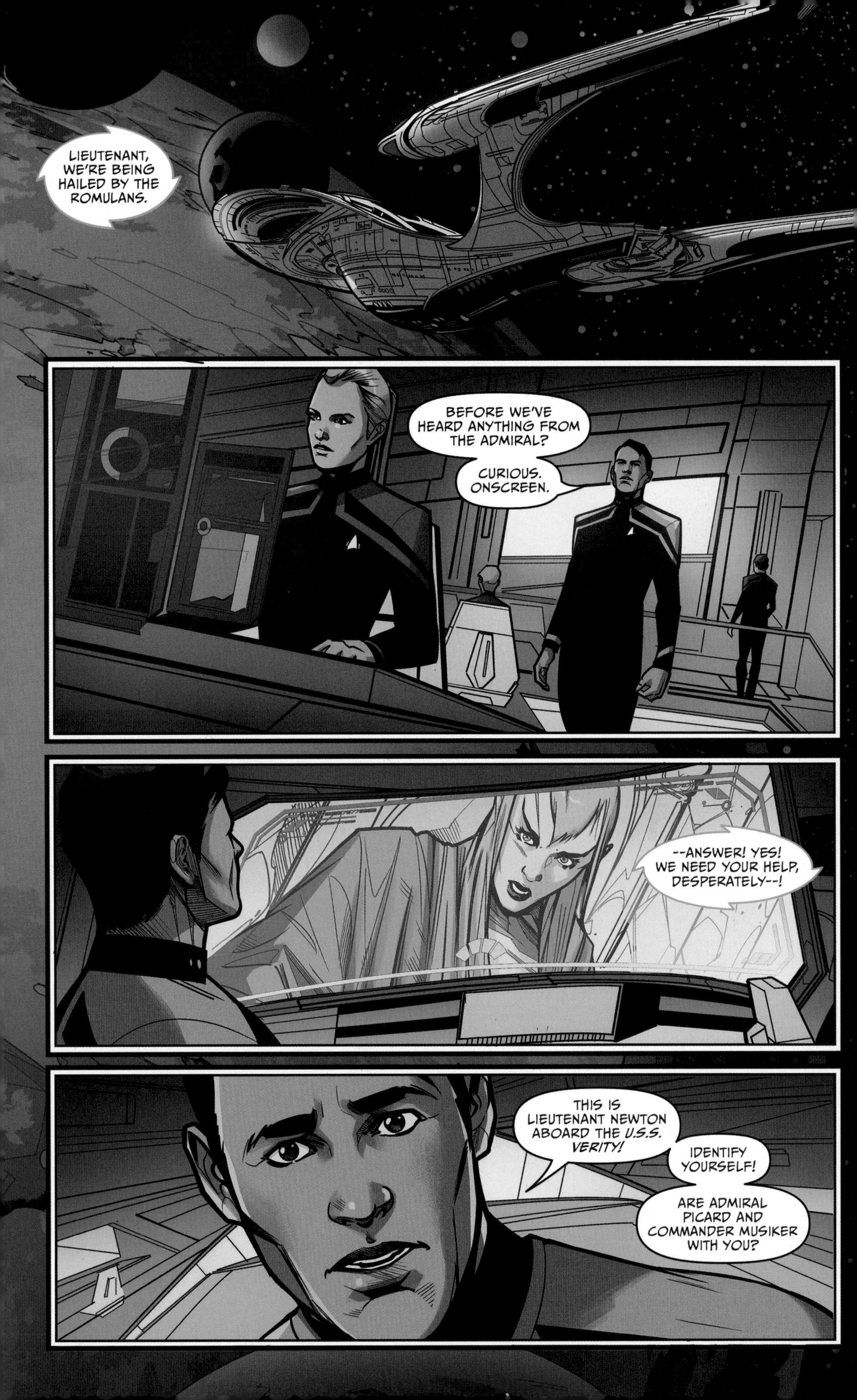
LIEUTENANT, WE'RE BEING HAILED BY THE ROMULANS.
BEFORE WE'VE HEARD ANYTHING FROM THE ADMIRAL?
CURIOUS. ONSCREEN.
--ANSWER! YES! WE NEED YOUR HELP, DESPERATELY--!
THIS IS LIEUTENANT NEWTON ABOARD THE *U.S.S. VERITY!*
IDENTIFY YOURSELF!
ARE ADMIRAL PICARD AND COMMANDER MUSIKER WITH YOU?

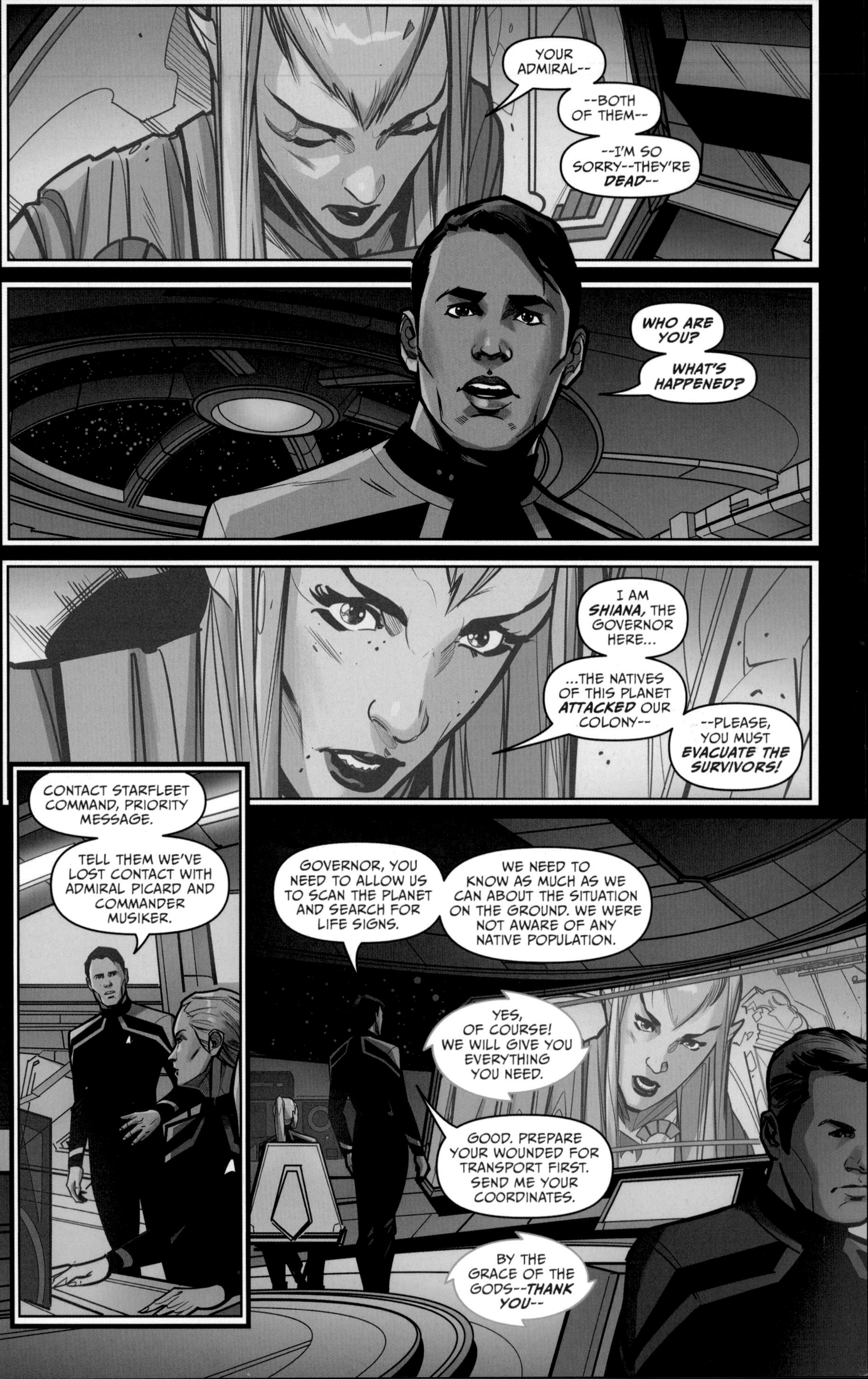

YOUR ADMIRAL--
--BOTH OF THEM--
--I'M SO SORRY--THEY'RE *DEAD*--
WHO ARE YOU?
WHAT'S HAPPENED?
I AM *SHIANA,* THE GOVERNOR HERE...
...THE NATIVES OF THIS PLANET *ATTACKED* OUR COLONY--
--PLEASE, YOU MUST *EVACUATE THE SURVIVORS!*
CONTACT STARFLEET COMMAND, PRIORITY MESSAGE.
TELL THEM WE'VE LOST CONTACT WITH ADMIRAL PICARD AND COMMANDER MUSIKER.
GOVERNOR, YOU NEED TO ALLOW US TO SCAN THE PLANET AND SEARCH FOR LIFE SIGNS.
WE NEED TO KNOW AS MUCH AS WE CAN ABOUT THE SITUATION ON THE GROUND. WE WERE NOT AWARE OF ANY NATIVE POPULATION.
YES, OF COURSE! WE WILL GIVE YOU EVERYTHING YOU NEED.
GOOD. PREPARE YOUR WOUNDED FOR TRANSPORT FIRST. SEND ME YOUR COORDINATES.
BY THE GRACE OF THE GODS--*THANK YOU*--

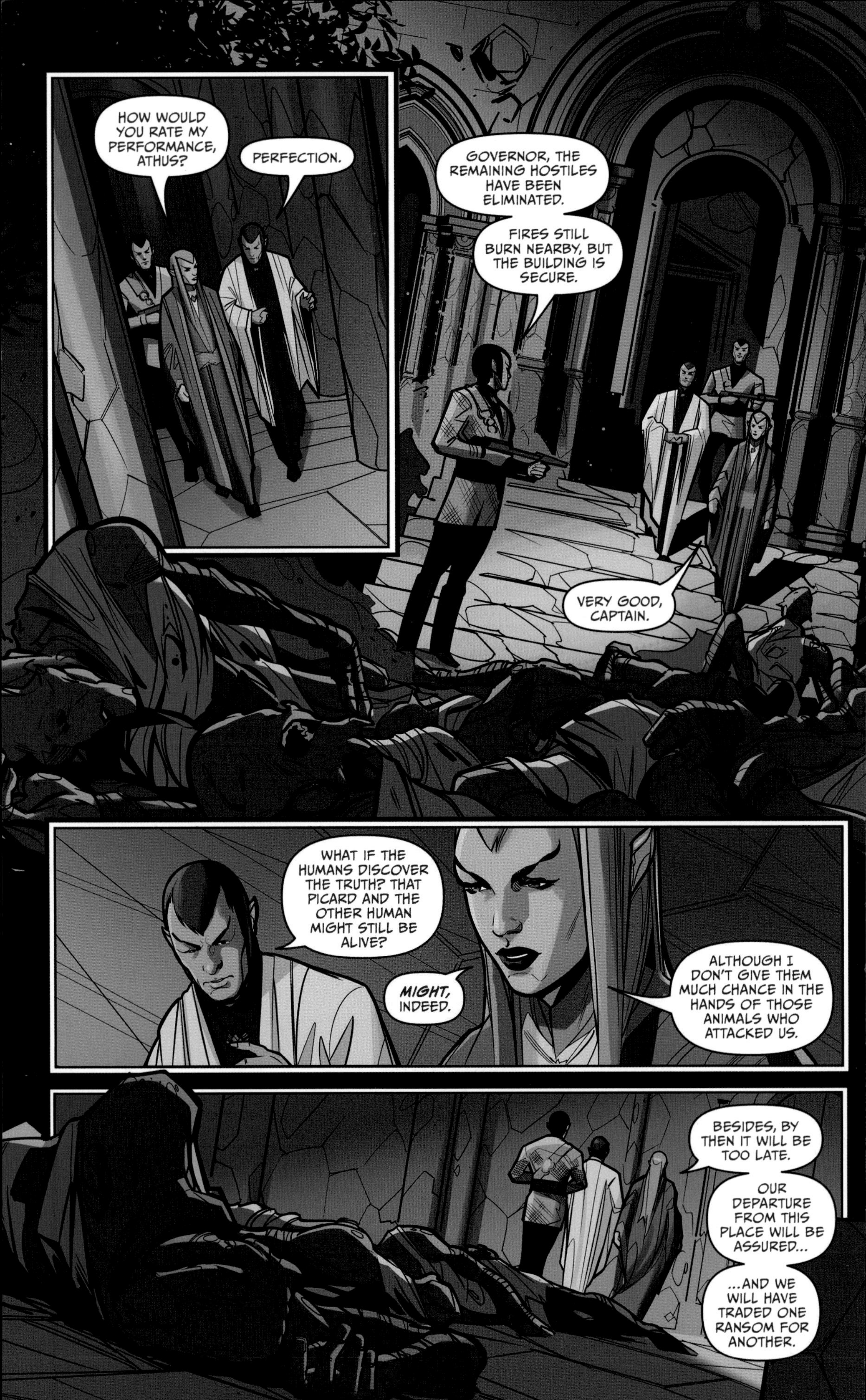
HOW WOULD YOU RATE MY PERFORMANCE, ATHUS?
PERFECTION.
GOVERNOR, THE REMAINING HOSTILES HAVE BEEN ELIMINATED.
FIRES STILL BURN NEARBY, BUT THE BUILDING IS SECURE.
VERY GOOD, CAPTAIN.
WHAT IF THE HUMANS DISCOVER THE TRUTH? THAT PICARD AND THE OTHER HUMAN MIGHT STILL BE ALIVE?
MIGHT, INDEED.
ALTHOUGH I DON'T GIVE THEM MUCH CHANCE IN THE HANDS OF THOSE ANIMALS WHO ATTACKED US.
BESIDES, BY THEN IT WILL BE TOO LATE.
OUR DEPARTURE FROM THIS PLACE WILL BE ASSURED...
...AND WE WILL HAVE TRADED ONE RANSOM FOR ANOTHER.

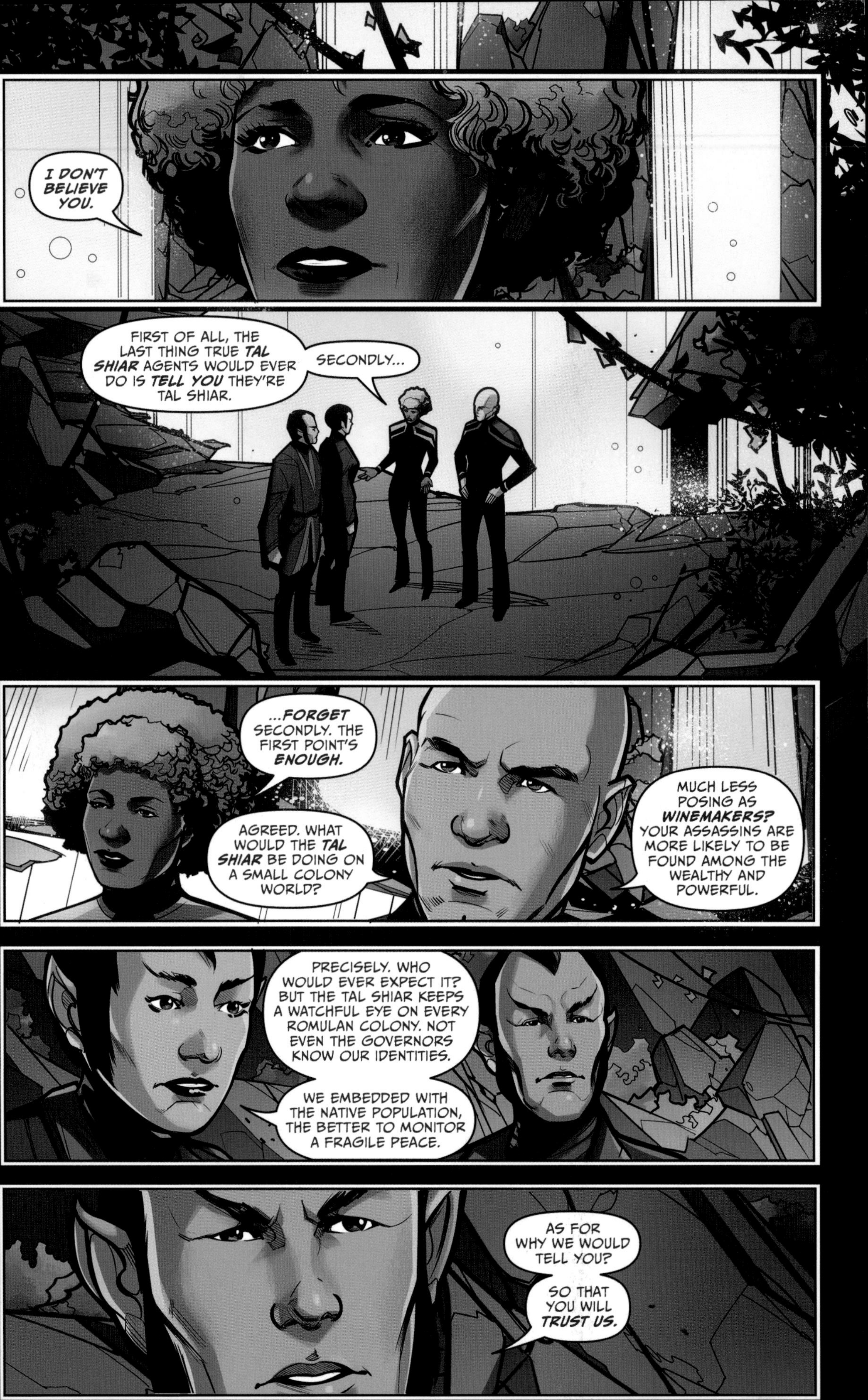
I DON'T BELIEVE YOU.
FIRST OF ALL, THE LAST THING TRUE TAL SHIAR AGENTS WOULD EVER DO IS TELL YOU THEY'RE TAL SHIAR.
SECONDLY...
...FORGET SECONDLY. THE FIRST POINT'S ENOUGH.
AGREED. WHAT WOULD THE TAL SHIAR BE DOING ON A SMALL COLONY WORLD?
MUCH LESS POSING AS WINEMAKERS? YOUR ASSASSINS ARE MORE LIKELY TO BE FOUND AMONG THE WEALTHY AND POWERFUL.
PRECISELY. WHO WOULD EVER EXPECT IT? BUT THE TAL SHIAR KEEPS A WATCHFUL EYE ON EVERY ROMULAN COLONY. NOT EVEN THE GOVERNORS KNOW OUR IDENTITIES.
WE EMBEDDED WITH THE NATIVE POPULATION, THE BETTER TO MONITOR A FRAGILE PEACE.
AS FOR WHY WE WOULD TELL YOU?
SO THAT YOU WILL TRUST US.

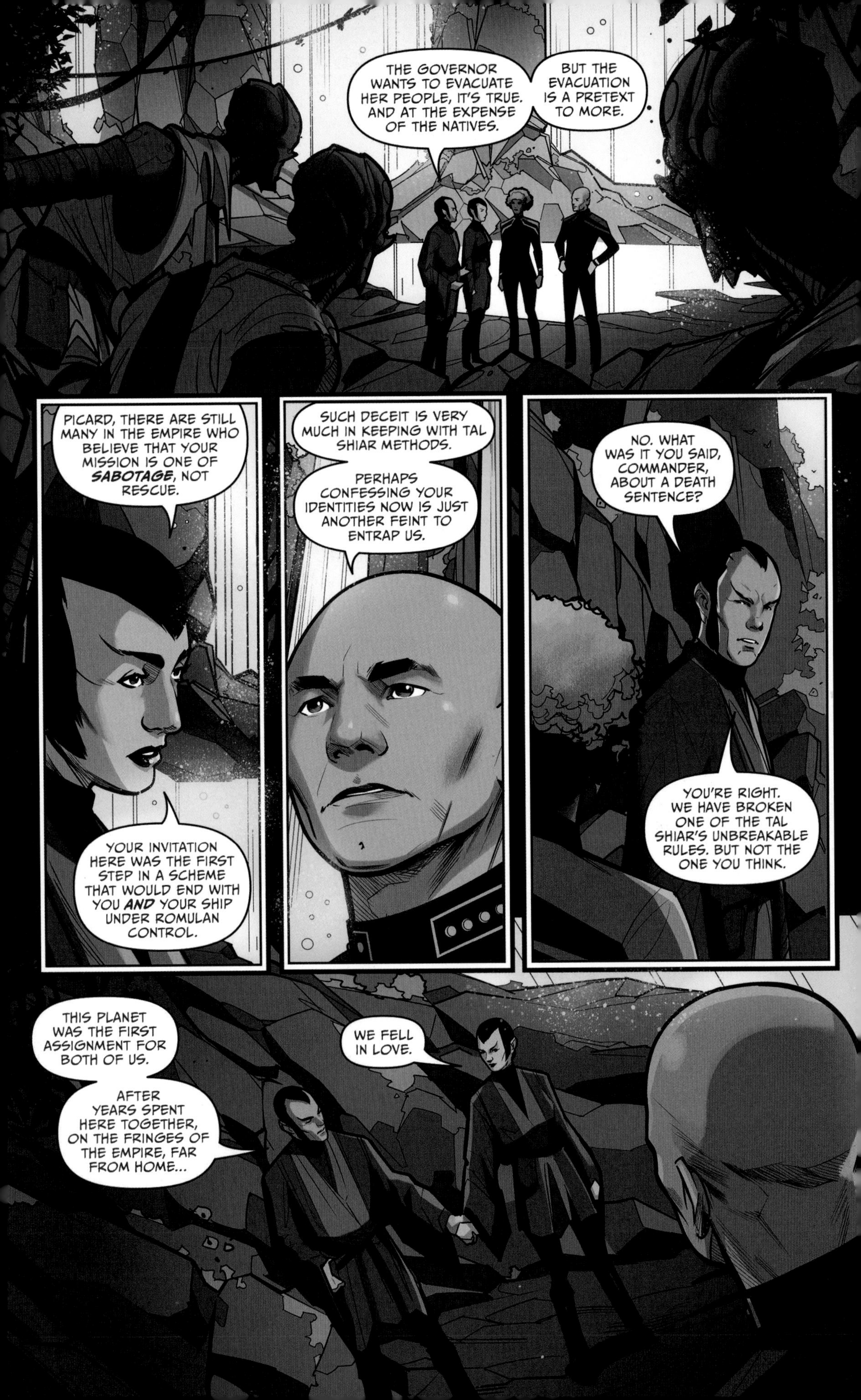
THE GOVERNOR WANTS TO EVACUATE HER PEOPLE, IT'S TRUE. AND AT THE EXPENSE OF THE NATIVES.
BUT THE EVACUATION IS A PRETEXT TO MORE.
PICARD, THERE ARE STILL MANY IN THE EMPIRE WHO BELIEVE THAT YOUR MISSION IS ONE OF *SABOTAGE*, NOT RESCUE.
YOUR INVITATION HERE WAS THE FIRST STEP IN A SCHEME THAT WOULD END WITH YOU *AND* YOUR SHIP UNDER ROMULAN CONTROL.
SUCH DECEIT IS VERY MUCH IN KEEPING WITH TAL SHIAR METHODS.
PERHAPS CONFESSING YOUR IDENTITIES NOW IS JUST ANOTHER FEINT TO ENTRAP US.
NO. WHAT WAS IT YOU SAID, COMMANDER, ABOUT A DEATH SENTENCE?
YOU'RE RIGHT. WE HAVE BROKEN ONE OF THE TAL SHIAR'S UNBREAKABLE RULES. BUT NOT THE ONE YOU THINK.
THIS PLANET WAS THE FIRST ASSIGNMENT FOR BOTH OF US.
AFTER YEARS SPENT HERE TOGETHER, ON THE FRINGES OF THE EMPIRE, FAR FROM HOME...
WE FELL IN LOVE.

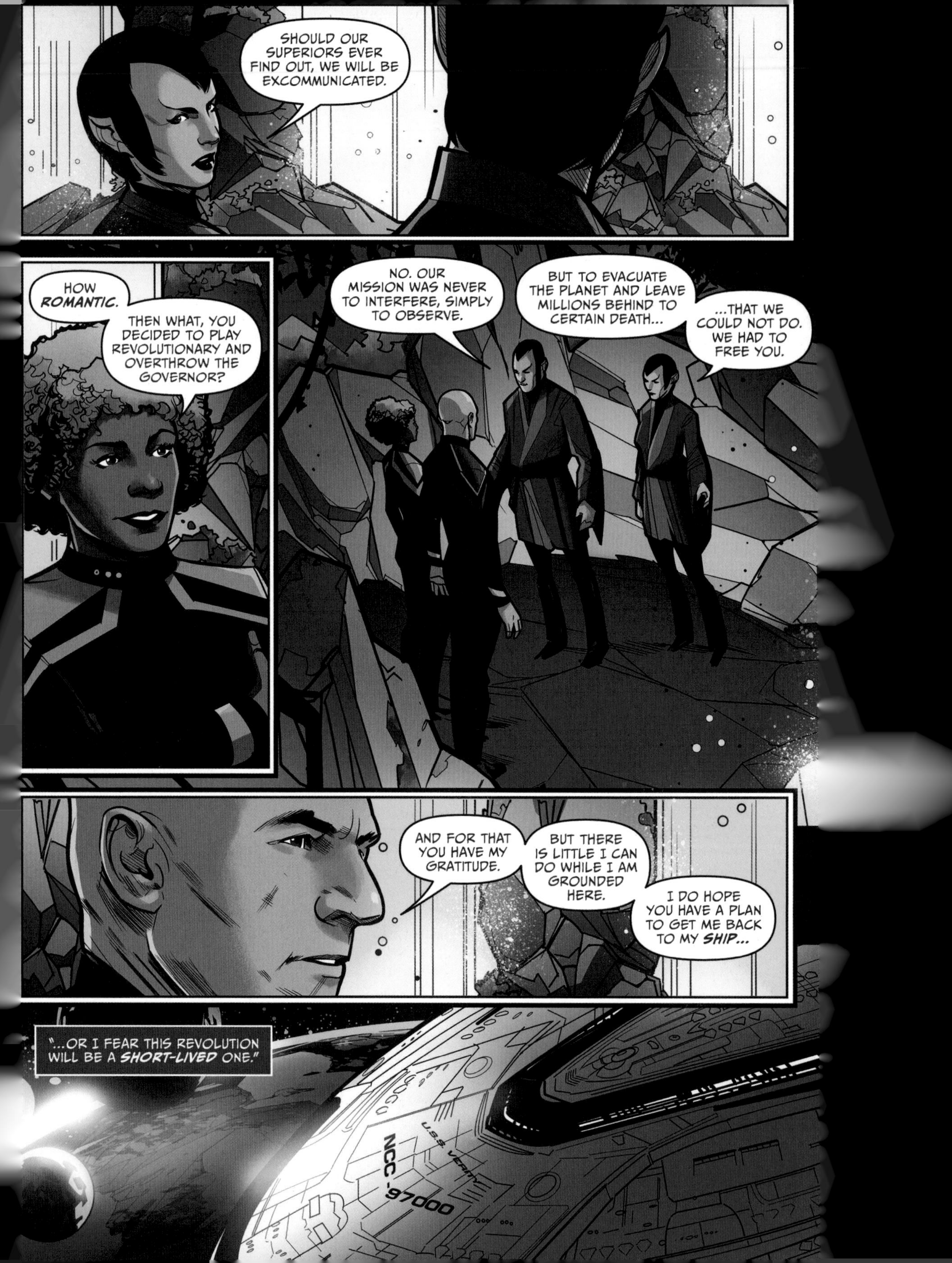
SHOULD OUR SUPERIORS EVER FIND OUT, WE WILL BE EXCOMMUNICATED.
HOW *ROMANTIC*.
THEN WHAT, YOU DECIDED TO PLAY REVOLUTIONARY AND OVERTHROW THE GOVERNOR?
NO. OUR MISSION WAS NEVER TO INTERFERE, SIMPLY TO OBSERVE.
BUT TO EVACUATE THE PLANET AND LEAVE MILLIONS BEHIND TO CERTAIN DEATH...
...THAT WE COULD NOT DO. WE HAD TO FREE YOU.
AND FOR THAT YOU HAVE MY GRATITUDE.
BUT THERE IS LITTLE I CAN DO WHILE I AM GROUNDED HERE.
I DO HOPE YOU HAVE A PLAN TO GET ME BACK TO MY *SHIP*...
"...OR I FEAR THIS REVOLUTION WILL BE A *SHORT-LIVED* ONE."
U.S.S. VERITY
NCC-97000

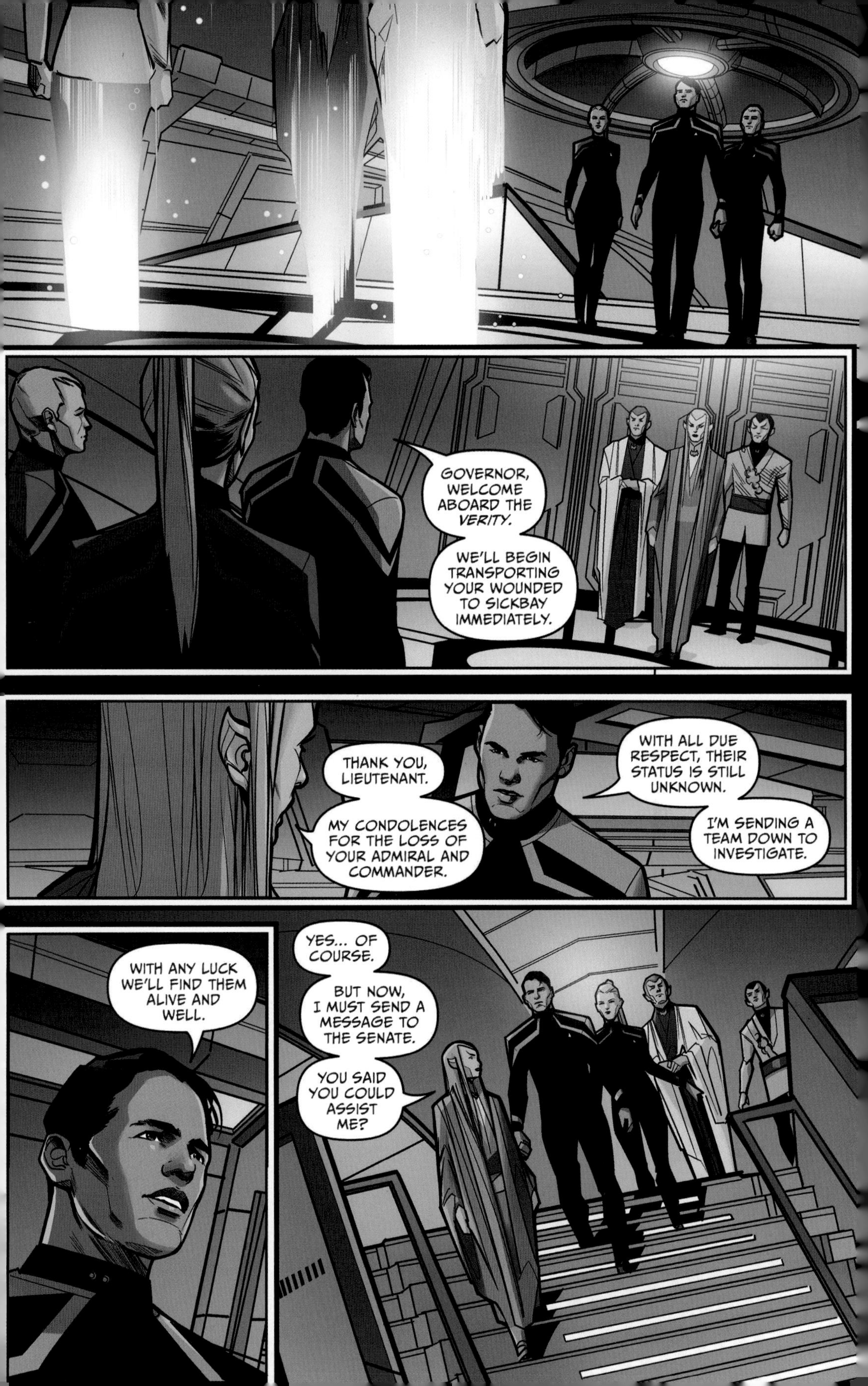
GOVERNOR, WELCOME ABOARD THE *VERITY*.
WE'LL BEGIN TRANSPORTING YOUR WOUNDED TO SICKBAY IMMEDIATELY.
THANK YOU, LIEUTENANT.
MY CONDOLENCES FOR THE LOSS OF YOUR ADMIRAL AND COMMANDER.
WITH ALL DUE RESPECT, THEIR STATUS IS STILL UNKNOWN.
I'M SENDING A TEAM DOWN TO INVESTIGATE.
WITH ANY LUCK WE'LL FIND THEM ALIVE AND WELL.
YES... OF COURSE.
BUT NOW, I MUST SEND A MESSAGE TO THE SENATE.
YOU SAID YOU COULD ASSIST ME?

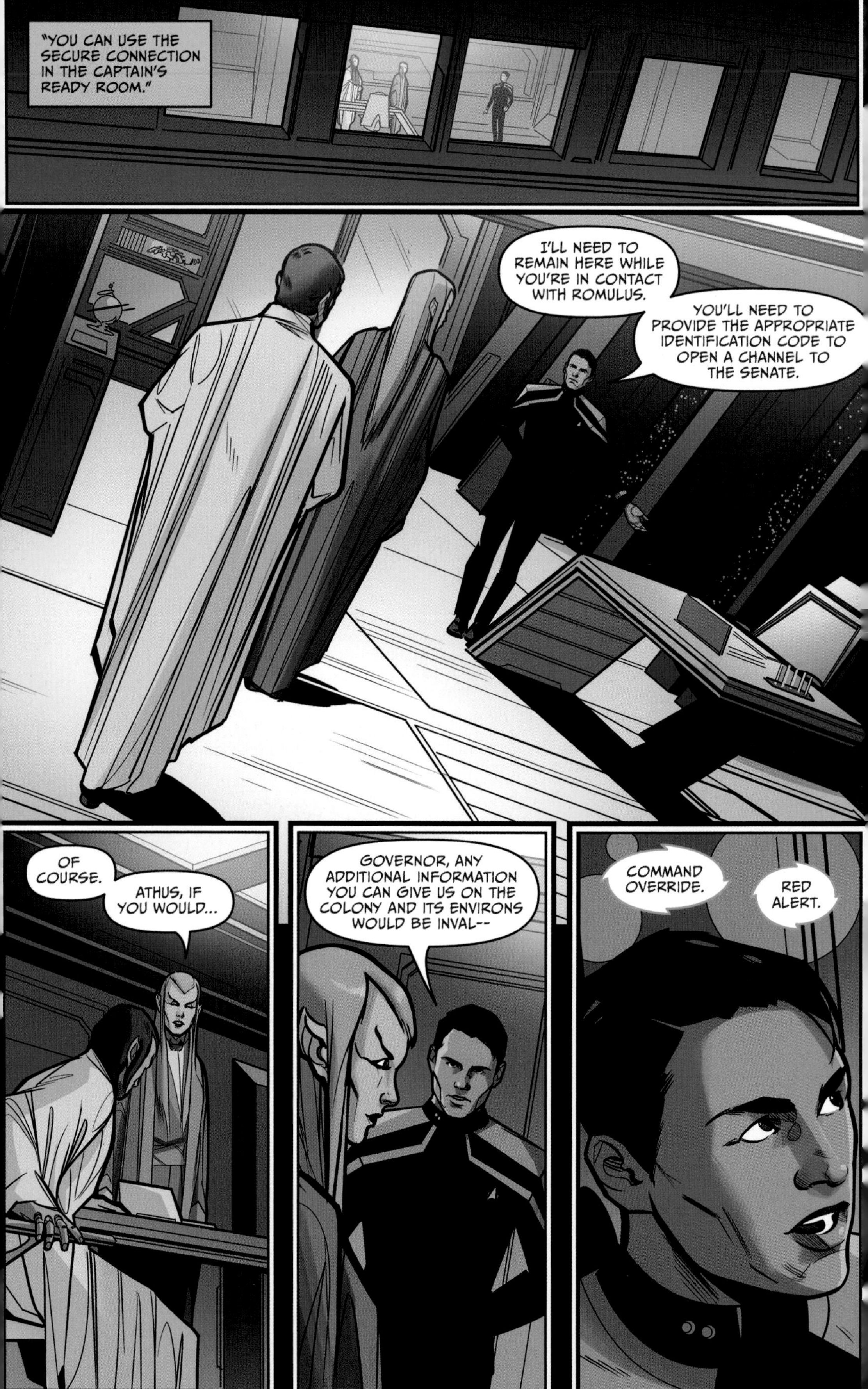
"YOU CAN USE THE SECURE CONNECTION IN THE CAPTAIN'S READY ROOM."
I'LL NEED TO REMAIN HERE WHILE YOU'RE IN CONTACT WITH ROMULUS.
YOU'LL NEED TO PROVIDE THE APPROPRIATE IDENTIFICATION CODE TO OPEN A CHANNEL TO THE SENATE.
OF COURSE.
ATHUS, IF YOU WOULD...
GOVERNOR, ANY ADDITIONAL INFORMATION YOU CAN GIVE US ON THE COLONY AND ITS ENVIRONS WOULD BE INVAL--
COMMAND OVERRIDE.
RED ALERT.

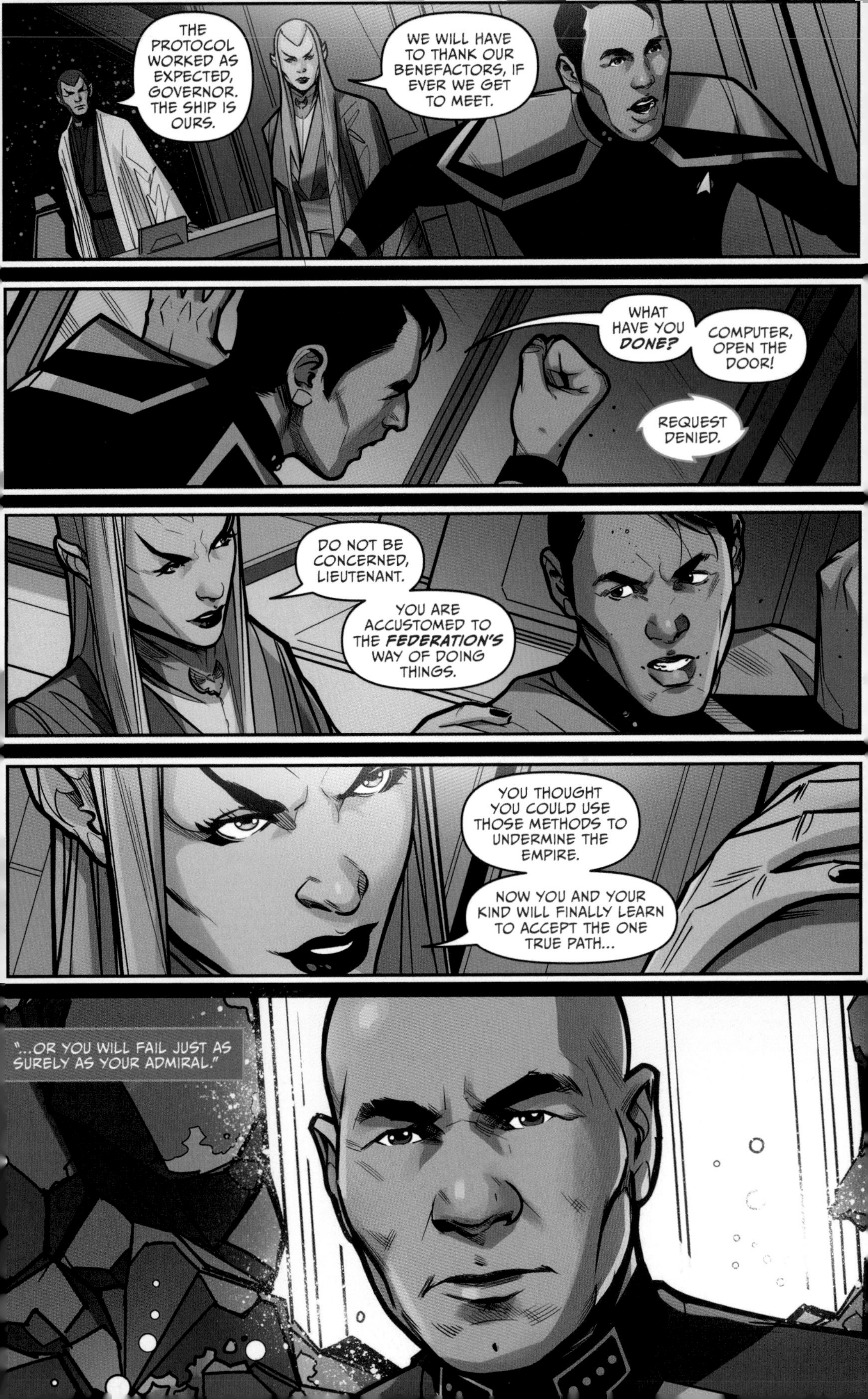
THE PROTOCOL WORKED AS EXPECTED, GOVERNOR. THE SHIP IS OURS.
WE WILL HAVE TO THANK OUR BENEFACTORS, IF EVER WE GET TO MEET.
WHAT HAVE YOU DONE?
COMPUTER, OPEN THE DOOR!
REQUEST DENIED.
DO NOT BE CONCERNED, LIEUTENANT.
YOU ARE ACCUSTOMED TO THE FEDERATION'S WAY OF DOING THINGS.
YOU THOUGHT YOU COULD USE THOSE METHODS TO UNDERMINE THE EMPIRE.
NOW YOU AND YOUR KIND WILL FINALLY LEARN TO ACCEPT THE ONE TRUE PATH...
"...OR YOU WILL FAIL JUST AS SURELY AS YOUR ADMIRAL."

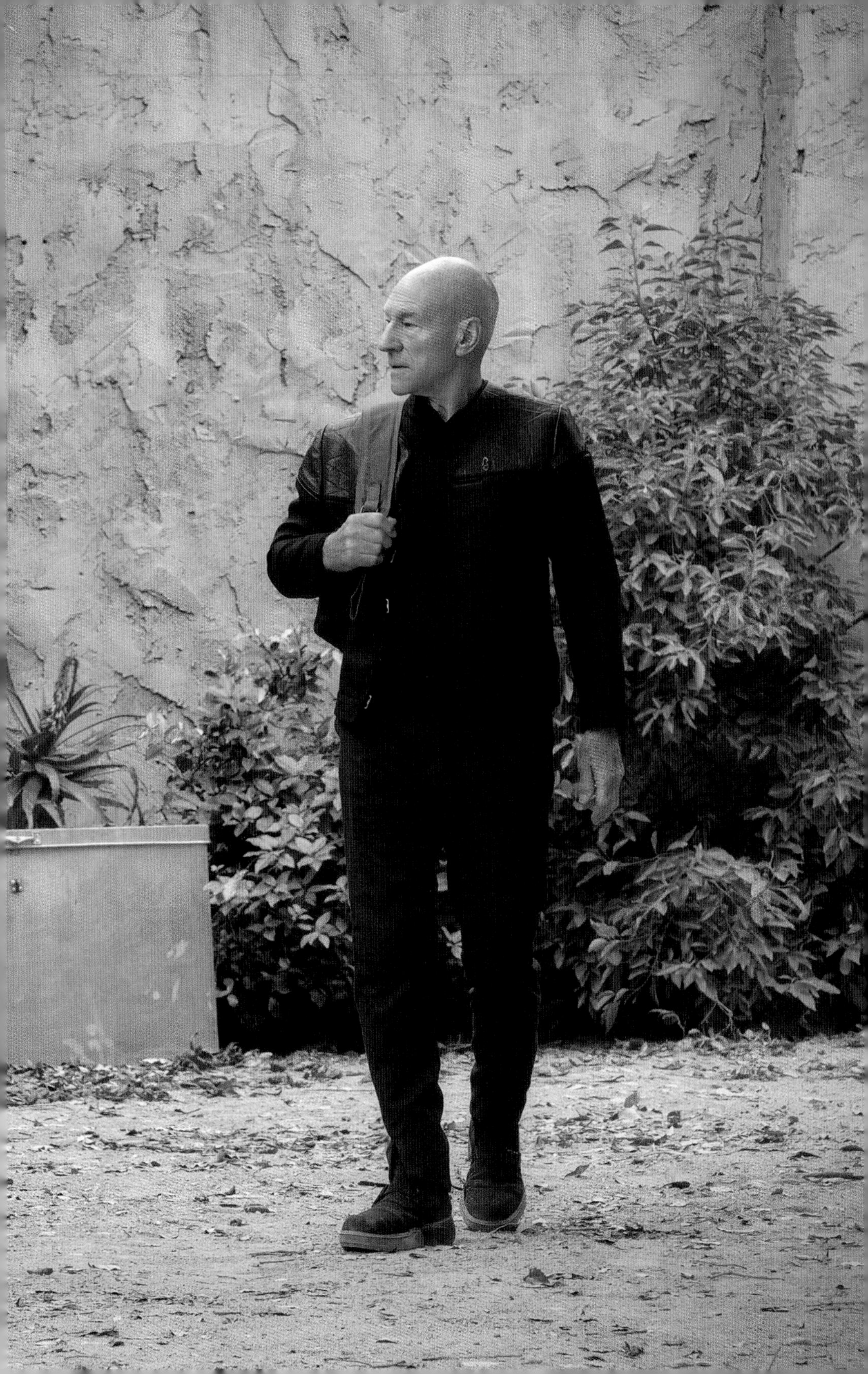

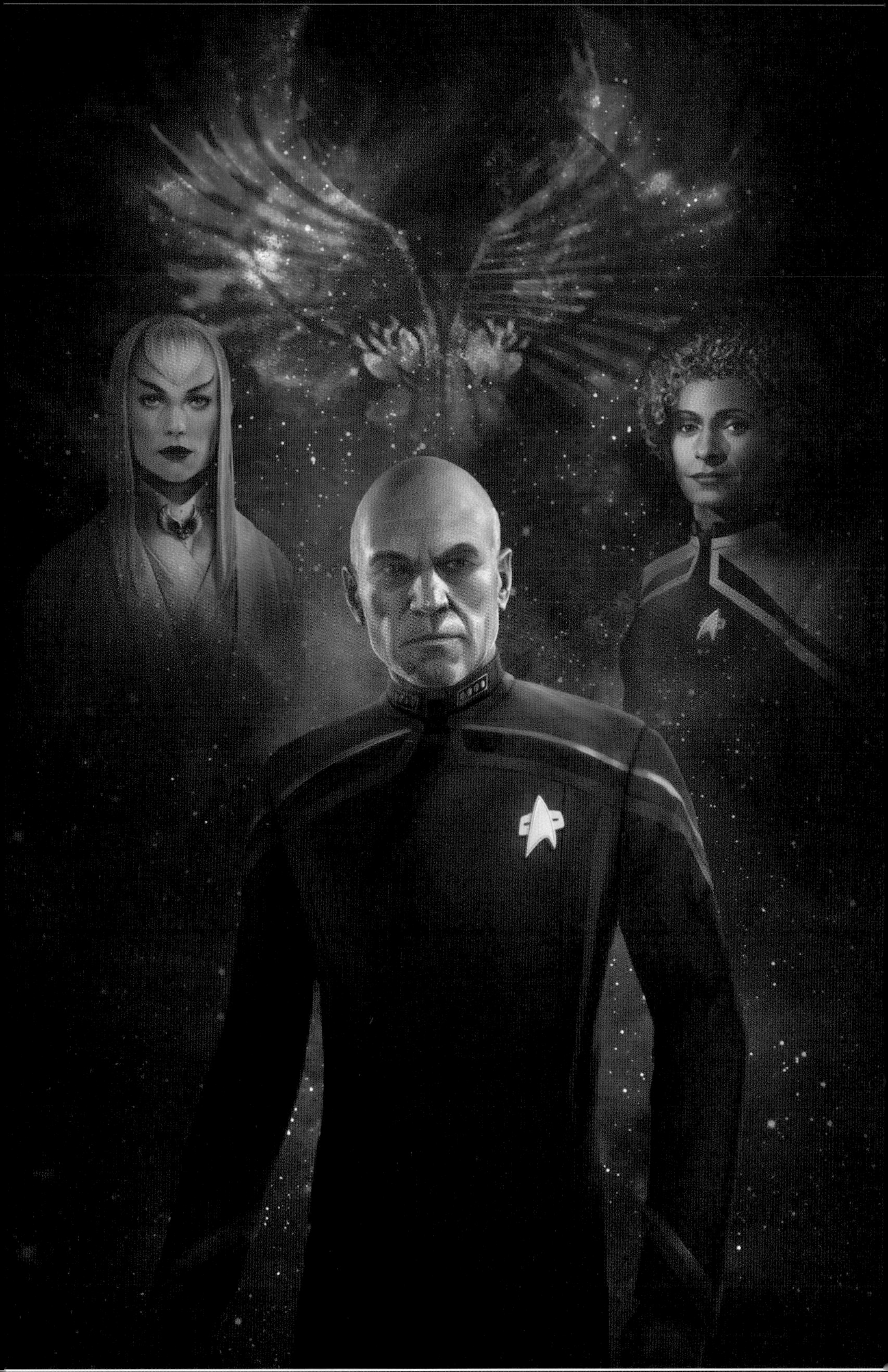

art by SARA PITRE-DUROCHER

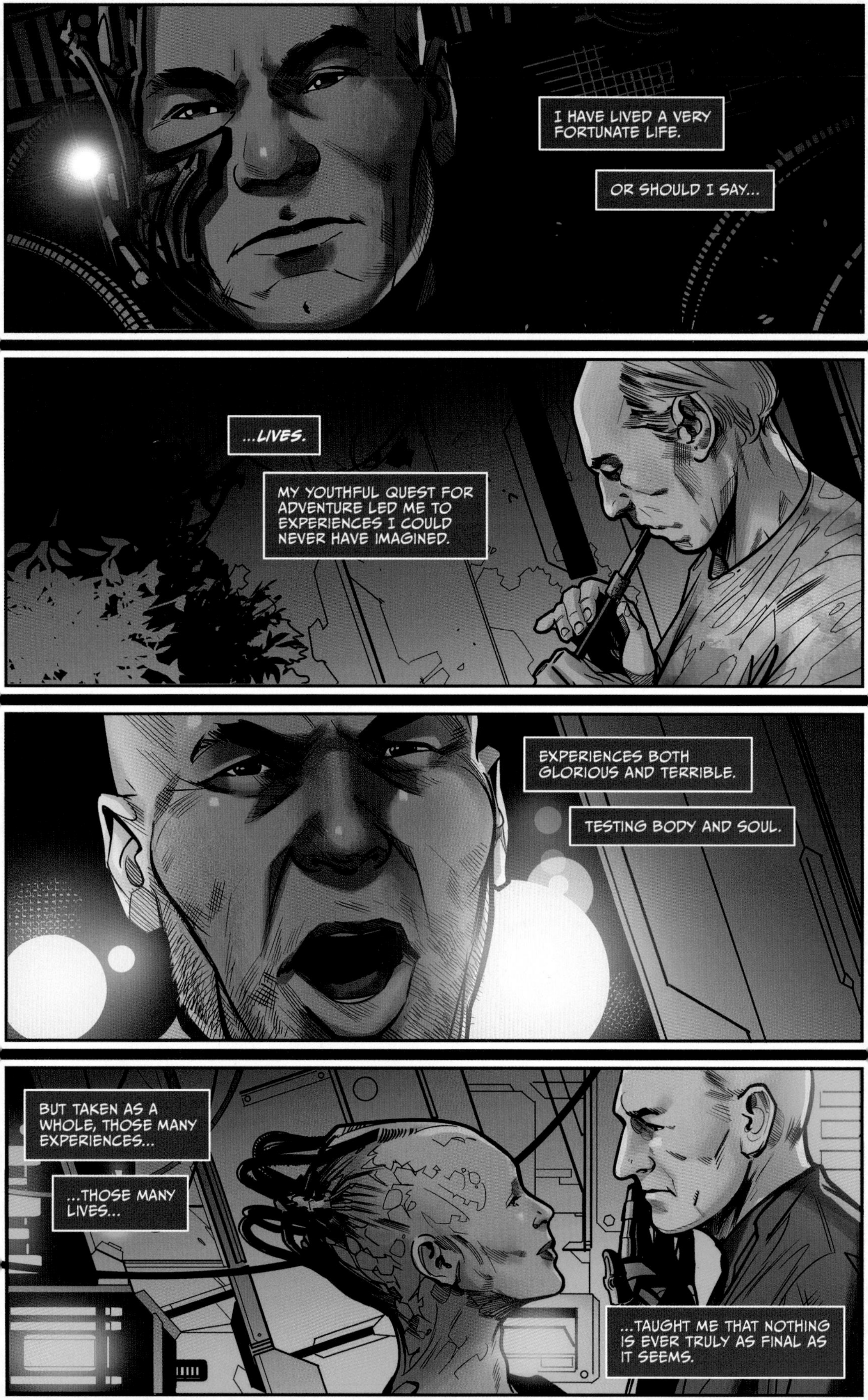
I HAVE LIVED A VERY FORTUNATE LIFE.
OR SHOULD I SAY...
...LIVES.
MY YOUTHFUL QUEST FOR ADVENTURE LED ME TO EXPERIENCES I COULD NEVER HAVE IMAGINED.
EXPERIENCES BOTH GLORIOUS AND TERRIBLE.
TESTING BODY AND SOUL.
BUT TAKEN AS A WHOLE, THOSE MANY EXPERIENCES...
...THOSE MANY LIVES...
...TAUGHT ME THAT NOTHING IS EVER TRULY AS FINAL AS IT SEEMS.

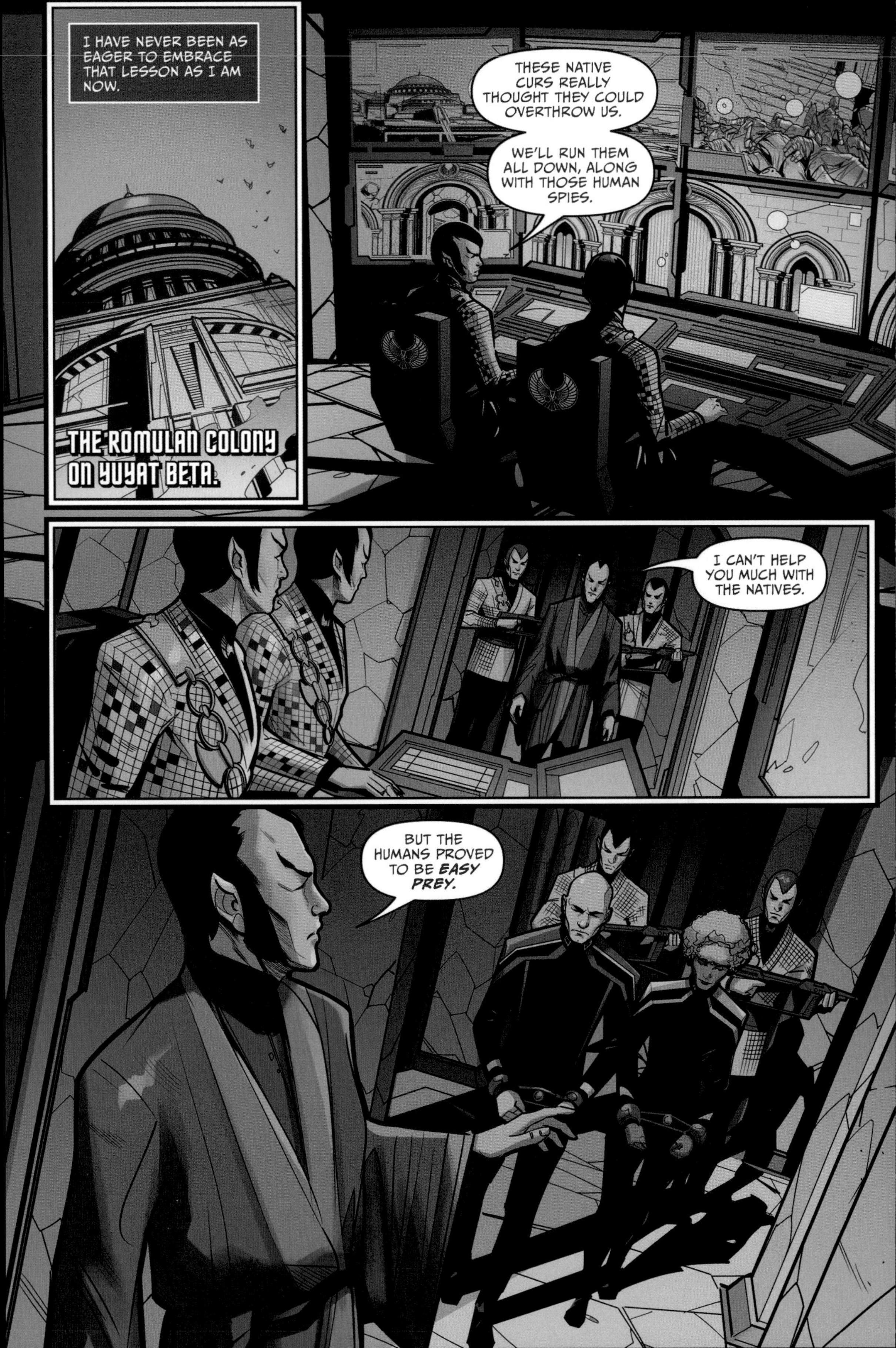
I HAVE NEVER BEEN AS EAGER TO EMBRACE THAT LESSON AS I AM NOW.
THE ROMULAN COLONY ON YUYAT BETA.
THESE NATIVE CURS REALLY THOUGHT THEY COULD OVERTHROW US.
WE'LL RUN THEM ALL DOWN, ALONG WITH THOSE HUMAN SPIES.
I CAN'T HELP YOU MUCH WITH THE NATIVES.
BUT THE HUMANS PROVED TO BE *EASY PREY.*

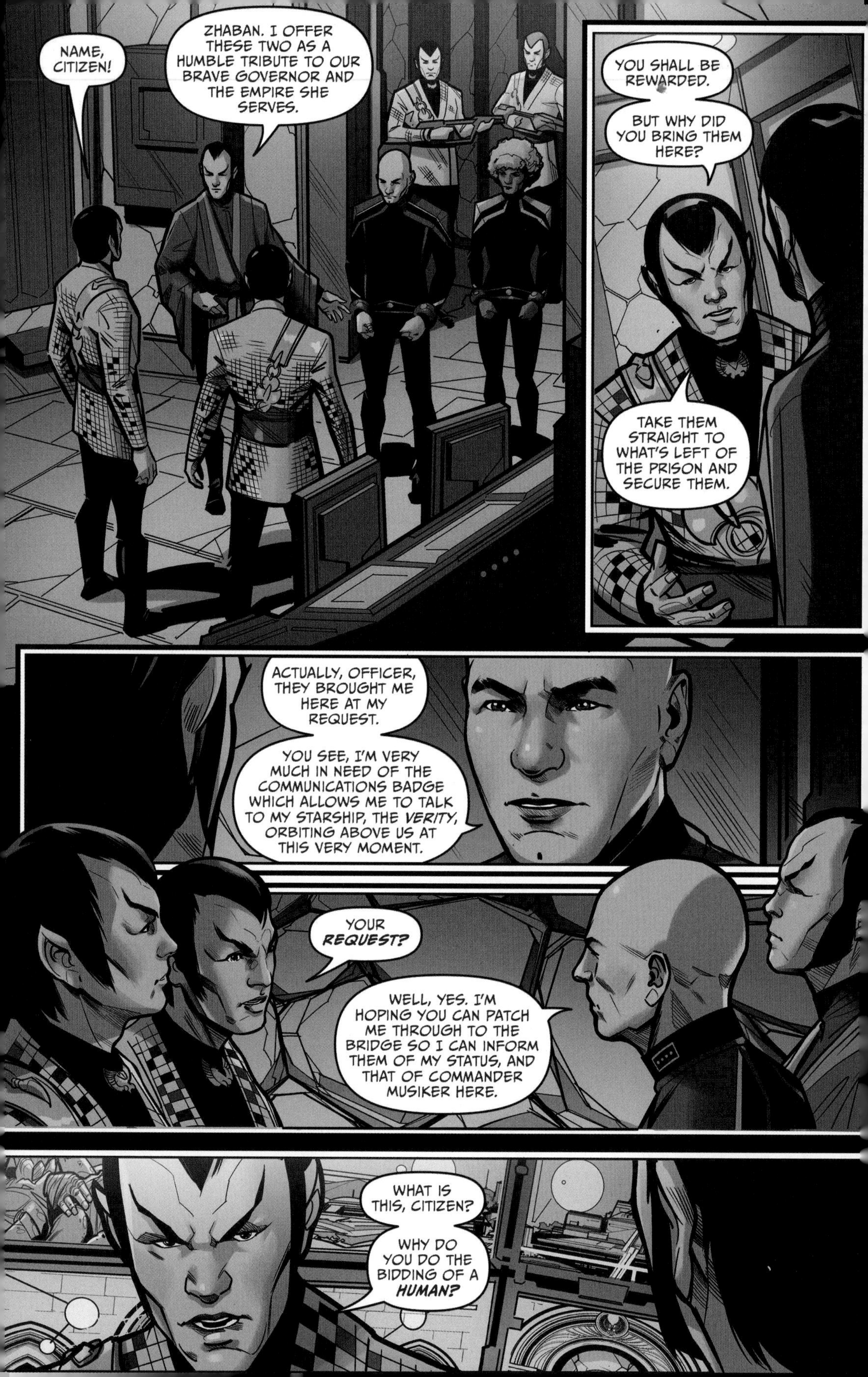
NAME, CITIZEN!
ZHABAN. I OFFER THESE TWO AS A HUMBLE TRIBUTE TO OUR BRAVE GOVERNOR AND THE EMPIRE SHE SERVES.
YOU SHALL BE REWARDED.
BUT WHY DID YOU BRING THEM HERE?
TAKE THEM STRAIGHT TO WHAT'S LEFT OF THE PRISON AND SECURE THEM.
ACTUALLY, OFFICER, THEY BROUGHT ME HERE AT MY REQUEST.
YOU SEE, I'M VERY MUCH IN NEED OF THE COMMUNICATIONS BADGE WHICH ALLOWS ME TO TALK TO MY STARSHIP, THE *VERITY*, ORBITING ABOVE US AT THIS VERY MOMENT.
YOUR **REQUEST?**
WELL, YES. I'M HOPING YOU CAN PATCH ME THROUGH TO THE BRIDGE SO I CAN INFORM THEM OF MY STATUS, AND THAT OF COMMANDER MUSIKER HERE.
WHAT IS THIS, CITIZEN?
WHY DO YOU DO THE BIDDING OF A **HUMAN?**

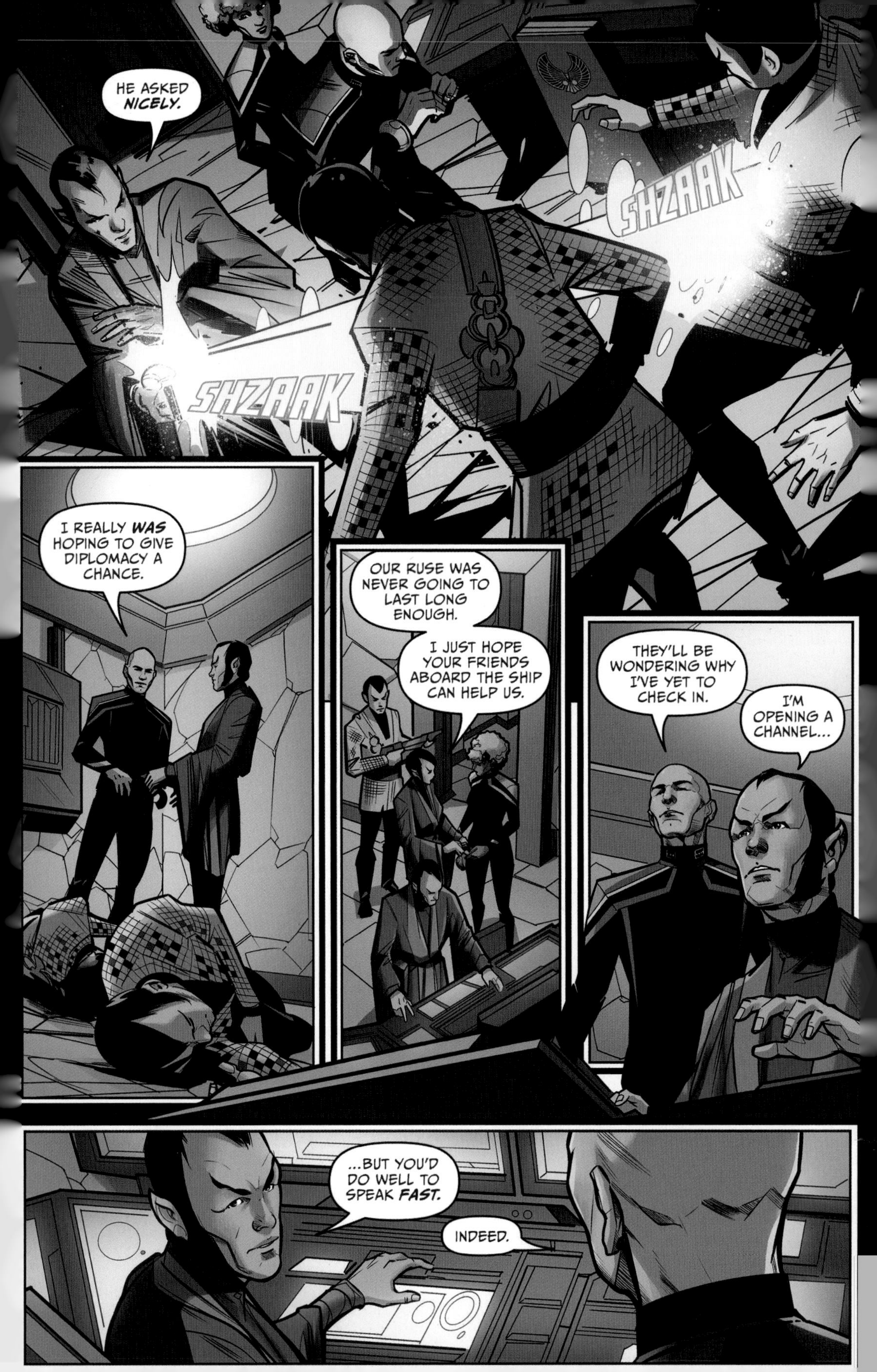
HE ASKED NICELY.
SHZAAK
SHZAAK
I REALLY WAS HOPING TO GIVE DIPLOMACY A CHANCE.
OUR RUSE WAS NEVER GOING TO LAST LONG ENOUGH.
I JUST HOPE YOUR FRIENDS ABOARD THE SHIP CAN HELP US.
THEY'LL BE WONDERING WHY I'VE YET TO CHECK IN.
I'M OPENING A CHANNEL...
...BUT YOU'D DO WELL TO SPEAK FAST.
INDEED.

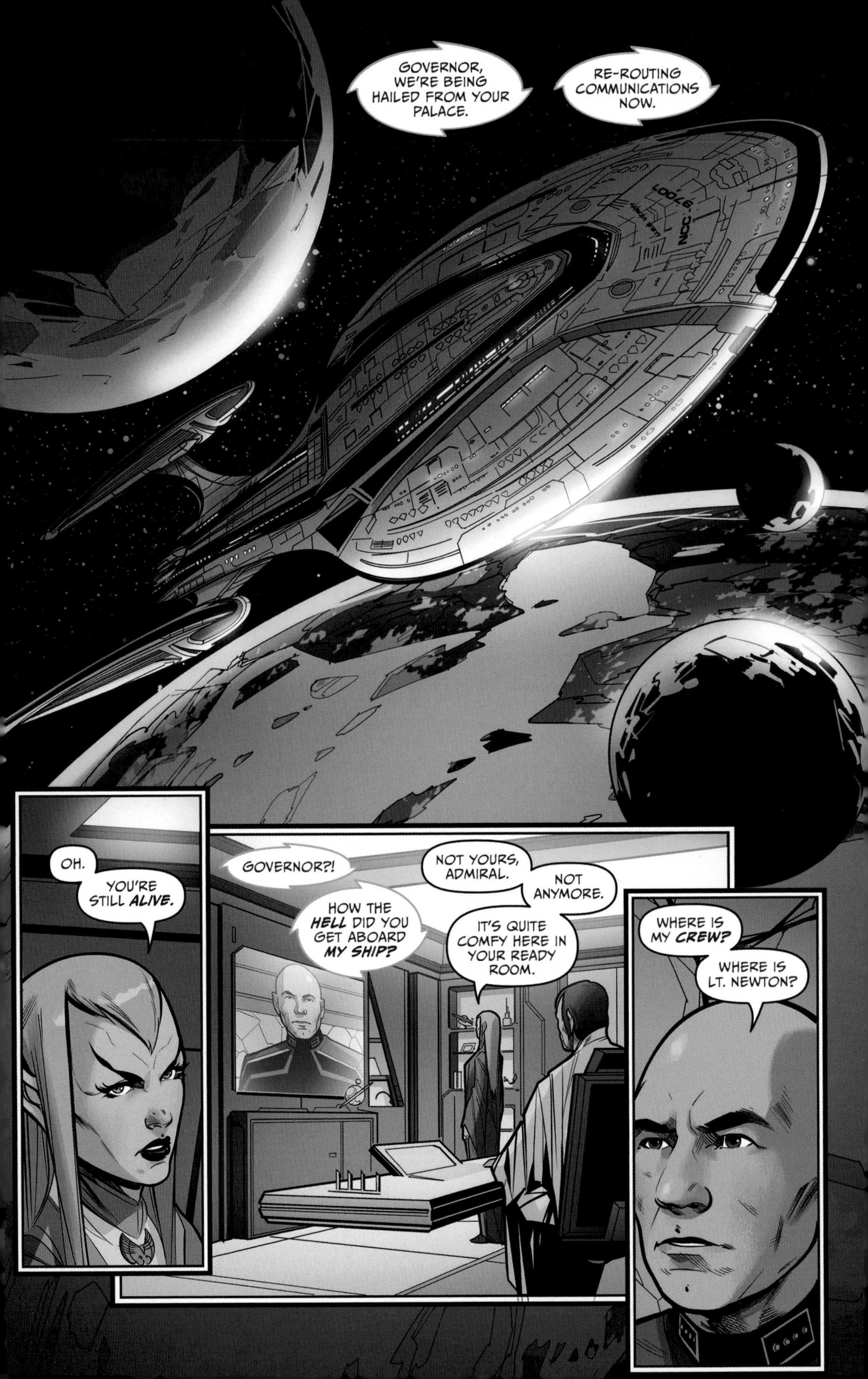
GOVERNOR, WE'RE BEING HAILED FROM YOUR PALACE.
RE-ROUTING COMMUNICATIONS NOW.
OH.
YOU'RE STILL ALIVE.
GOVERNOR?!
HOW THE HELL DID YOU GET ABOARD MY SHIP?
NOT YOURS, ADMIRAL.
NOT ANYMORE.
IT'S QUITE COMFY HERE IN YOUR READY ROOM.
WHERE IS MY CREW?
WHERE IS LT. NEWTON?

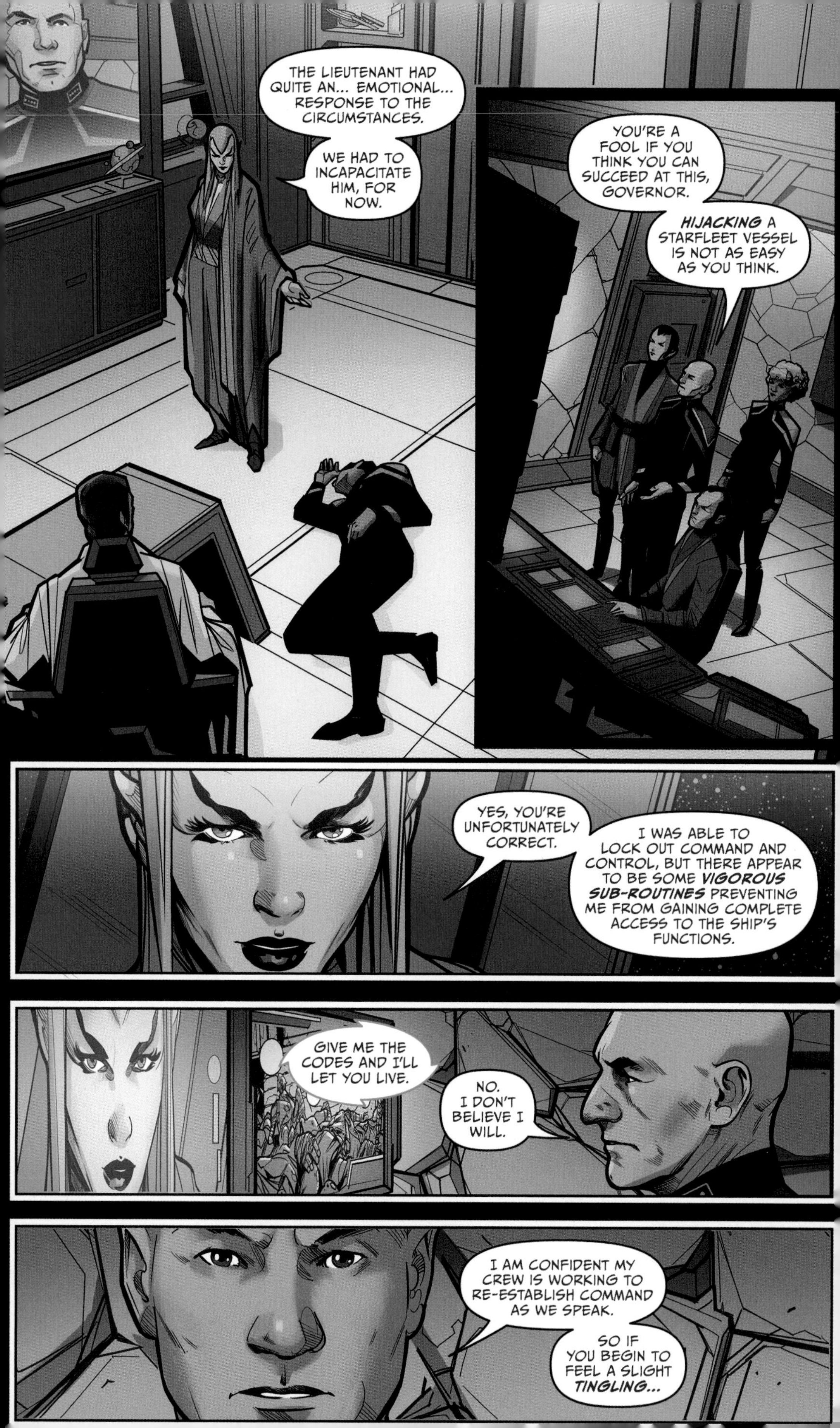
THE LIEUTENANT HAD QUITE AN... EMOTIONAL... RESPONSE TO THE CIRCUMSTANCES.
WE HAD TO INCAPACITATE HIM, FOR NOW.
YOU'RE A FOOL IF YOU THINK YOU CAN SUCCEED AT THIS, GOVERNOR.
HIJACKING A STARFLEET VESSEL IS NOT AS EASY AS YOU THINK.
YES, YOU'RE UNFORTUNATELY CORRECT.
I WAS ABLE TO LOCK OUT COMMAND AND CONTROL, BUT THERE APPEAR TO BE SOME *VIGOROUS SUB-ROUTINES* PREVENTING ME FROM GAINING COMPLETE ACCESS TO THE SHIP'S FUNCTIONS.
GIVE ME THE CODES AND I'LL LET YOU LIVE.
NO. I DON'T BELIEVE I WILL.
I AM CONFIDENT MY CREW IS WORKING TO RE-ESTABLISH COMMAND AS WE SPEAK.
SO IF YOU BEGIN TO FEEL A SLIGHT *TINGLING...*

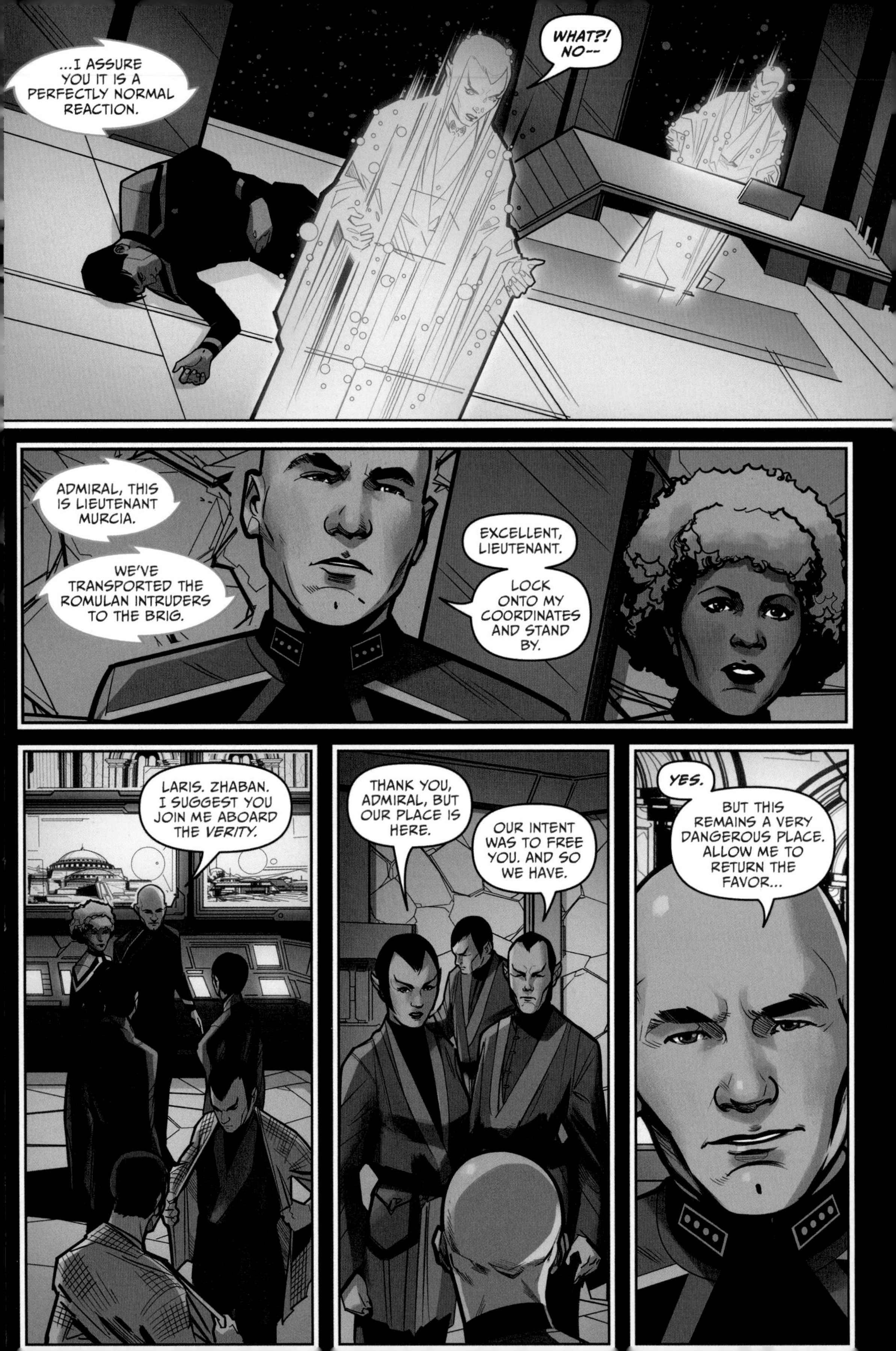
...I ASSURE YOU IT IS A PERFECTLY NORMAL REACTION.
WHAT?! NO--
ADMIRAL, THIS IS LIEUTENANT MURCIA.
WE'VE TRANSPORTED THE ROMULAN INTRUDERS TO THE BRIG.
EXCELLENT, LIEUTENANT.
LOCK ONTO MY COORDINATES AND STAND BY.
LARIS. ZHABAN. I SUGGEST YOU JOIN ME ABOARD THE *VERITY*.
THANK YOU, ADMIRAL, BUT OUR PLACE IS HERE.
OUR INTENT WAS TO FREE YOU. AND SO WE HAVE.
YES.
BUT THIS REMAINS A VERY DANGEROUS PLACE. ALLOW ME TO RETURN THE FAVOR...

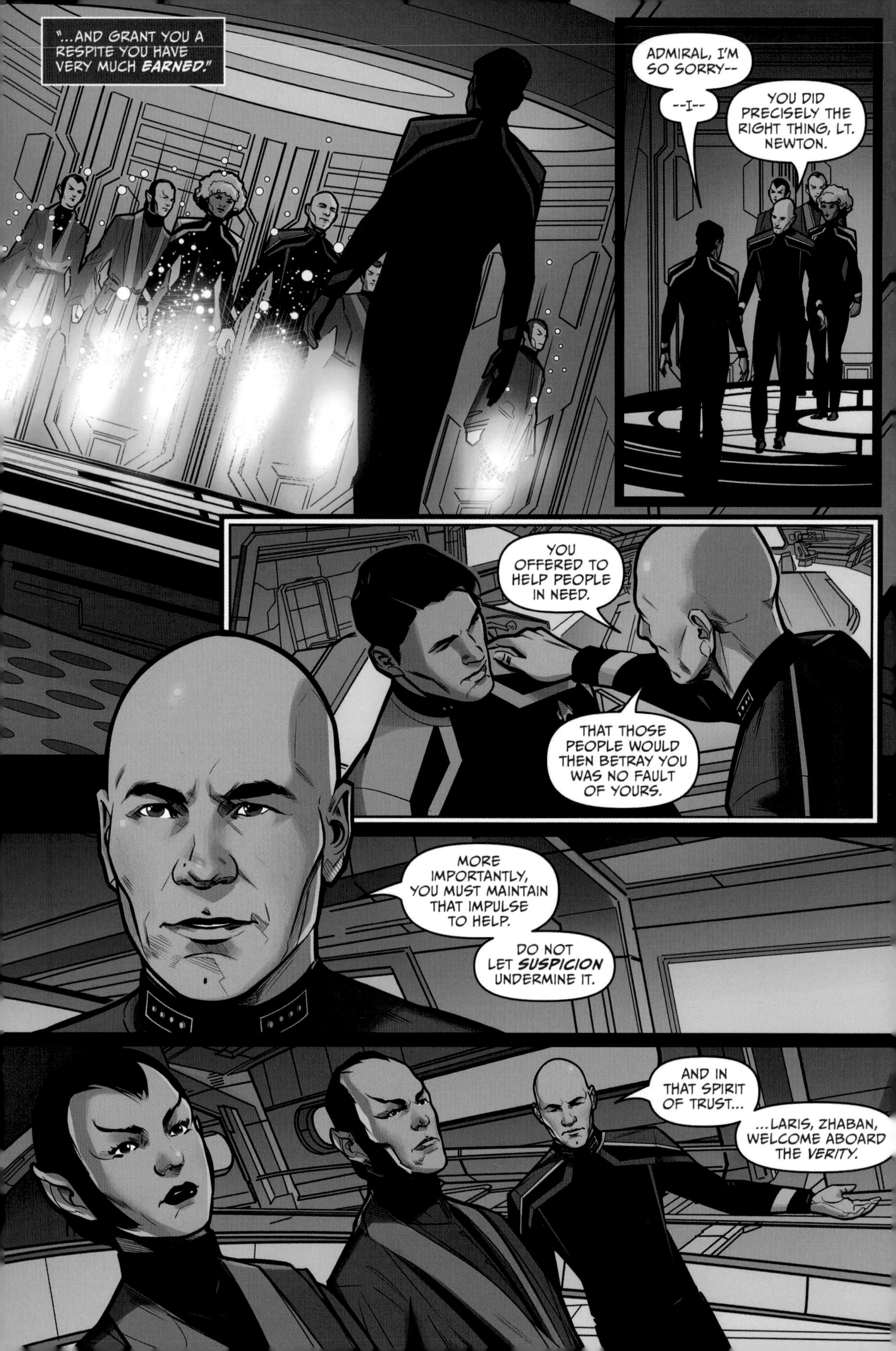
"...AND GRANT YOU A RESPITE YOU HAVE VERY MUCH *EARNED*."
ADMIRAL, I'M SO SORRY--
--I--
YOU DID PRECISELY THE RIGHT THING, LT. NEWTON.
YOU OFFERED TO HELP PEOPLE IN NEED.
THAT THOSE PEOPLE WOULD THEN BETRAY YOU WAS NO FAULT OF YOURS.
MORE IMPORTANTLY, YOU MUST MAINTAIN THAT IMPULSE TO HELP.
DO NOT LET *SUSPICION* UNDERMINE IT.
AND IN THAT SPIRIT OF TRUST...
...LARIS, ZHABAN, WELCOME ABOARD THE *VERITY*.

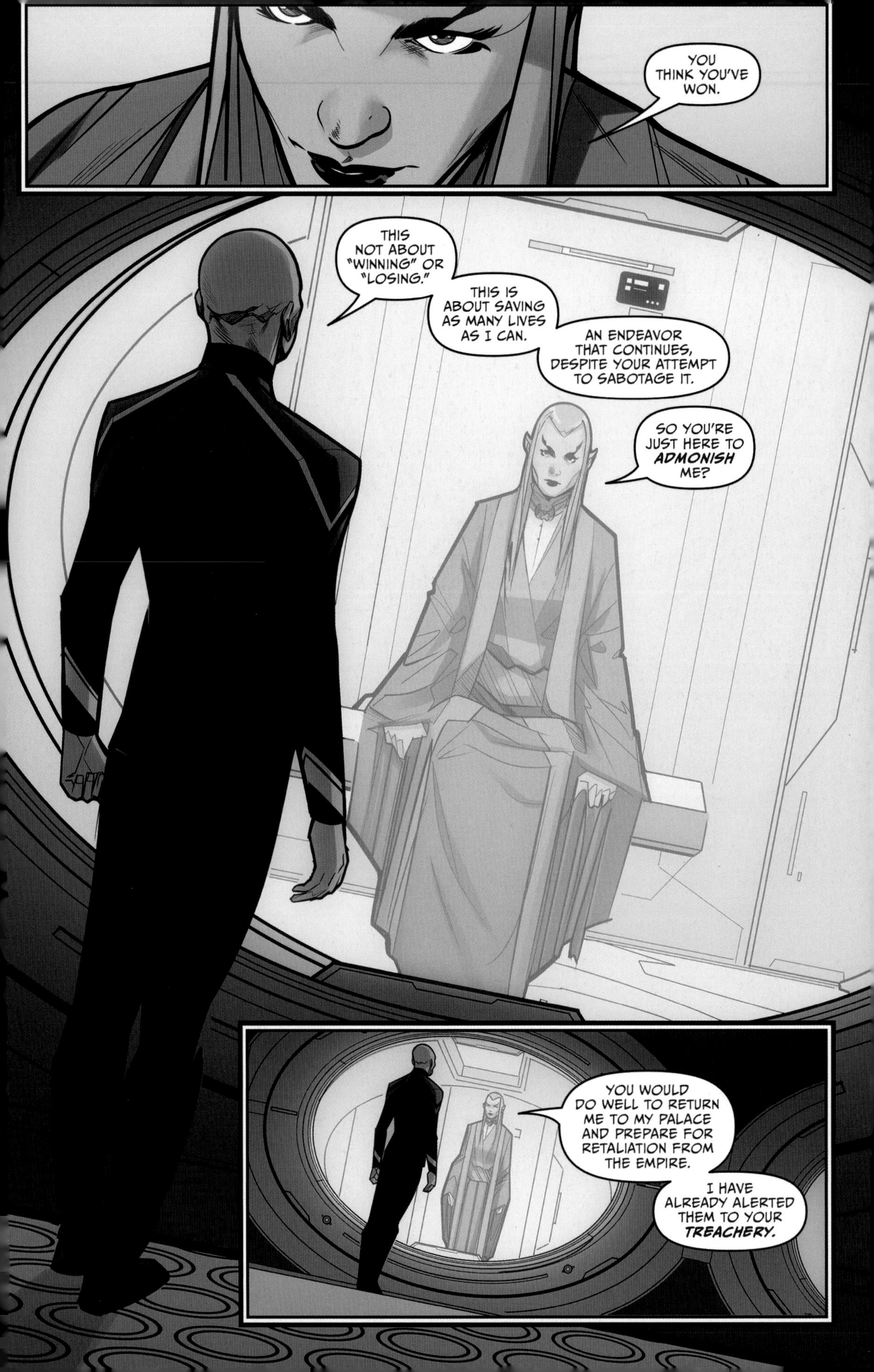
YOU THINK YOU'VE WON.
THIS NOT ABOUT "WINNING" OR "LOSING."
THIS IS ABOUT SAVING AS MANY LIVES AS I CAN.
AN ENDEAVOR THAT CONTINUES, DESPITE YOUR ATTEMPT TO SABOTAGE IT.
SO YOU'RE JUST HERE TO ***ADMONISH*** ME?
YOU WOULD DO WELL TO RETURN ME TO MY PALACE AND PREPARE FOR RETALIATION FROM THE EMPIRE.
I HAVE ALREADY ALERTED THEM TO YOUR ***TREACHERY.***

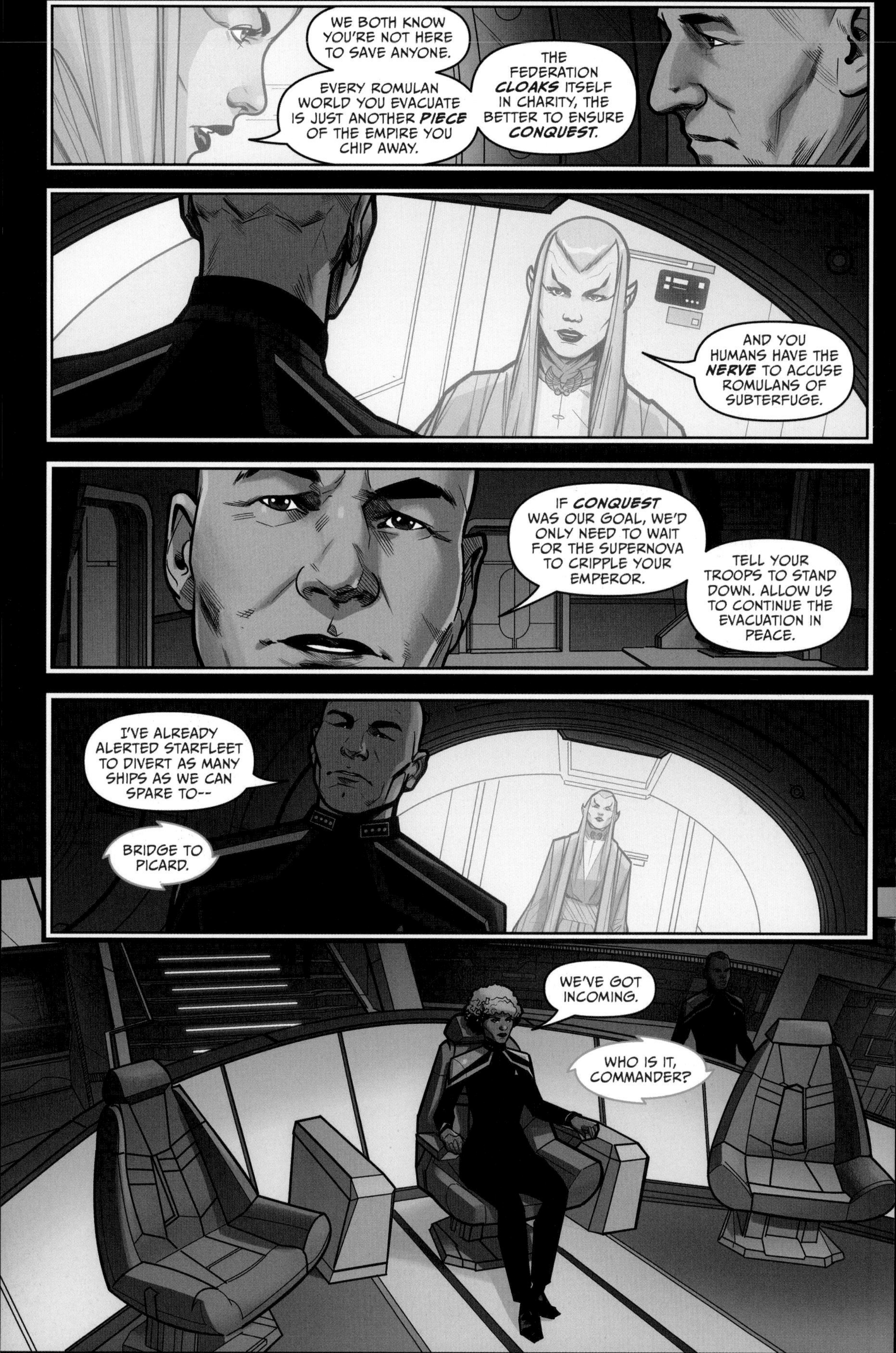
WE BOTH KNOW YOU'RE NOT HERE TO SAVE ANYONE.
EVERY ROMULAN WORLD YOU EVACUATE IS JUST ANOTHER PIECE OF THE EMPIRE YOU CHIP AWAY.
THE FEDERATION CLOAKS ITSELF IN CHARITY, THE BETTER TO ENSURE CONQUEST.
AND YOU HUMANS HAVE THE NERVE TO ACCUSE ROMULANS OF SUBTERFUGE.
IF CONQUEST WAS OUR GOAL, WE'D ONLY NEED TO WAIT FOR THE SUPERNOVA TO CRIPPLE YOUR EMPEROR.
TELL YOUR TROOPS TO STAND DOWN. ALLOW US TO CONTINUE THE EVACUATION IN PEACE.
I'VE ALREADY ALERTED STARFLEET TO DIVERT AS MANY SHIPS AS WE CAN SPARE TO--
BRIDGE TO PICARD.
WE'VE GOT INCOMING.
WHO IS IT, COMMANDER?

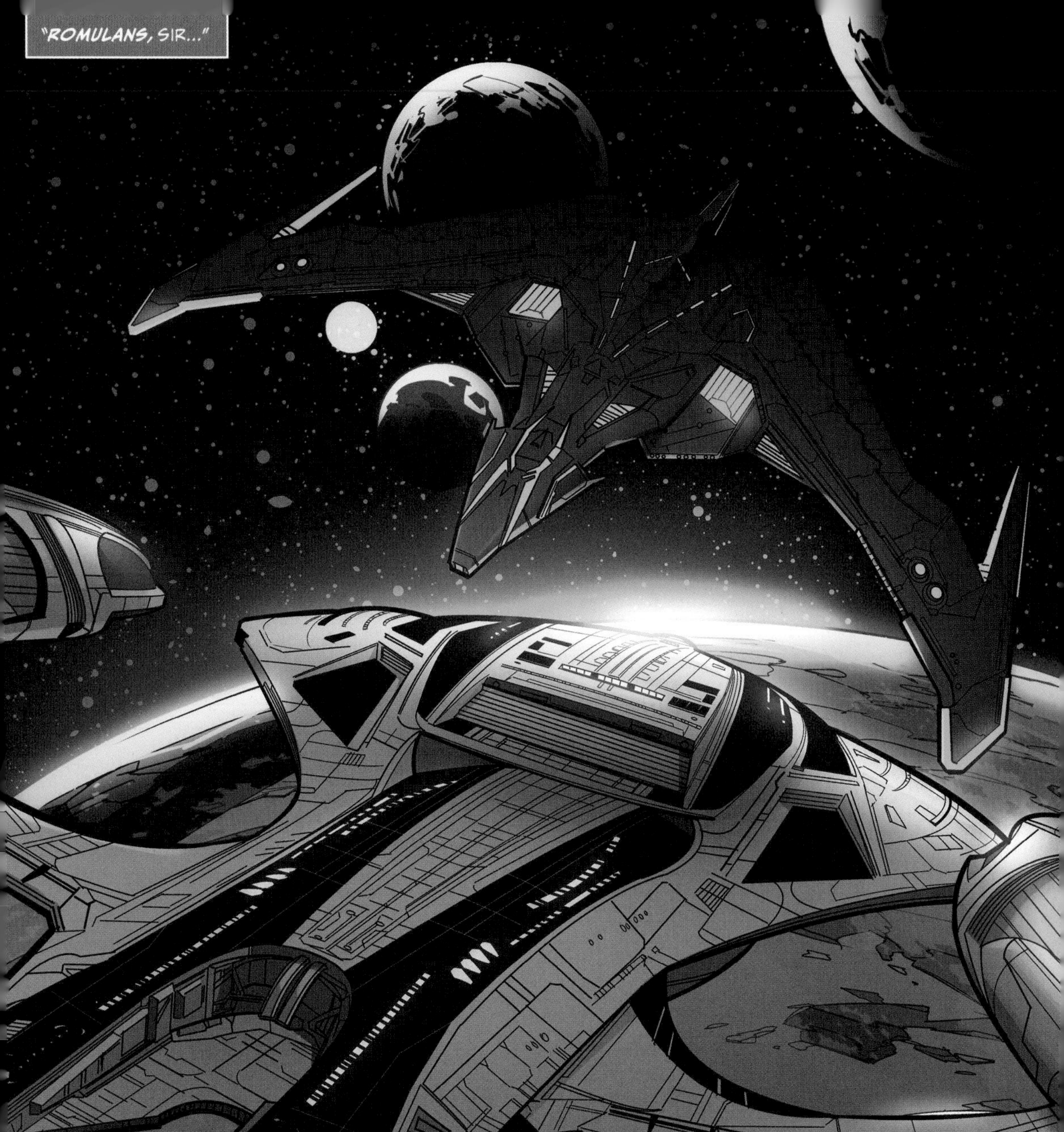
"ROMULANS, SIR..."

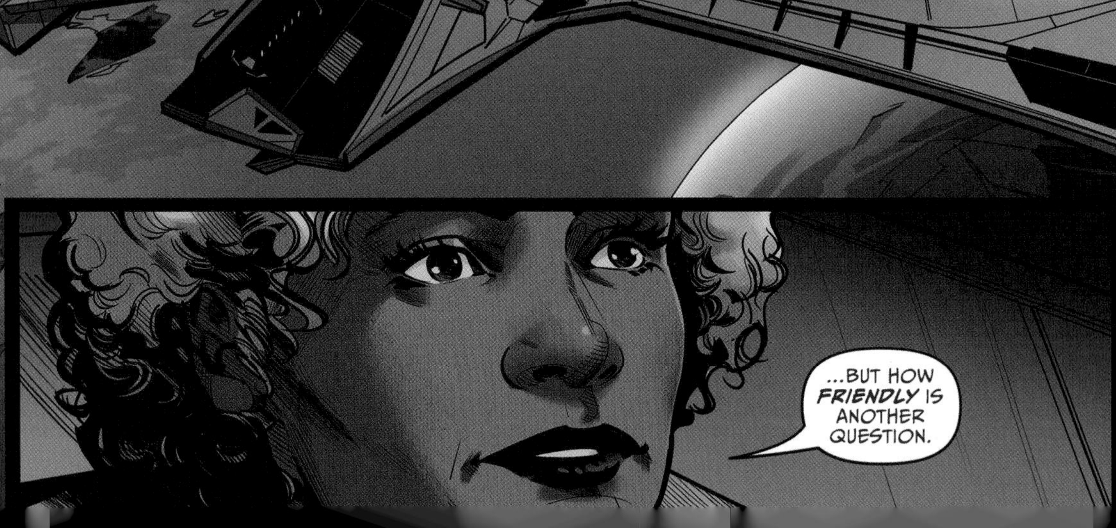
...BUT HOW FRIENDLY IS ANOTHER QUESTION.

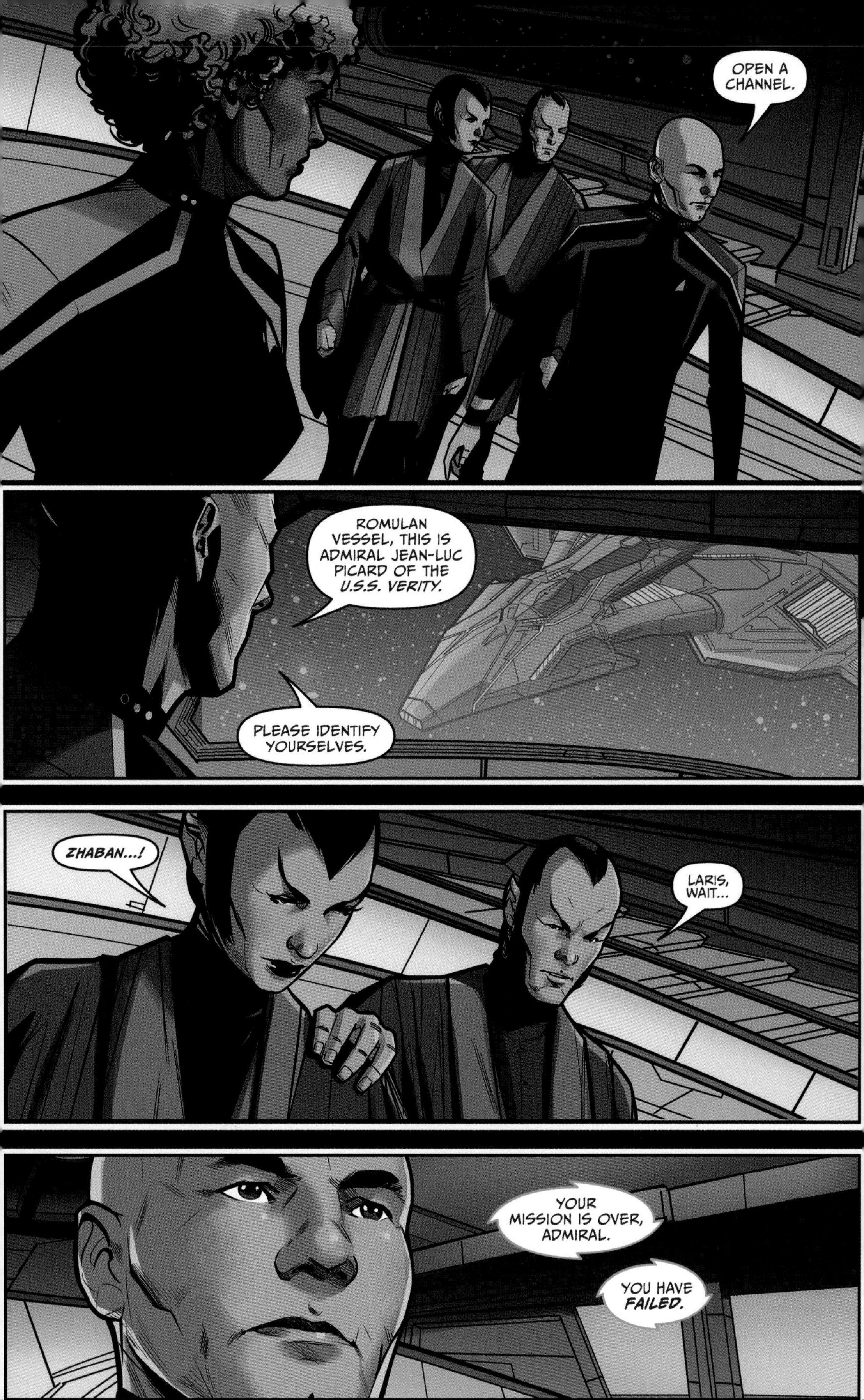
OPEN A CHANNEL.
ROMULAN VESSEL, THIS IS ADMIRAL JEAN-LUC PICARD OF THE *U.S.S. VERITY.*
PLEASE IDENTIFY YOURSELVES.
ZHABAN...!
LARIS, WAIT...
YOUR MISSION IS OVER, ADMIRAL.
YOU HAVE ***FAILED.***

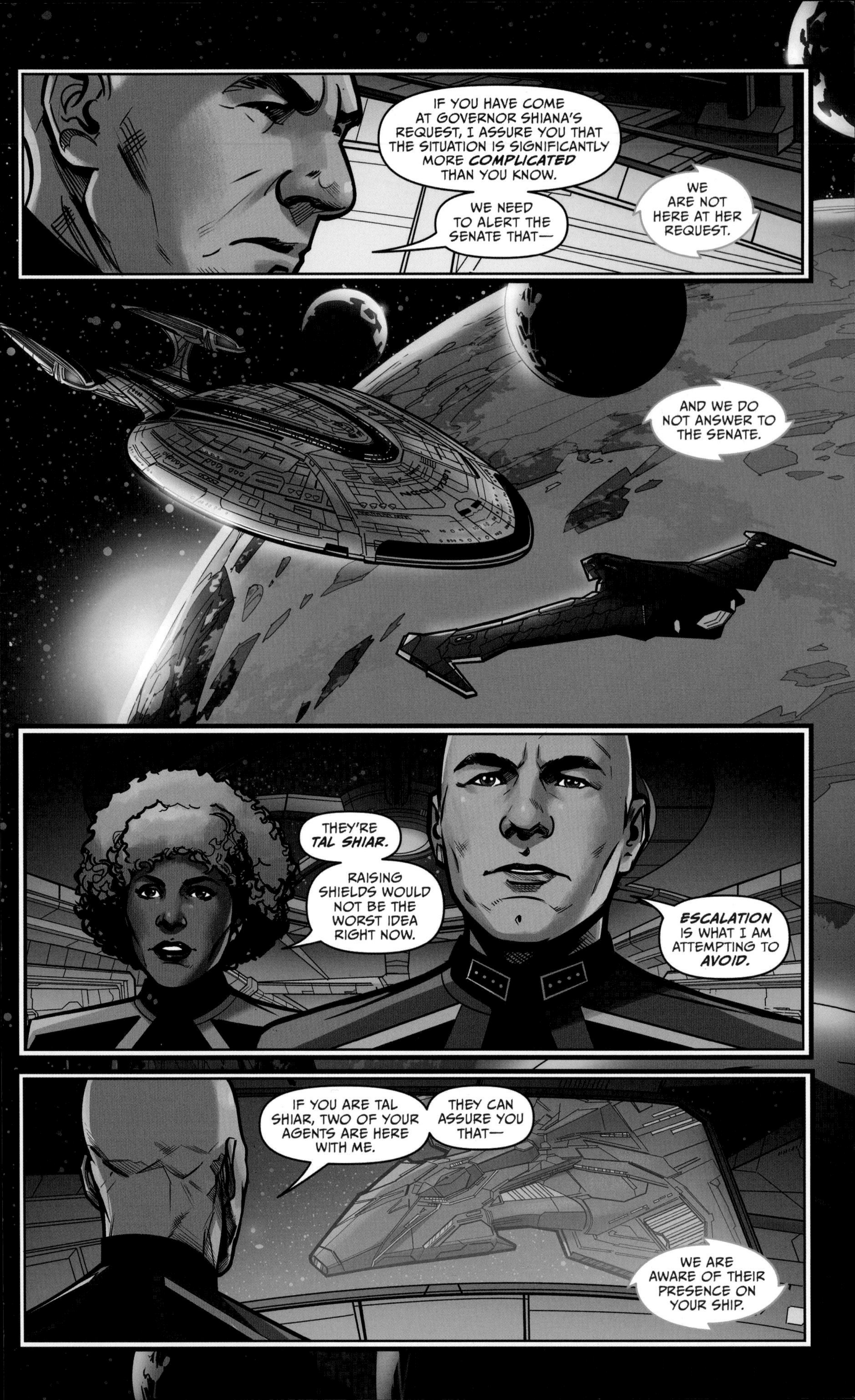
IF YOU HAVE COME AT GOVERNOR SHIANA'S REQUEST, I ASSURE YOU THAT THE SITUATION IS SIGNIFICANTLY MORE COMPLICATED THAN YOU KNOW.
WE NEED TO ALERT THE SENATE THAT—
WE ARE NOT HERE AT HER REQUEST.
AND WE DO NOT ANSWER TO THE SENATE.
THEY'RE TAL SHIAR.
RAISING SHIELDS WOULD NOT BE THE WORST IDEA RIGHT NOW.
ESCALATION IS WHAT I AM ATTEMPTING TO AVOID.
IF YOU ARE TAL SHIAR, TWO OF YOUR AGENTS ARE HERE WITH ME.
THEY CAN ASSURE YOU THAT—
WE ARE AWARE OF THEIR PRESENCE ON YOUR SHIP.

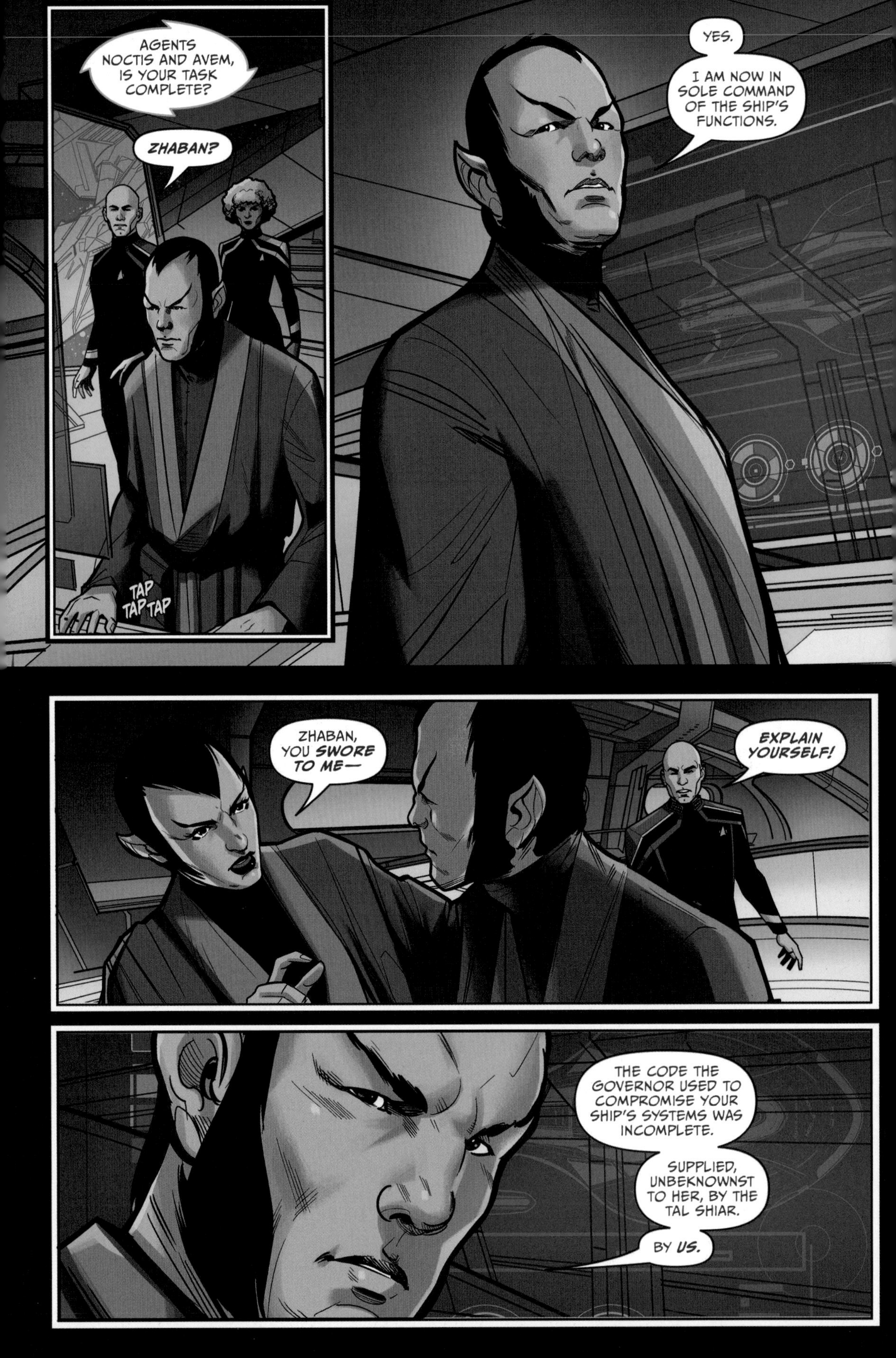
AGENTS NOCTIS AND AVEM, IS YOUR TASK COMPLETE?
ZHABAN?
TAP TAP TAP
YES.
I AM NOW IN SOLE COMMAND OF THE SHIP'S FUNCTIONS.
ZHABAN, YOU SWORE TO ME—
EXPLAIN YOURSELF!
THE CODE THE GOVERNOR USED TO COMPROMISE YOUR SHIP'S SYSTEMS WAS INCOMPLETE.
SUPPLIED, UNBEKNOWNST TO HER, BY THE TAL SHIAR.
BY US.

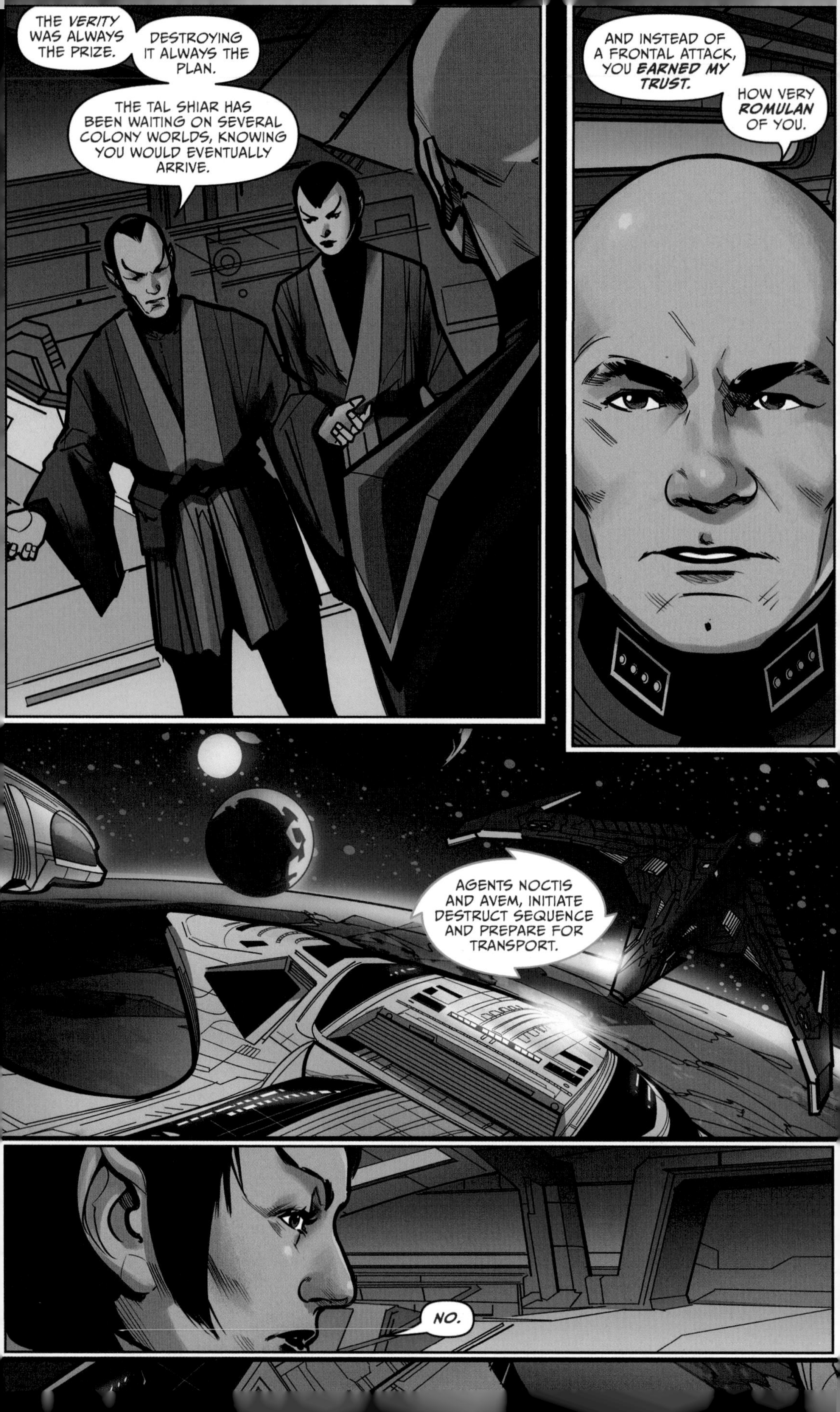
THE VERITY WAS ALWAYS THE PRIZE.
DESTROYING IT ALWAYS THE PLAN.
THE TAL SHIAR HAS BEEN WAITING ON SEVERAL COLONY WORLDS, KNOWING YOU WOULD EVENTUALLY ARRIVE.
AND INSTEAD OF A FRONTAL ATTACK, YOU EARNED MY TRUST.
HOW VERY ROMULAN OF YOU.
AGENTS NOCTIS AND AVEM, INITIATE DESTRUCT SEQUENCE AND PREPARE FOR TRANSPORT.
NO.

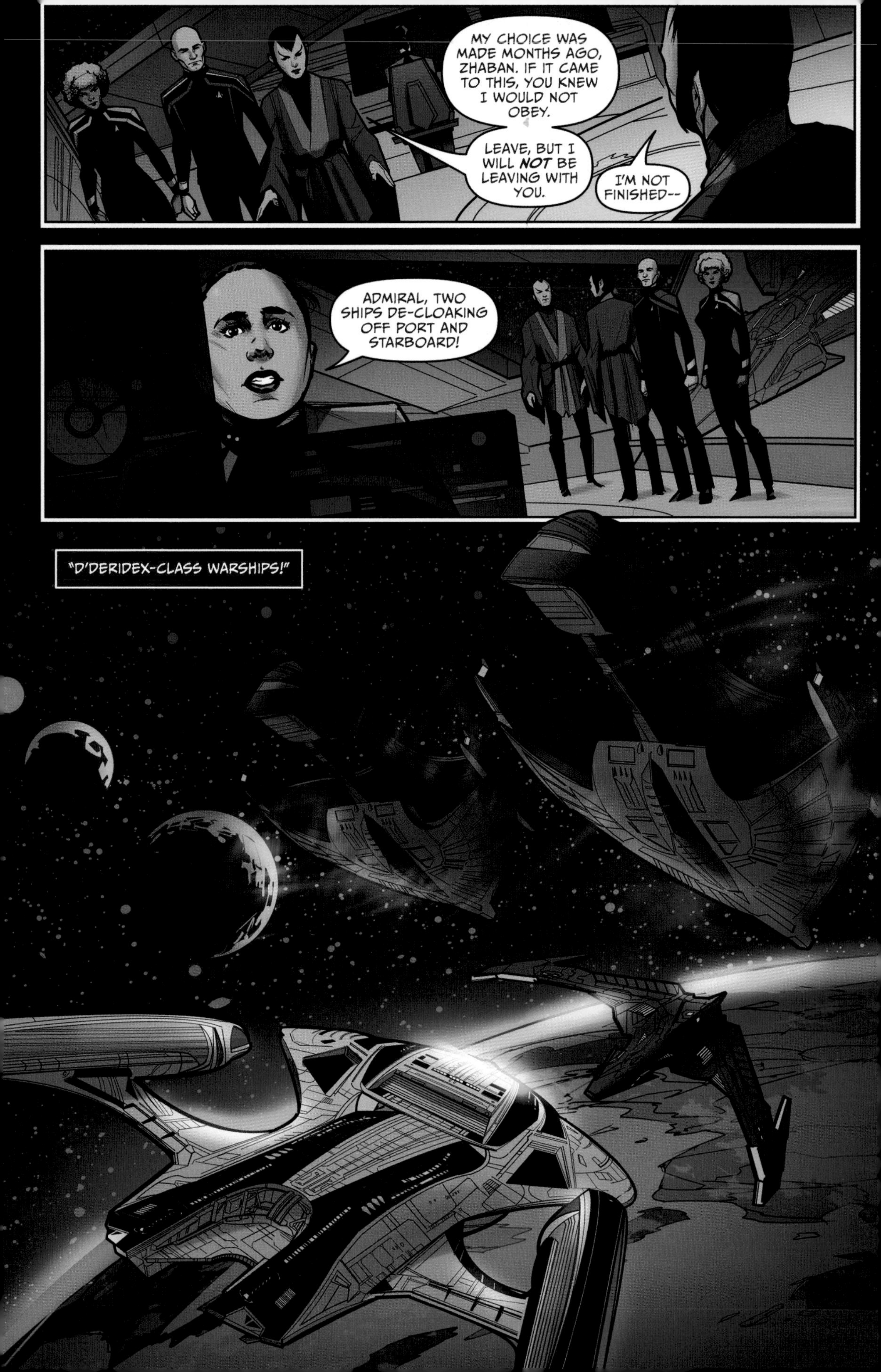
MY CHOICE WAS MADE MONTHS AGO, ZHABAN. IF IT CAME TO THIS, YOU KNEW I WOULD NOT OBEY.
LEAVE, BUT I WILL **NOT** BE LEAVING WITH YOU.
I'M NOT FINISHED--
ADMIRAL, TWO SHIPS DE-CLOAKING OFF PORT AND STARBOARD!
"D'DERIDEX-CLASS WARSHIPS!"

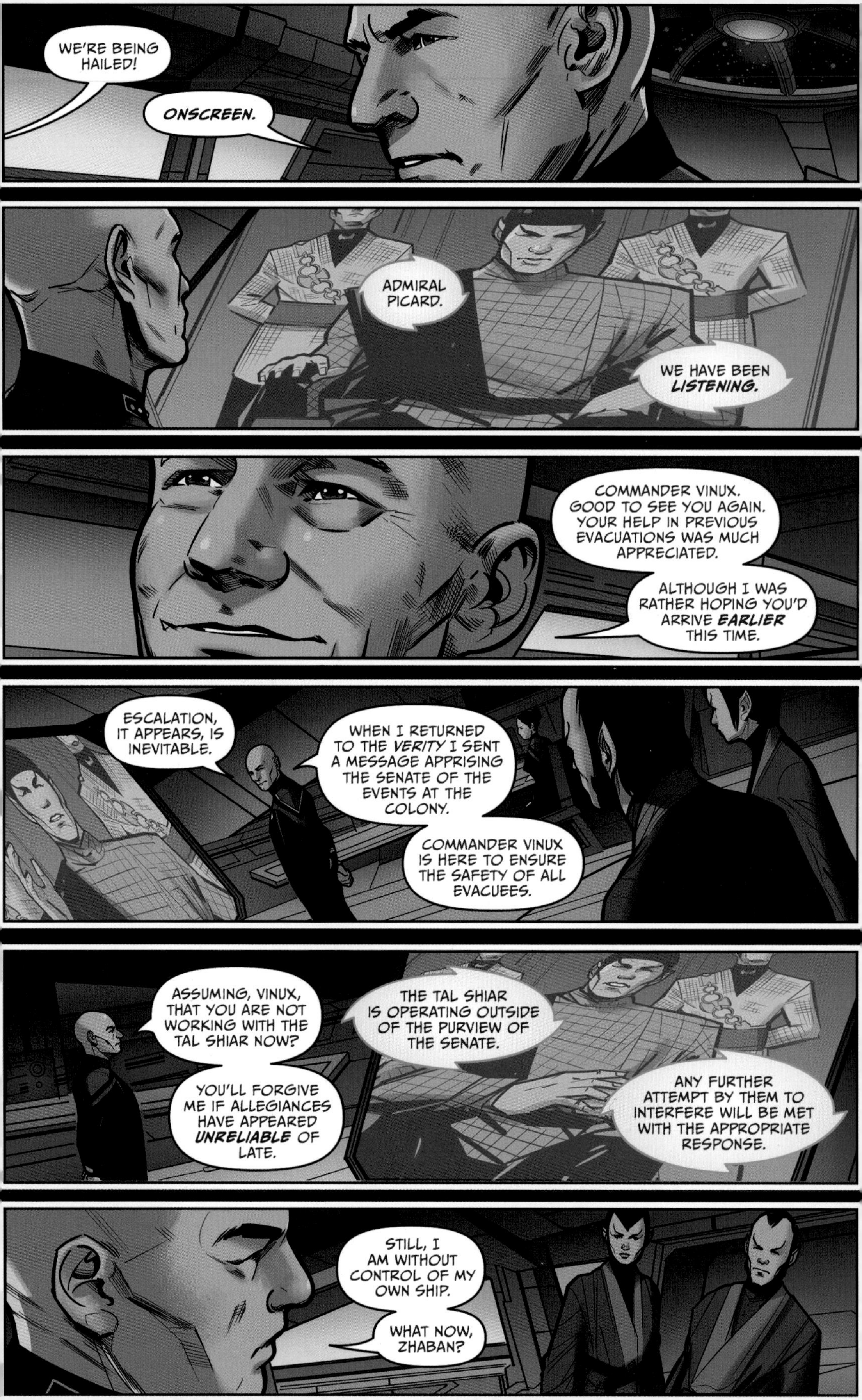

WE'RE BEING HAILED!
ONSCREEN.
ADMIRAL PICARD.
WE HAVE BEEN LISTENING.
COMMANDER VINUX. GOOD TO SEE YOU AGAIN. YOUR HELP IN PREVIOUS EVACUATIONS WAS MUCH APPRECIATED.
ALTHOUGH I WAS RATHER HOPING YOU'D ARRIVE EARLIER THIS TIME.
ESCALATION, IT APPEARS, IS INEVITABLE.
WHEN I RETURNED TO THE VERITY I SENT A MESSAGE APPRISING THE SENATE OF THE EVENTS AT THE COLONY.
COMMANDER VINUX IS HERE TO ENSURE THE SAFETY OF ALL EVACUEES.
ASSUMING, VINUX, THAT YOU ARE NOT WORKING WITH THE TAL SHIAR NOW?
YOU'LL FORGIVE ME IF ALLEGIANCES HAVE APPEARED UNRELIABLE OF LATE.
THE TAL SHIAR IS OPERATING OUTSIDE OF THE PURVIEW OF THE SENATE.
ANY FURTHER ATTEMPT BY THEM TO INTERFERE WILL BE MET WITH THE APPROPRIATE RESPONSE.
STILL, I AM WITHOUT CONTROL OF MY OWN SHIP.
WHAT NOW, ZHABAN?

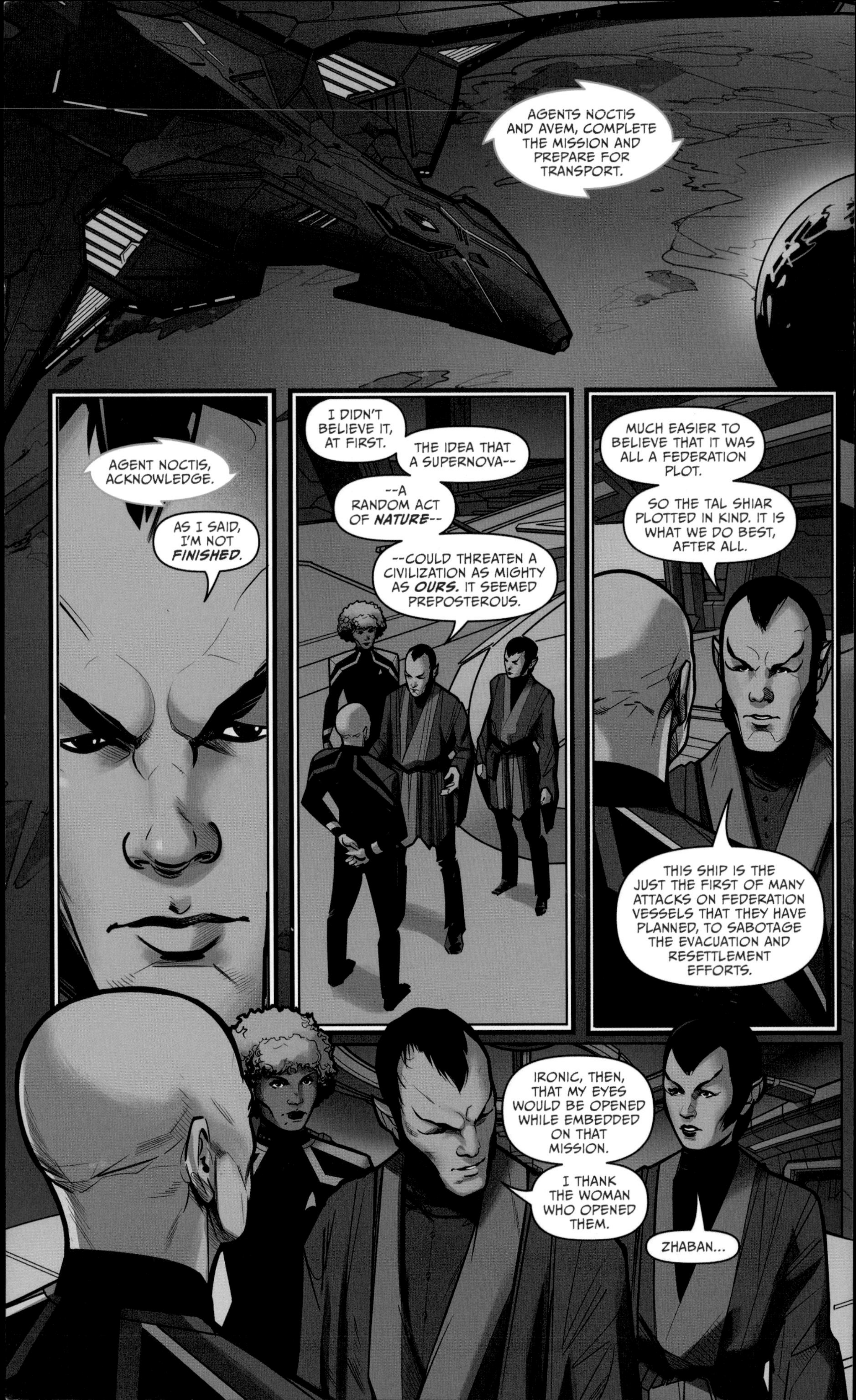
AGENTS NOCTIS AND AVEM, COMPLETE THE MISSION AND PREPARE FOR TRANSPORT.
AGENT NOCTIS, ACKNOWLEDGE.
AS I SAID, I'M NOT FINISHED.
I DIDN'T BELIEVE IT, AT FIRST.
THE IDEA THAT A SUPERNOVA--
--A RANDOM ACT OF NATURE--
--COULD THREATEN A CIVILIZATION AS MIGHTY AS OURS. IT SEEMED PREPOSTEROUS.
MUCH EASIER TO BELIEVE THAT IT WAS ALL A FEDERATION PLOT.
SO THE TAL SHIAR PLOTTED IN KIND. IT IS WHAT WE DO BEST, AFTER ALL.
THIS SHIP IS THE JUST THE FIRST OF MANY ATTACKS ON FEDERATION VESSELS THAT THEY HAVE PLANNED, TO SABOTAGE THE EVACUATION AND RESETTLEMENT EFFORTS.
IRONIC, THEN, THAT MY EYES WOULD BE OPENED WHILE EMBEDDED ON THAT MISSION.
I THANK THE WOMAN WHO OPENED THEM.
ZHABAN...

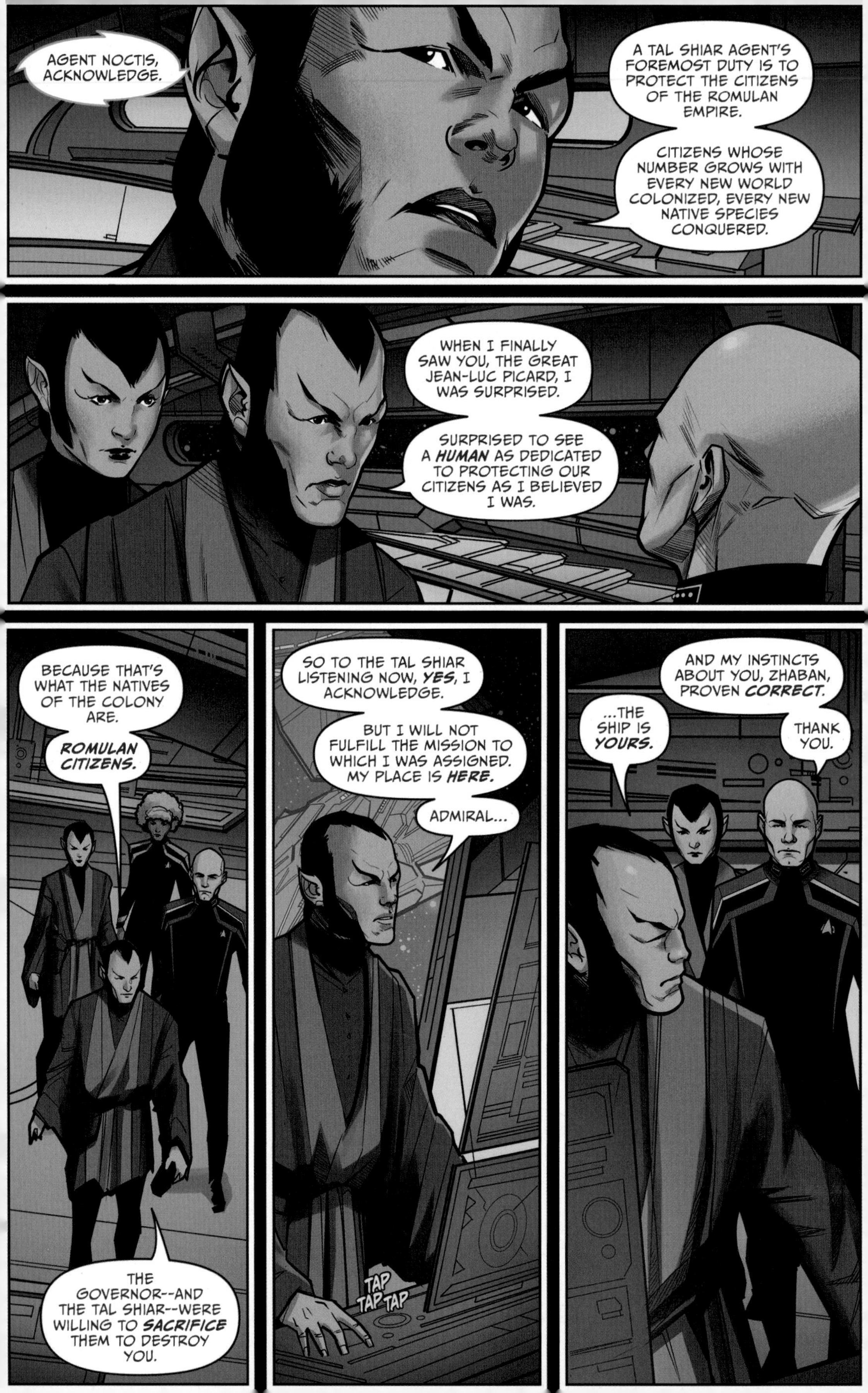
AGENT NOCTIS, ACKNOWLEDGE.
A TAL SHIAR AGENT'S FOREMOST DUTY IS TO PROTECT THE CITIZENS OF THE ROMULAN EMPIRE.
CITIZENS WHOSE NUMBER GROWS WITH EVERY NEW WORLD COLONIZED, EVERY NEW NATIVE SPECIES CONQUERED.
WHEN I FINALLY SAW YOU, THE GREAT JEAN-LUC PICARD, I WAS SURPRISED.
SURPRISED TO SEE A ***HUMAN*** AS DEDICATED TO PROTECTING OUR CITIZENS AS I BELIEVED I WAS.
BECAUSE THAT'S WHAT THE NATIVES OF THE COLONY ARE.
ROMULAN CITIZENS.
THE GOVERNOR--AND THE TAL SHIAR--WERE WILLING TO ***SACRIFICE*** THEM TO DESTROY YOU.
SO TO THE TAL SHIAR LISTENING NOW, ***YES***, I ACKNOWLEDGE.
BUT I WILL NOT FULFILL THE MISSION TO WHICH I WAS ASSIGNED. MY PLACE IS ***HERE.***
ADMIRAL...
TAP TAP TAP
...THE SHIP IS ***YOURS.***
AND MY INSTINCTS ABOUT YOU, ZHABAN, PROVEN ***CORRECT.***
THANK YOU.

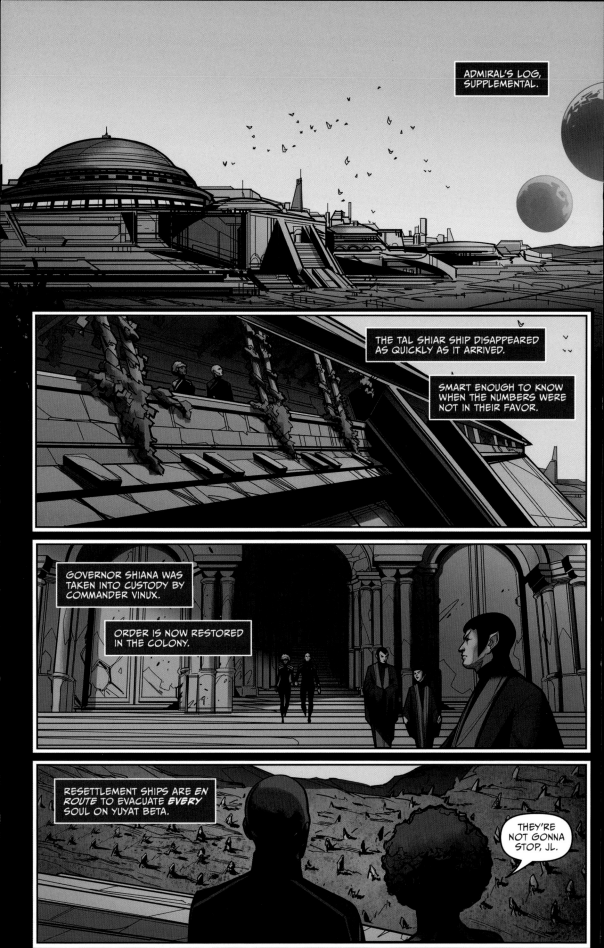

ADMIRAL'S LOG,
SUPPLEMENTAL.

THE TAL SHIAR SHIP DISAPPEARED
AS QUICKLY AS IT ARRIVED.

SMART ENOUGH TO KNOW
WHEN THE NUMBERS WERE
NOT IN THEIR FAVOR.

GOVERNOR SHIANA WAS
TAKEN INTO CUSTODY BY
COMMANDER VINUX.

ORDER IS NOW RESTORED
IN THE COLONY.

RESETTLEMENT SHIPS ARE *EN
ROUTE* TO EVACUATE *EVERY*
SOUL ON YUYAT BETA.

THEY'RE
NOT GONNA
STOP, JL.

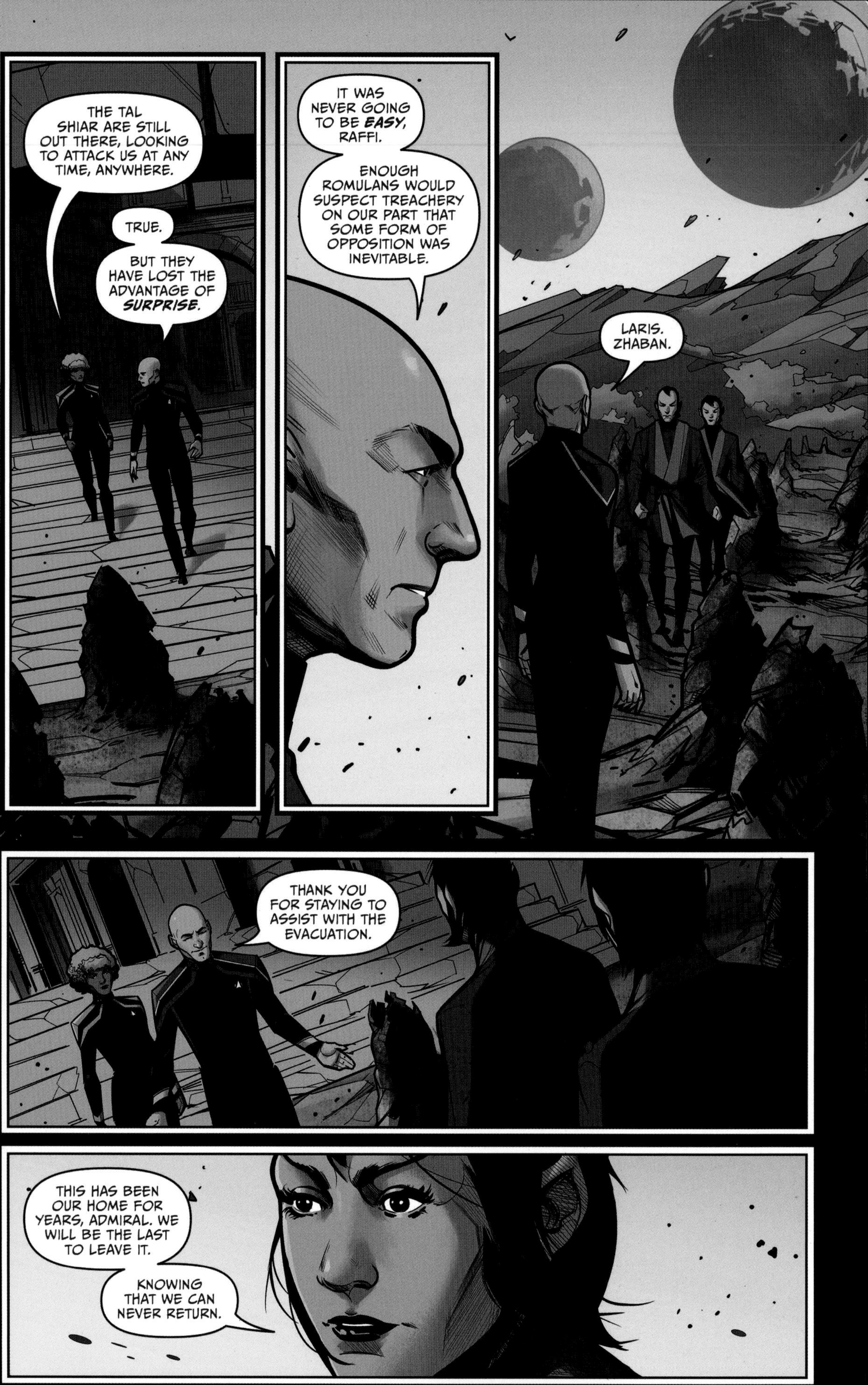
THE TAL SHIAR ARE STILL OUT THERE, LOOKING TO ATTACK US AT ANY TIME, ANYWHERE.
TRUE.
BUT THEY HAVE LOST THE ADVANTAGE OF *SURPRISE*.
IT WAS NEVER GOING TO BE *EASY*, RAFFI.
ENOUGH ROMULANS WOULD SUSPECT TREACHERY ON OUR PART THAT SOME FORM OF OPPOSITION WAS INEVITABLE.
LARIS. ZHABAN.
THANK YOU FOR STAYING TO ASSIST WITH THE EVACUATION.
THIS HAS BEEN OUR HOME FOR YEARS, ADMIRAL. WE WILL BE THE LAST TO LEAVE IT.
KNOWING THAT WE CAN NEVER RETURN.

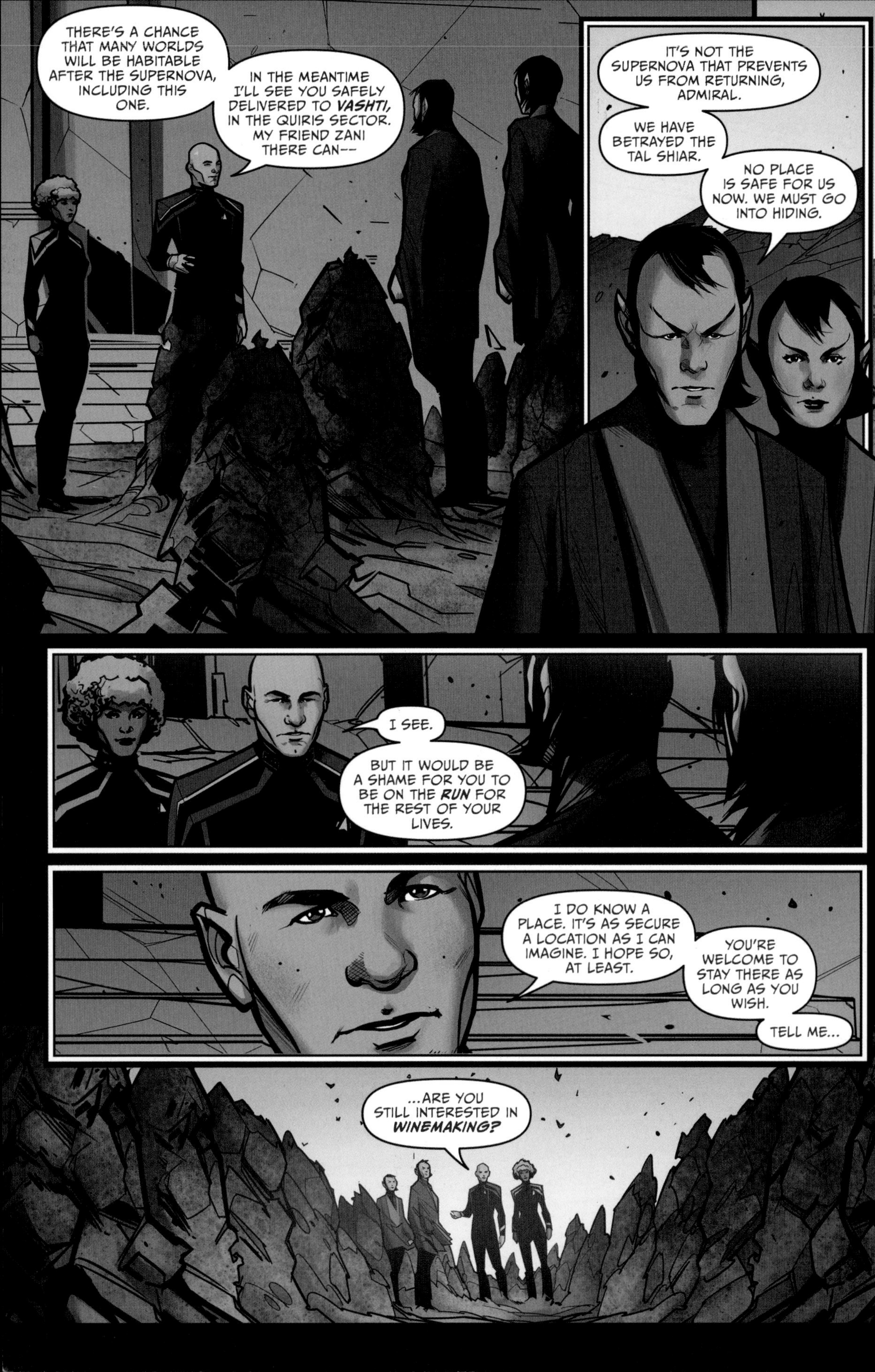
THERE'S A CHANCE THAT MANY WORLDS WILL BE HABITABLE AFTER THE SUPERNOVA, INCLUDING THIS ONE.
IN THE MEANTIME I'LL SEE YOU SAFELY DELIVERED TO **VASHTI**, IN THE QUIRIS SECTOR. MY FRIEND ZANI THERE CAN--
IT'S NOT THE SUPERNOVA THAT PREVENTS US FROM RETURNING, ADMIRAL.
WE HAVE BETRAYED THE TAL SHIAR.
NO PLACE IS SAFE FOR US NOW. WE MUST GO INTO HIDING.
I SEE.
BUT IT WOULD BE A SHAME FOR YOU TO BE ON THE **RUN** FOR THE REST OF YOUR LIVES.
I DO KNOW A PLACE. IT'S AS SECURE A LOCATION AS I CAN IMAGINE. I HOPE SO, AT LEAST.
YOU'RE WELCOME TO STAY THERE AS LONG AS YOU WISH.
TELL ME...
...ARE YOU STILL INTERESTED IN **WINEMAKING?**

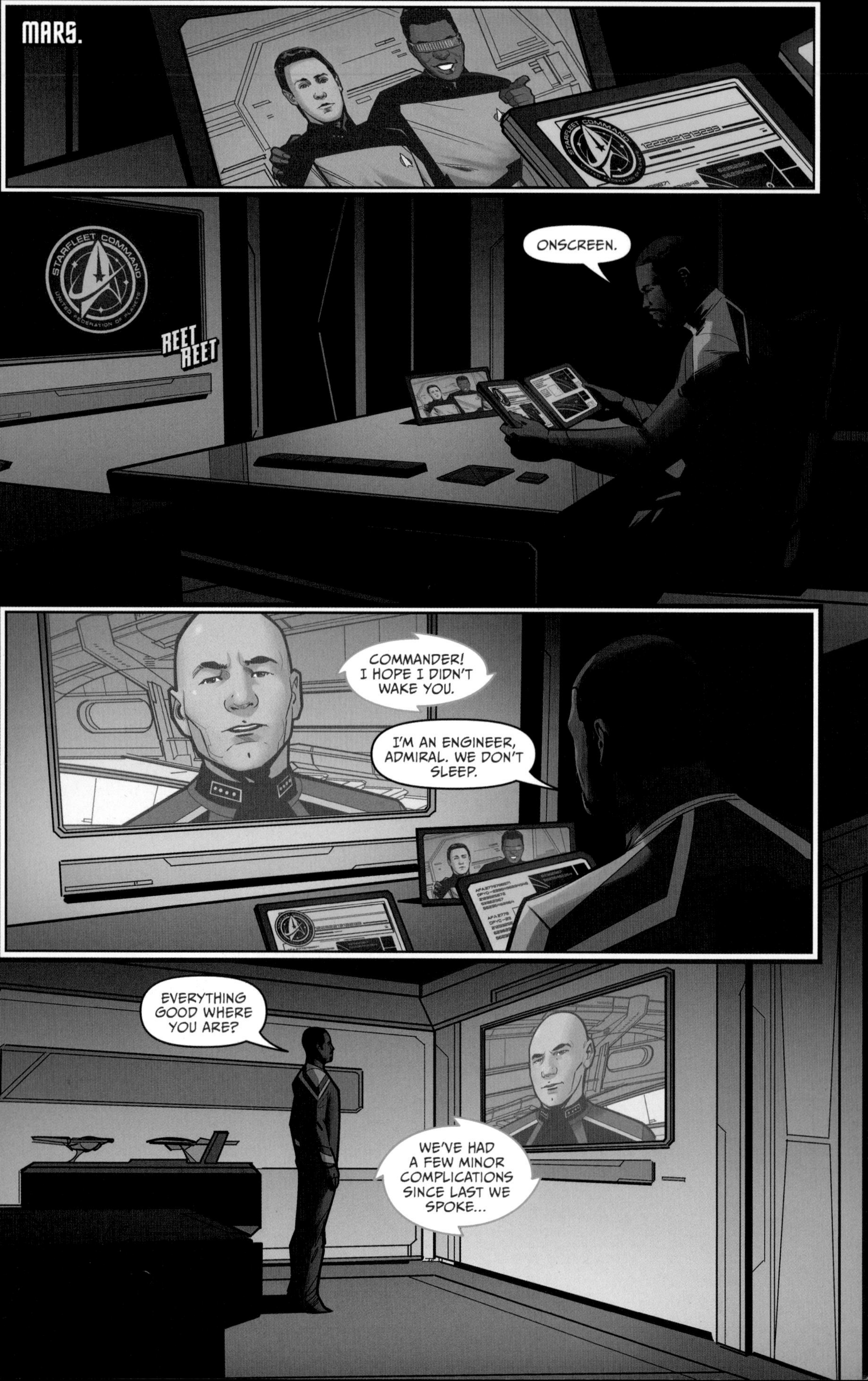
MARS.
ONSCREEN.
REET REET
COMMANDER! I HOPE I DIDN'T WAKE YOU.
I'M AN ENGINEER, ADMIRAL. WE DON'T SLEEP.
EVERYTHING GOOD WHERE YOU ARE?
WE'VE HAD A FEW MINOR COMPLICATIONS SINCE LAST WE SPOKE...

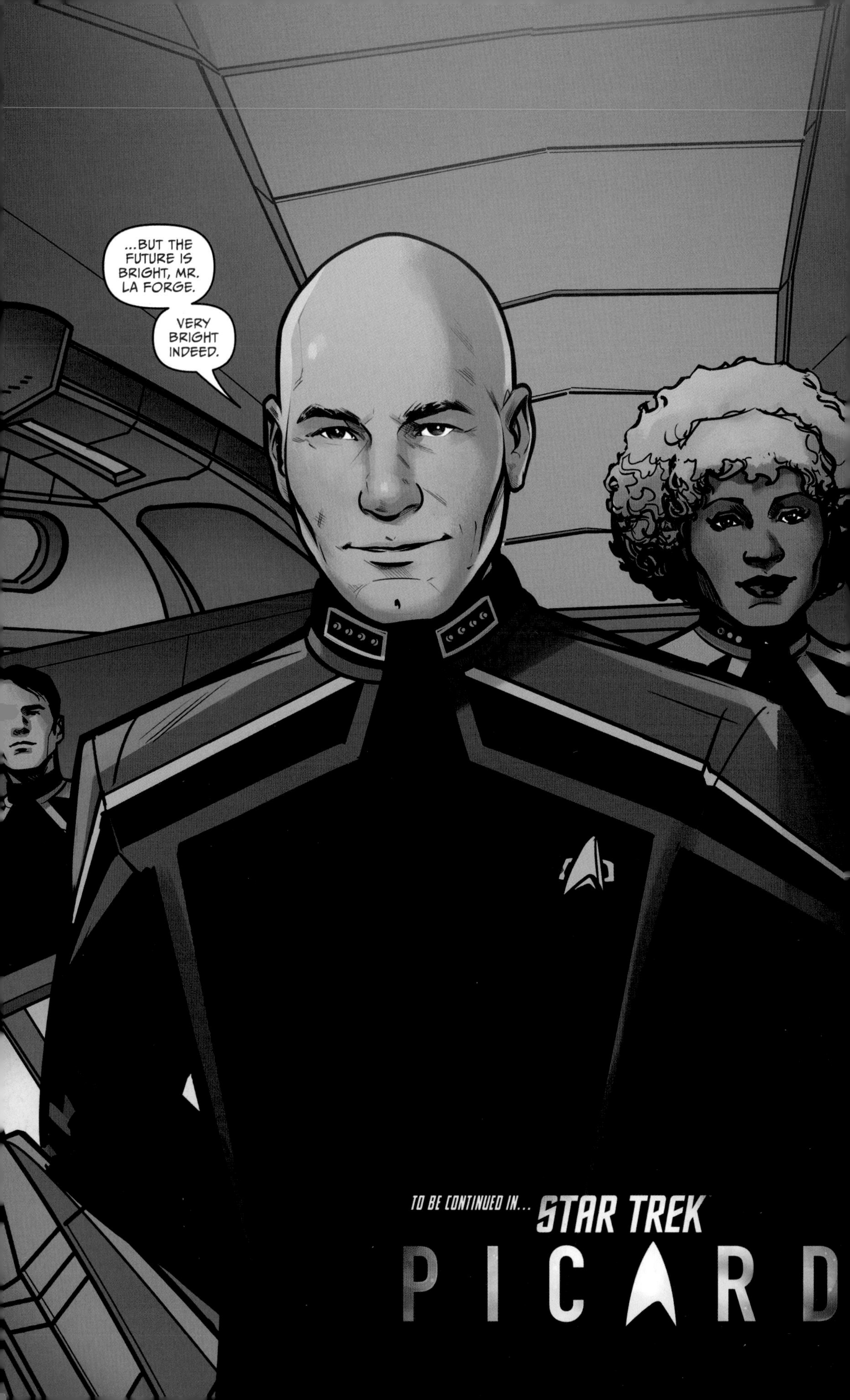
...BUT THE FUTURE IS BRIGHT, MR. LA FORGE.
VERY BRIGHT INDEED.
TO BE CONTINUED IN... STAR TREK
PICARD

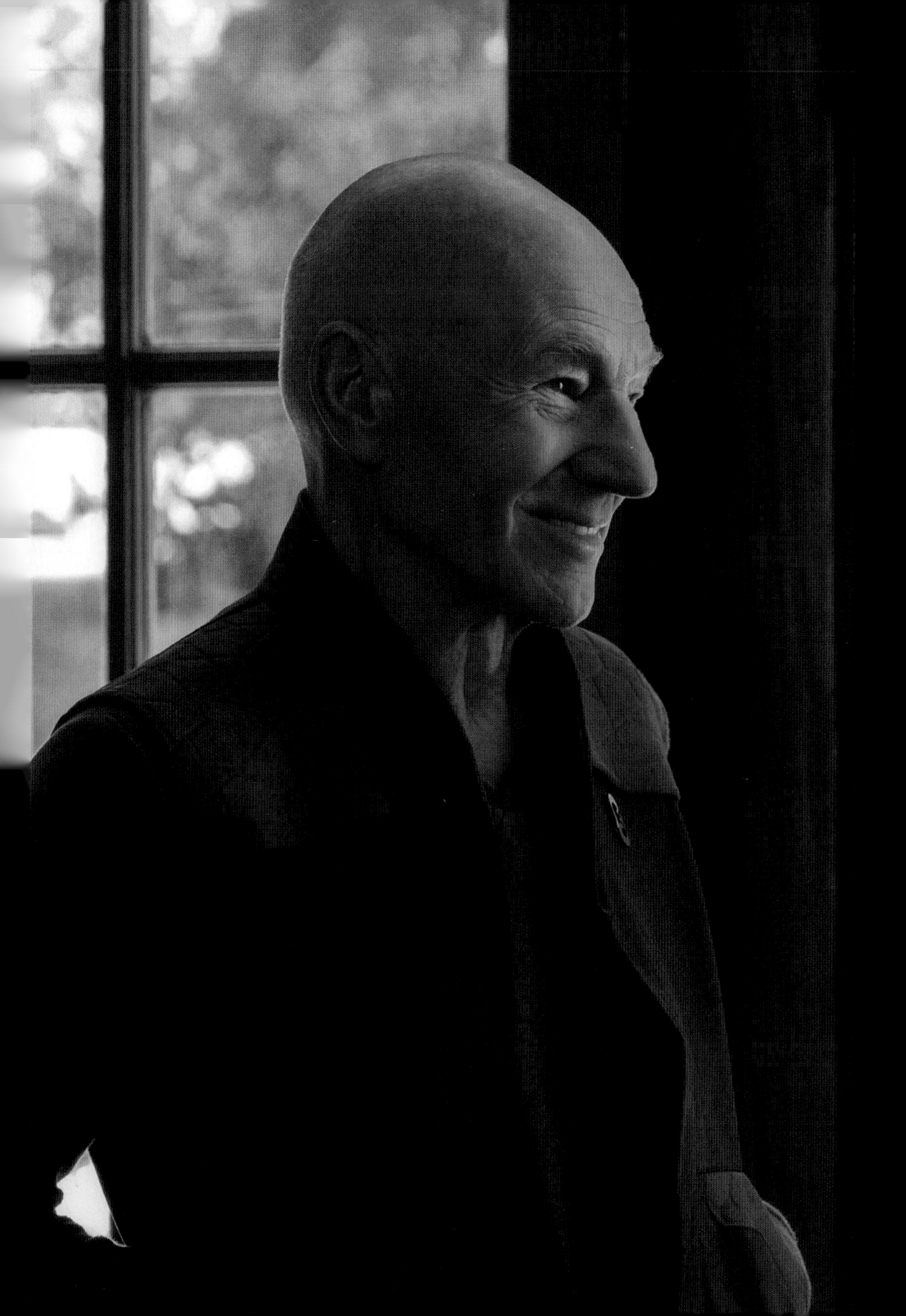

CAPTAIN'S LOG

An Interview with Kirsten Beyer
Co-Creator/Supervising Producer on *Picard*

CAPTAIN'S LOG: A new *Star Trek* series featuring the continuing adventures of Jean-Luc Picard has been a dream of fans for decades, but for years Patrick Stewart was adamant that it would never happen. Can you tell us a bit about how you were able to bring *Star Trek: Picard* to life and what makes it different from ideas that were turned down before?

KIRSTEN BEYER: The most critical difference was our desire to move beyond the structure and type of storytelling of *Trek*'s previous iterations and uncover aspects of the character that Sir Patrick had never before been able to explore. It wasn't that he was uninterested in *Star Trek* or Picard as a character. It was that none of us intended to retread well-worn territory or relationships. There had to be something new to say, and it needed to be relevant to this moment in time.

CL: When *Star Trek: Picard* was announced at *Star Trek* Las Vegas 2018, it was a massive surprise. How long had the show been in development when you finally got to reveal it to the world, and what was it like keeping that secret for so long?

KB: Our earliest work on what would become *Star Trek: Picard* had begun eight months prior to the announcement. It wasn't a hard secret to keep. Passionate as we all were about the possibility, until all of the details had been worked out, there was nothing to tell. My favorite part about that day, because I could not be present for the announcement, was a text from Alex Kurtzman just after he got offstage. Two words: "It's real."

CL: Unlike *Star Trek: The Next Generation*, Patrick Stewart is an executive producer on *Star Trek: Picard* and is actively involved in

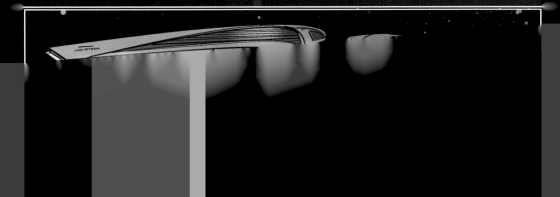

the creative process. What has it been like working with him?

KB: What do you do when your real life exceeds your expectations? (Besides, keep it to yourself?) I never really dared to dream of this happening. Sir Patrick is a generous and brilliant collaborator, and because he demands the best of those with whom he surrounds himself, you try to rise to that occasion. It's exhausting and exhilarating, and I wouldn't trade it for the world.

CL: You've been in the writer's rooms for both *Discovery* and *Picard.* Are there a lot of differences in the creation process for each show, or do you find that there are a lot of similarities?

KB: The biggest difference has been the individual personalities on the projects, as well as the stated goals of each. *Discovery*'s focus is more action-oriented, while *Picard* is entirely character driven. This means that the work in the rooms crafting the story and the writing is very different, but that's a great thing, and I have enjoyed it tremendously.

CL: Is there anything that's happened during *Star Trek: Picard*'s first season that you were surprised you actually got to do, or any major moments that stand out to you as your favorite?

KB: By far my greatest joy was having Jonathan Frakes direct the episode I wrote. We had met several times on the first

two seasons of *Discovery*, but it was such a delight to be on set with him. Whether he is or not, he appears to be incredibly relaxed and keeps everyone's spirits so high during the long shooting days. When you find ways to elevate moments that he loves, small choices that add to the overall performances, it's absolutely exhilarating.

CL: With *Star Trek: Picard* renewed for a second season, is there anything you can tease as to where we may see Picard's adventures take him next?

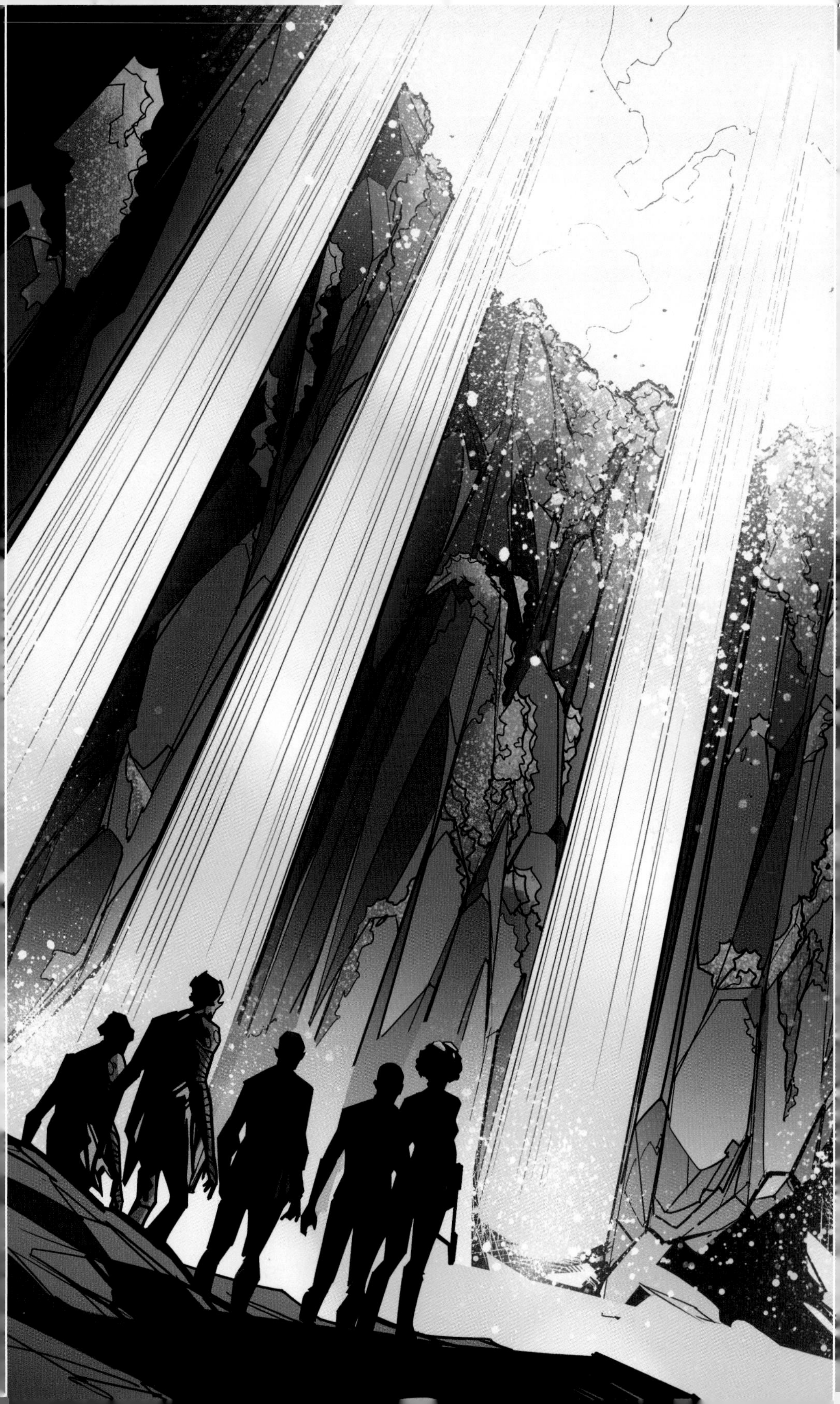

KB: No, but nice try.

CL: How did you determine what area of backstory to explore for the prequel comic? Did you know you wanted it to introduce Laris and Zhaban, or were there other stories you considered exploring before landing on this one?

KB: There is no getting around the fact that there are 20 years of material between the last time we saw Picard and the start of the series. So in a way, narrowing the focus was a challenge. That said, the events most closely related to the series had to be connected to the Romulan rescue mission and the new characters. Laris and Zhaban's story felt like the absolute right size for the prequel and also one that was compelling given how very important they become to Picard.

CL: What was your writing process with Mike Johnson like for this story? Was it similar to your collaboration on the *Discovery* series the two of you have done for IDW Publishing, or was it different because the show was not yet on air while this comic was being written?

KB: The first comic we wrote together for *Discovery* was created well before the show was on the air. This is just how we roll now. We create the story together, then Mike goes away and turns it into a brilliant comic book. I am fortunate indeed in my collaboration with Mike. He is a treasure, and I absolutely adore working with him.

CL: When approaching a comic book storyline, do you have a different process or set of considerations you take into account than when creating a storyline for an episode of TV?

KB: Yes, merely as a matter of form. Comics require a certain focus and balance of action and character development. Television episodes do as well, but it feels like they have more room to breathe. We had ten episodes to tell one Picard story on TV. We

had three issues, the equivalent of a little more than one television episode in terms of page count, to tell our *Picard: Countdown* story. The process of developing a story isn't that different, but the comics feel like they have to be tighter—almost like poetry instead of prose.

CL: Was there anything that you had hoped would make it into the comic that ultimately did not fit?

KB: Not that I can recall. Mike?

MIKE JOHNSON [pops head out of turbolift]: No, I think we got it all!

CL: You've now written *Star Trek* stories for novels, television, and comic books. Is there a medium that you think of as your favorite to work in? How about one you'd still like to try your hand at?

KB: Interpretive dance? Comics are the most fun because of Mike. Really, he is just carrying me along on his coattails. I still love novels but they are inordinately time consuming when I am also working on television so, for now, they feel so very hard to do properly. I have come to love television writing, but still have a long way to go. Working that craft daily, however, is a joyful challenge.

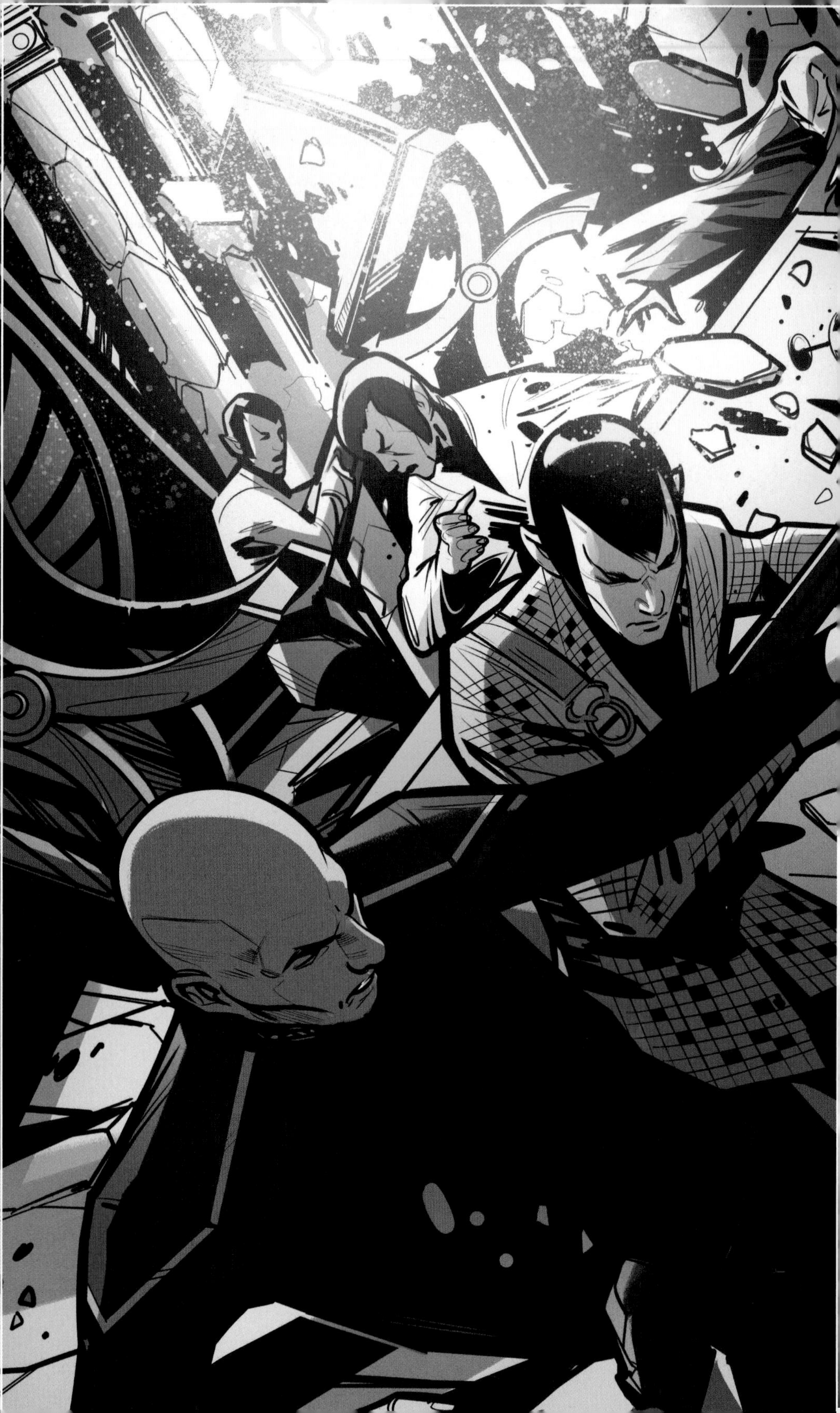

VISUALIZING THE *VERITY*

CRYPTIC STUDIOS AND IDW COMICS TEAM UP TO BRING THE *U.S.S. VERITY* TO LIFE

by **Thomas Marrone** Lead Ship & UI Artist, *Star Trek Online*

After almost two decades, it was time for Jean-Luc Picard to leave the bridge of the *U.S.S. Enterprise*, put on admiral's pips, and take command of a brand-new ship. Named the *U.S.S. Verity*, it was scheduled to appear in the IDW comic *Picard: Countdown* #1. The *Verity* would be Picard's flagship for the rescue operation meant to save billions of Romulans from a looming supernova and serve as a symbol of cooperation and hope to both the Romulans and the Federation.

The *Verity*'s role in the story had been well established, but there's more to a comic book than words. IDW needed to create a visual design for Picard's new ship. The design needed to show a progression from the ships of *The Next Generation*, *Deep Space Nine*, and *Voyager* era, while still feeling distinctly Starfleet. This was a design challenge that had been solved many times before by another team used to telling visual stories in the *Star Trek* Universe: the developers at Cryptic Studios, creators of *Star Trek Online*.

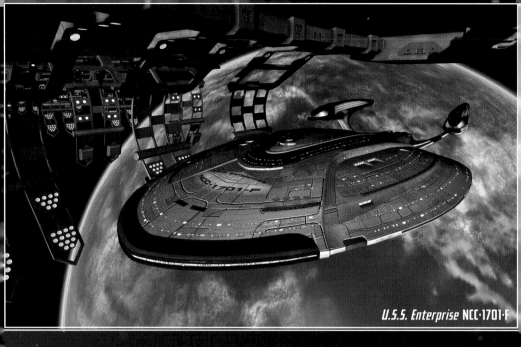

For almost a decade, *Star Trek Online* was one of the only multimedia ways to experience the *Star Trek* Universe as it existed after the events of the final *Next Generation* feature film, *Star Trek: Nemesis*. As a unique iteration of the *Star Trek* franchise, *Star Trek Online* also has its own designs for Starfleet uniforms, hand phasers, communicators, and, of course, starships. *STO*'s most famous starship continues the *Star Trek* legacy of ships named *Enterprise*.

This *U.S.S. Enterprise* NCC·1701·F is designated an *Odyssey*-class Star Cruiser. Its design was a collaboration of *Star Trek Online*'s developers at Cryptic Studios and *Star Trek* fans themselves. Cryptic, along with CBS, conducted a "Design the *Enterprise*" contest to allow fans to contribute to the newest version of the iconic starship. The winning ship, designed by Adam Ihle, would inspire Cryptic's own artists to create a sleek new design language for Starfleet ships in *STO*'s

25th century that showed a progression past the *Galaxy*, *Intrepid*, and *Sovereign*-class ships of the late 24th century.

This new *Enterprise* appears as a key player in the story of *Star Trek Online*. In the game, players take the role of a new captain and explore a galaxy still wracked in turmoil after the destruction of Romulus upended the galactic status quo. If that sounds a little familiar, that's because the newest *Star Trek* series, *Star Trek: Picard*, also deals with the fallout of Romulus' destruction.

While *STO* has spent years since its 2010 launch writing its own lore about the state of the *Star Trek* universe after 2387, the team at Cryptic Studios was excited for the opportunities to work with CBS and other *Star Trek* partners like IDW to leverage the new canon *Star Trek: Picard* is writing. With a decade of stories, characters, and ships to draw from, it was only natural for IDW and

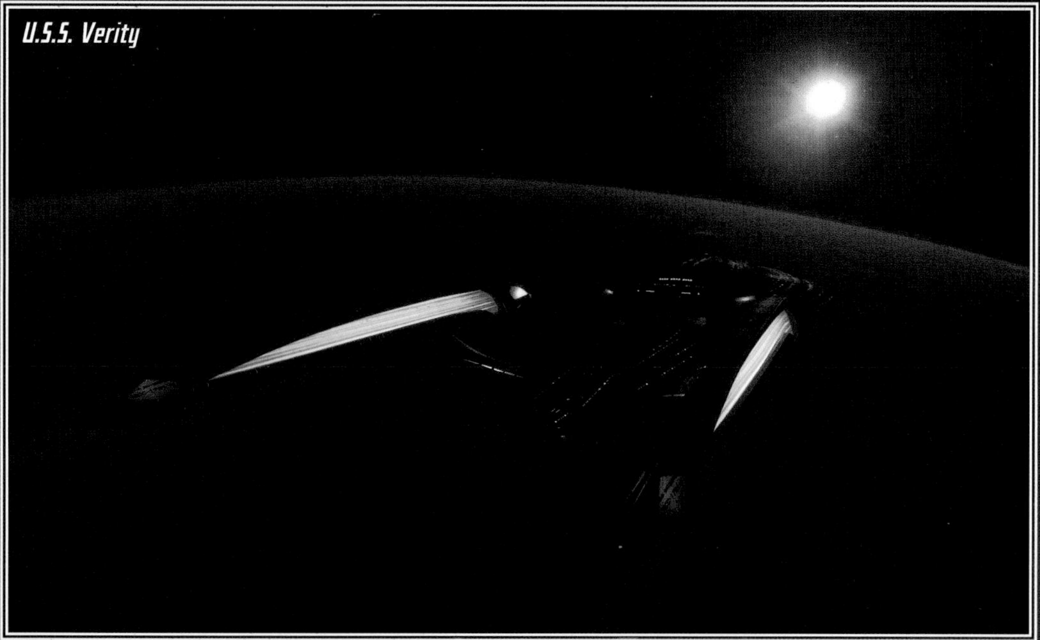
U.S.S. Verity

Cryptic to join forces and bring the *Odyssey* class from *STO* into the *Picard* universe as the *U.S.S. Verity*.

TROUBLED PAST: AN IN-UNIVERSE LOOK AT THE HISTORY OF THE *U.S.S. VERITY* AND THE *ODYSSEY* CLASS OF STARSHIPS

During Shinzon's coup of the Romulan Star Empire, the *U.S.S. Enterprise*, NCC-1701-E, encountered the massive Reman flagship *Scimitar*. Romulan starships had always skewed larger than Federation ships, but the *Scimitar* was in a class of tonnage and destructive power all its own. A few years before, Starfleet cruisers and escorts encountered giant Jem'Hadar battleships during the Dominion War that overpowered any rival starship in every respect. Following these events, Starfleet planners were concerned that the Federation's heavy cruisers were falling behind the curve on defensive and offensive capability. After coming face to face with several examples of super-capital starships from belligerent threat forces, the admiralty decided to invest in an ambitious design program. The goal was to create Starfleet's own iteration of a massive "star cruiser" that could compete with Romulan, Reman, and Jem'Hadar super-capital class starships.

The project called for two ships to be built in tandem: the prototype of the new class, the *U.S.S. Odyssey*, and a sister ship, the *U.S.S. Verity*. Construction began on the *Odyssey* first, with the keel on the *Verity* being laid down a few months later.

Then, in 2381, the Romulans asked for help. Their scientists discovered a supernova was imminent, and it would threaten Romulus, Remus, and dozens of other worlds. After

a fierce debate, the Federation decided to create a rescue plan. This ambitious plan called for hundreds of new ships and an entirely new infrastructure incorporating synthetic labor. Tapped to lead it was Jean-Luc Picard, now promoted to Admiral.

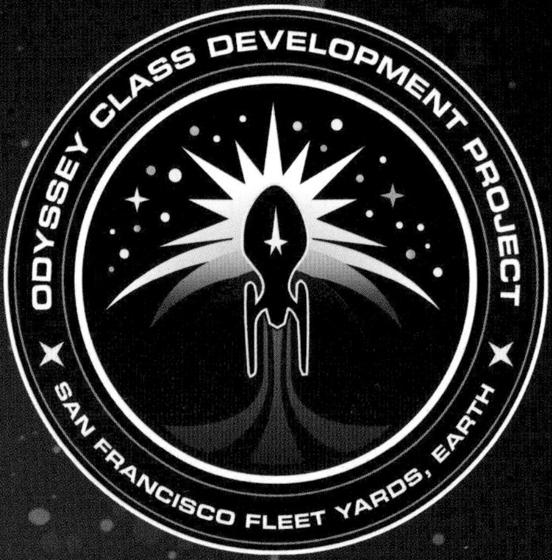
ODYSSEY CLASS DEVELOPMENT PROJECT
SAN FRANCISCO FLEET YARDS, EARTH

The ambitious plan meant a major shift in the construction priorities at Utopia Planitia, Starfleet's biggest shipyard. Advanced Starship Design Bureau engineers evaluated both *Odyssey*-class ships to determine how they might serve the rescue effort. Their massive internal volume, large powerplant, and fleet of auxiliary craft made them ideal candidates to lead the mission as its flagship. The *U.S.S. Odyssey* was further along in its construction, and most of its internal compartments and power systems were already laid down. Comparatively, the *U.S.S. Verity* was not as far along, meaning there was still time to adjust her design to accommodate the specific needs of the new rescue plan.

The admiralty decided to halt all production on the *U.S.S. Odyssey* and shift the staffing and material resources over to the *Verity* project, implementing several changes to the base design that increased passenger space, engine endurance, and communications capabilities. With a breakneck construction and testing program, the *Verity* was launched by the end of 2381 under the command of Admiral Jean-Luc Picard.

As the rescue plan matured, Starfleet Command decided to defer the resumption of the *Odyssey* until the fleet of rescue transports was finished. Its space frame was moved from Utopia Planitia to a "boneyard" in Jupiter orbit to make room for rescue ship construction. The scale of the *U.S.S. Odyssey* presented a potential investment of a tremendous amount of material and labor, and Starfleet planners simply needed those resources elsewhere if the rescue plan were to succeed.

As history records, it failed. A surprise attack by the synth labor force on Utopia Planitia destroyed the shipyards, the transport armada, and the Federation's political will to act in one fell swoop. Picard would resign his commission, the *Verity* would be mothballed, and the *Odyssey* forgotten as Starfleet re-aligned its priorities to respond to an isolationist civilian administration.

It wouldn't be until decades later, when a new generation of Starfleet officers needed a flagship, that the *U.S.S. Odyssey* would finally take to the skies. An escalating conflict with the Klingons in 2405 required Starfleet to return to the idea of the super-capital class starship and bring the

Odyssey project back online. Its systems were upgraded to 25th-century technology, and it finally launched in 2409. It was the vanguard for a new class of Federation starships that could compete at the super-capital level, and, of course, the sister ship of the next vessel to bear the name *U.S.S. Enterprise*, NCC-1701-F.

DESIGNING THE
ODYSSEY CLASS

Cryptic Studios worked with *Star Trek* fans to create the next version of the *Enterprise*. Creating a new iteration of the *U.S.S. Enterprise* is no small task. Any of the artists who have done this over the course of *Star Trek*'s history will tell you how the *Enterprise* is more than just a ship: the *Enterprise* is a companion, a home, and a guardian. She is there alongside the other characters throughout *Star Trek*'s many incarnations and has earned the status of a character in her own right.

When Cryptic decided it was time to add a new *Enterprise* to *Star Trek Online*, they went to CBS to discuss how such an important process should be handled. Dan Stahl, executive producer of *STO* at the time, recalls: "That discussion is what directly led to the 'Design the Next *Enterprise*' contest. Cryptic Studios believes in involving our players with the direction of the game, and we are regularly listening for feedback and comments as we develop new features and content."

Cryptic launched the "Design the Next *Enterprise*" contest in December 2010, just before the one-year anniversary of *Star Trek Online*'s launch. The winner of the contest would receive a lifetime subscription to the game, a 3D model of their ship, and have the honor of their design becoming the next incarnation of the *U.S.S. Enterprise*, the NCC-1701-F.

Thousands of entries were submitted to the contest, and the *Star Trek Online* team had

hen work cut out for them. After harrowing the field down to 25, and then to four finalists, the process of selecting a winner began. Stahl describes the discussions as passionate: "At that point the debate was intense over which ship should claim the honors. It is no easy task to select something so important to the *Star Trek* mythos. There is a strong history to follow. We were conscious of this fact as we entered the selection process."

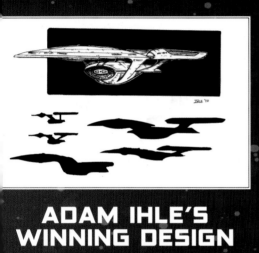

ADAM IHLE'S WINNING DESIGN

"We all agreed that our finalists felt familiar and strongly corresponded to established designs," Stahl says, discussing the team's final decision, "but Adam Ihle's design pushed the evolution of the ship in a bold new direction. When we compared this ship to our other finalists, the Ihle sketch sparked the most creative discussions. We all wanted to know more about this ship. It conjured debates about why Starfleet had moved in this direction. We felt it had the potential to be an excellent new design. It was our winner."

Jeremy Mattson, *STO*'s Art Lead at the time, remembers: "There were a few things

we really liked about Ihle's design; it was big and majestic, there were design cues from the *Galaxy* and *Sovereign* that made it feel familiar but that double neck was the icing on the cake. It was the thing that really made a statement and set it apart evolutionarily. We were all a little scared of it, but we were also very intrigued."

For Adam Ihle, the chance to design an *Enterprise* was one he could not pass up. A lifetime *Star Trek* fan and professional artist, Ihle knew that designing a new *Enterprise* was just as much about the past as it was about the future. "It had to fit into the lineage," he says. "I started by going back and looking at Matt Jefferies' original design and then down the history of the ship, from Andrew Probert's *Enterprise*-D to Doug Drexler's *Enterprise*-J. I knew it had to fit in yet be different enough to stand on its own."

Ihle says he went through about two dozen iterations while working through the design but the signature dual neck of the ship came to him early in the process. "In all honesty, I don't think I really knew if I was going in the right direction," Ihle remembers, but his grasp of the *Enterprise* as a signature character and his bold dual-neck approach were exactly what the developers at Cryptic were looking for.

FROM SKETCH TO SCREEN

With the winner chosen, it was up to *Star Trek Online*'s team of artists to adapt Ihle's

THINNER
SAUCER FORWARD
LONGER HULL
THICKER BASE
THICKER BASE & CURVIER

STAR TREK ONLINE - "ENTERPRISE F" - PROOF OF CONCEPT ROUGH 02

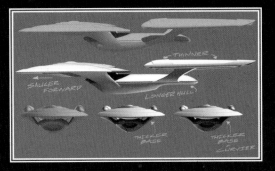

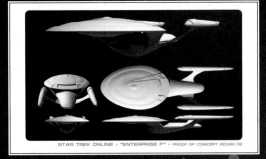

drawing to an actual 3D model for the game. While choosing a winner was a challenge for the team, taking that winner's design and developing it even further would pose an entirely new set of challenges. Dan Stahl recounts the next step in the process, "Now that we had our winner, the first order of business was to create a 3D model that showed the ship at various angles."

This task fell to *Star Trek Online*'s Art Lead, Jeremy Mattson. Mattson developed a rough "clay model" of the ship, determining its general proportions. Ihle's drawing of the ship was crisp and professional, but it left a lot of room for Cryptic's artist to develop the design, as it only showed the ship from one angle. Mattson says, "Since we only had a front view of the ship we still had some extrapolation to do. We actually liked the fact that there was room left for us to get our hands dirty in the design."

After weeks of discussion, sketching, and preliminary modeling by others on the team, *STO*'s ship artist Adam Williams had to synthesize everything done previously into the final vision for *Star Trek Online*'s *U.S.S. Enterprise*. Williams started by quickly blocking out the basic shapes of the ship. "After getting all of the general forms figured out," Williams recalls, "we began iterating on the overall design on a daily basis. It was during this period where we decided to really take the 'sleek and elegant' concept to the next level."

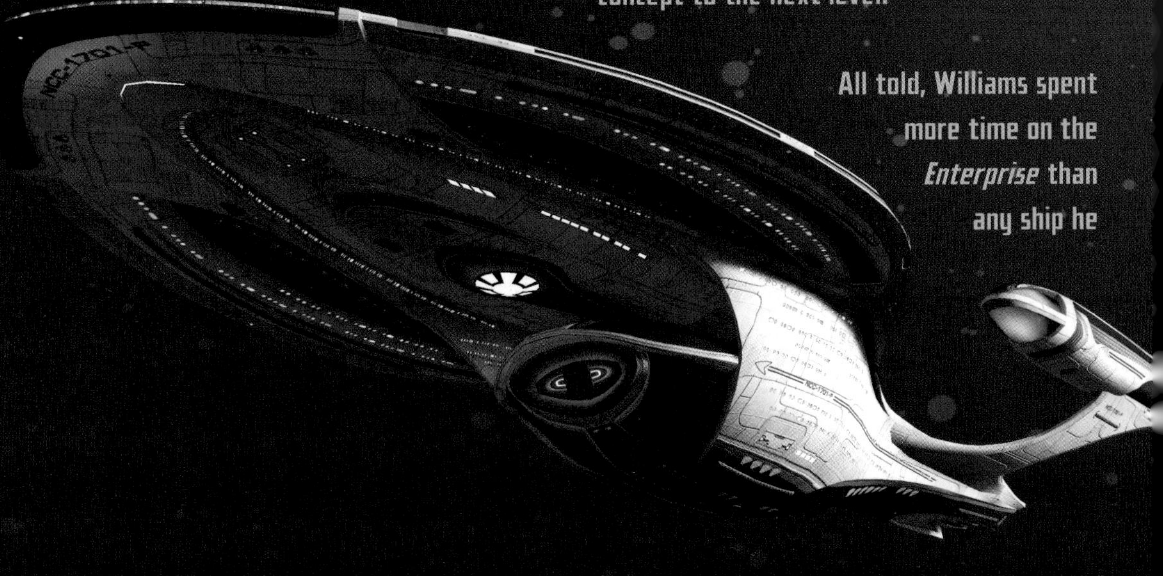

All told, Williams spent more time on the *Enterprise* than any ship he

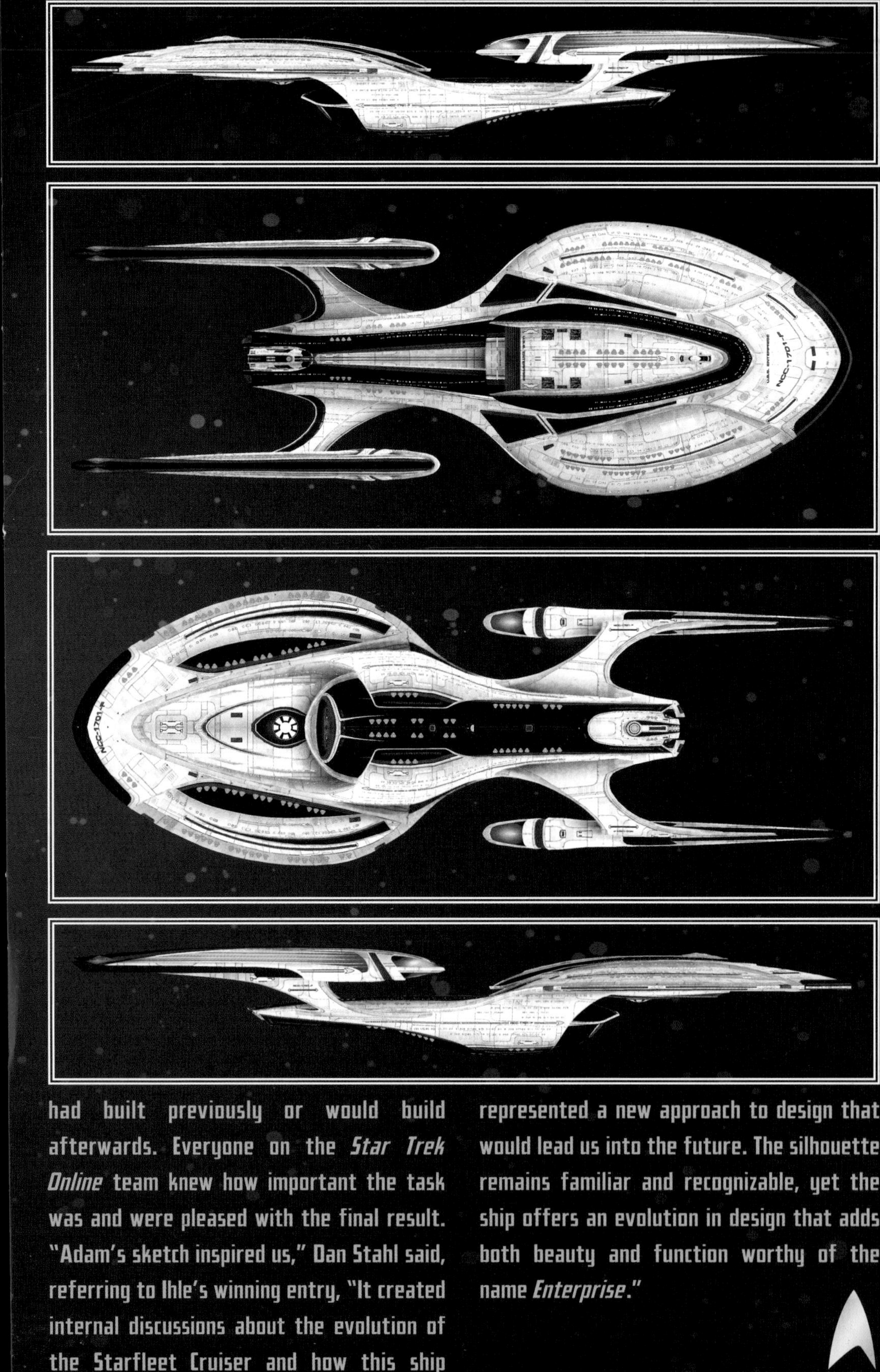
NCC-1701-F
NCC-1701-F
U.S.S. ENTERPRISE
NCC-1701-F

had built previously or would build afterwards. Everyone on the *Star Trek Online* team knew how important the task was and were pleased with the final result. "Adam's sketch inspired us," Dan Stahl said, referring to Ihle's winning entry, "It created internal discussions about the evolution of the Starfleet Cruiser and how this ship represented a new approach to design that would lead us into the future. The silhouette remains familiar and recognizable, yet the ship offers an evolution in design that adds both beauty and function worthy of the name *Enterprise*."

STAR TREK

PICARD

COUNTDOWN